BOTTOM FEEDER BLUES

A SAM LASKA CRIME THRILLER

RICHARD RYBICKI

HOLLOW POINT

PRESS

For Wes

What goes around, comes around.

- Unknown

1

DESILVA

Six miles southwest of Arcadia, Florida on Highway 17 - somewhere between Nocatee and Fort Ogden - a silver-grey Ford Crown Victoria pulled onto the shoulder of the road. The tires crunched on the hard-packed gravel as it slowed to a stop. Detective Lieutenant Kathleen DeSilva stepped from the cool air-conditioned car into the thick air.

She fanned away the stink of manure and vegetation with a hand and surveyed the scene. Yellow crime scene tape hung from scrub palmettos, snaked around temporary barricades and was finally tied off to some other weedy bush. The ribbon of yellow encircled another Ford Crown Vic, this one black in color, on the same shoulder of the road. It was hard not to notice the blue on white United States

Government license plates. They stood out like a stripper pole in the Vatican. The car's engine was still running.

DeSilva weaved her way around a disorganized mess of DeSoto County squad cars, their roof lights still flashing red and blue, and ducked under the yellow tape. She bee-lined to the small group of deputies gathered on the driver's side of the black auto.

In unison, the deputies straightened up as she approached. One of the group, a tall, lanky man with sergeant's chevrons on his sleeves, stepped forward. The brass nametag on his shirt read 'Hauser'. He nodded to DeSilva, "Lieutenant," he said.

"What do we have?" DeSilva said.

"Driver and passenger, both DOA. Both shot multiple times." Hauser took a step back and invited DeSilva to take a look with another nod of his head.

DeSilva moved in and peered into the car through the open driver's side window. "Wounds all on the left side. Shot by someone standing outside this window," she said. Without looking up she said, "How'd we get this?"

"Deputy Burns came on the car while on patrol," Hauser said.

"No one else around?"

"He didn't see anyone."

DeSilva poked her head up and scanned the farm fields on both sides of the road. It was the start of the September planting season and the fields were dotted with neat rows of young tomato plants. "Not a building in sight. I doubt anyone was even close enough to hear the shots," she said.

"Lieutenant?" Hauser said.

DeSilva peered back into the car, looking over the two bodies, the wounds, blood spatter, the floors, console, and dashboard. She scanned the pavement and gravel around the car. Trying to take it all in.

"Lieutenant?" Hauser said again.

Without looking up DeSilva answered. "Yeah?"

"You saw the plates?"

"Yeah," she said.

"This is some bad shit, Lieutenant. A real bucket of bad shit."

"Not for us. It's the FBI's bucket of shit. It's their investigation. All we need to do is secure and protect the scene until they get here."

"You think these are FBI agents?"

"I'm not sure. We'd have to check for ID's and badges on the bodies. But like I said, it's the FBI's scene. They have jurisdiction when any federal agent is murdered so we shouldn't touch anything." DeSilva stooped and took another look into the car. Her eyes fell on a set of handcuffs lying on the floor in the rear passenger's compartment. *Please, no,* she thought to herself. She looked back to the front compartment and spied a paper tucked into the visor. She tilted her head and swiveled around to read what she could.

"Shit," she said.

"What?" Hauser said.

She ignored her own instruction not to touch anything and grabbed the paper. She stood staring at it. Hauser asked his next question with a look.

"This is a federal writ for transfer of custody," DeSilva said. "These are U.S. marshals doing a transport from our county jail to the federal building in Fort Myers."

DeSilva looked up at Hauser. She saw a dozen more questions in the expression on his face. "There's an escaped prisoner out there," DeSilva said. "I need you to get on the radio and get an APB out and you need to do it now."

Hauser pointed at the writ in DeSilva's hand. "Is there a name?" Hauser asked. "Do we know who we're looking for?"

"Jesse Nichols," she said. "Former DeSoto County Sheriff's detective Jesse Nichols."

"Jesus." Hauser said.

"Did you know him?" DeSilva asked.

"Only enough to say hello."

"Good, then you know his physical description for the APB. He's obviously armed and dangerous and responsible for the murder of two U.S. marshals. And he's likely in an unknown vehicle with at least one other person. Get to it."

"Yes ma'am," Hauser said and hustled off to his patrol car.

DeSilva rolled up the writ and stuck it in a pocket. She needed to call her chief and notify the marshal's Service and FBI. She pulled her phone out and paused, scanning the scene again. She looked over the black Crown Vic and then at each of the two victims. She stared at the faces. One after the other. She promised herself to remember each man.

"Jesse Nichols," she said to herself. "Fucking piece of shit."

DeSilva walked back to her car and made her calls. First to the Fort Meyer's offices of the FBI and the marshal's service. The marshals had more questions than she had answers while the FBI was typically tight-lipped. Both told her, as she already knew, to touch nothing until they arrived. She'd explain about the writ in the visor when they got there.

Her boss, the duly elected sheriff of DeSoto County, seemed more interested in the political ramifications. A double homicide of federal agents in sleepy DeSoto County didn't look good for him. Especially since the escaped prisoner involved was once one of his deputies. Typically, he tried to micromanage the scene from his telephone until DeSilva explained to him the FBI had jurisdiction. When he heard that, he decided to forego a personal appearance at the scene as he would invariably be taking a backseat to the feds running the investigation, and he was up for reelection. He actually told DeSilva it would make him look weak and inconsequential.

When she was finally able to excuse herself from the Sheriff, DeSilva slipped her phone back into her pocket. She saw Sergeant Hauser standing nearby waiting for her.

"APB sent?" she asked.

"Yes, ma'am."

"You know what to do now?"

"Yes, ma'am," he answered. "We'll secure and protect. Do you need anything else?"

DeSilva leaned back against the front of her car. Folding her arms, she said, "Yeah, Sarge. What do you think?' She nodded in the direction of the car containing the two dead marshals.

"Ma'am?"

"Why did they stop? Why did they pull over? They were on a prisoner transport. They know never to stop for anything. No stranded motorists, no hitchhiking half-naked Victoria's Secret models. Nothing. And why would they let someone just walk up on them once they did stop?"

"I don't know, Lieutenant."

"They didn't even have time to pull their weapons," she said more to herself than to Hauser.

"What do you think, Lieutenant?"

DeSilva shook her head. She didn't like the only reason she could think of.

A thump-thump-thump off in the distance

caught their attention. DeSilva looked up to the southwest sky and spied a pair of helicopters headed their way.

"Set up a roadblock and detour, Sarge," she said. "We need to close this section of the road."

2

LASKA

"You're gonna marry her." Nosmo King wasn't asking a question.

Sam Laska pulled a small black velvet box from his jacket pocket and set it on the table between them. "I asked her. She said no."

"What do you mean she said no?"

"Marley said no. She said she needs to think about it."

"What did you do?"

"Nothing, Nosmo. At least I don't think I did."

"What was her reaction when you asked her? Was she upset? Sad?"

"She seemed to be happy. I went all out. Dinner, champagne, I got down on one knee. She was surprised. Happy surprised. Not upset surprised. She smiled, kissed me and said she needed a little time to think before answering."

Nosmo King, a detective on the Sarasota Police Department, was Marley's uncle. He and his wife Victoria were childless and Marley, her parents both deceased, was the daughter they never had. He moved forward in his chair. His eyes narrowed and his jaw tightened. Nosmo sat back and drained his glass. He looked over and signaled the bartender to bring another round.

"Not working today?" Laska said.

He turned back to Laska. "You counting my drinks now? I get enough of that from my wife. Anyway, I'm on vacation." He leaned in closer. "Do you love her?"

Sam opened the velvet box and handed it to Nosmo. "That's my mother's ring. She wore it every day since the day my father gave it to her. She gave it to me before she died. She wanted me to give it to my one true love."

"Does Marley know that? Or does she think you only asked her because she's pregnant?"

"She knows how I feel. And she told me she loves me so I don't know what to think. I don't understand what's going on with her." Sam picked at the corner of the label on his beer bottle. "Maybe she's just overwhelmed. Maybe things have just moved too fast for her."

"Maybe if you had a job. No woman wants a man without a job. A woman needs to know her man can take care of her and her baby. I know this restaurant is doing good and she doesn't need money now, but all that can change. Today it's slammed, tomorrow it might be shuttered."

Sam took the small box from Nosmo and slipped it back into his pocket. "I'm on that. I put in an application with the State. I got my PI license. I rented an office."

Nosmo's chair moaned and creaked under the strain of his bulk as he leaned back. "Are you nuts? That's no kind of job. There's no steady income there. And what kind of cases do you think you're gonna get? If you get any at all. The best you're gonna get will have you peeping through motel windows at cheating husbands."

"There's more to it than that, Nosmo. There's process service and skip tracing. Plus, lawyers always need good investigators."

"Defense lawyers do. You'll be working for the other side."

Sam stared at his beer and fiddled with the label again. He looked up at Nosmo. "The truth doesn't take sides. And at least I'll be working. I already sent out a few feelers. I've got a few nibbles too." That part was a lie.

Nosmo eyed his empty glass. He pushed it aside with the back of a meaty paw. "Did you tell Marley?" he said.

"Yeah, she's okay with it."

"Just okay, huh?"

"She's not thrilled, but she knows investigative work is what I do best. I was a good detective in Chicago, Nosmo. I'm still good at it."

The bartender brought over their drinks, and after he left, Sam said, "I know she'd be happier if I kept the insurance investigator job but she understands why I passed on it. And, yeah, I guess she's not happy about me having a job where I carry a gun. It's not like being the police, but you know it's still scary for her. Your wife has gotta feel the same way."

"Every cop's family feels the same way." He took a sip of the brown liquid and smiled at the glass in his hand.

"Anyway, I doubt my career choice is what's holding her back," Sam said. He took a slug of his beer and set the bottle back down. "Maybe..."

"Maybe what?"

"Maybe it's the mixed-race thing."

"What kind of stupid thing is that to say? You know she don't care about that."

"Yeah, but maybe she cares what other people think. They look at us when we're together, Nosmo. They don't stare – well, some of them do. Mostly it's sideways glances, frowns, shaking heads. Then whispered conversations and more frowns."

"I get it. Believe me, I get it. Florida is the deep

south and lily white around these parts. But I'm sure Marley doesn't care what other people think. Did she ever say anything to you?"

"No, but it has to bother her. I mean, it bothers me."

"You can't let what other people think bother you. Don't waste an ounce of brain power on people like that. I learned that lesson a long time ago."

"What lesson?" A smiling Marley Jones walked up and stood next to Laska. She rested a hand on his shoulder. The other held a Styrofoam to-go box.

"Sam thinks you worry about what people think. The race thing," Nosmo answered.

Marley looked down at Laska. "Really? You think it bothers me?"

Laska shot Nosmo a look. "Well..."

Nosmo cut him off before he could finish his answer. "And what's this crap about you not wanting to get married?"

Marley pointed a finger and gave her uncle a look that could stop a charging alligator in its tracks. "You mind your own business," she said to him. Then to Laska, "And you, we'll talk at home later." She set the to-go box on the table. "Here's your lunch," she said and walked off.

"Wow," Nosmo said. "That smile evaporated fast."

Laska leaned forward and rested his elbows on the table. "Thanks for that."

Nosmo smiled. "You're welcome."

Laska stood and grabbed the Styrofoam box. "Just for that, you can get the bill."

"We don't pay in Marley's place. You know that," Nosmo said.

"We might be paying today. She looks pretty angry. Leave a good tip."

Laska turned and headed for the door. When he hit the sidewalk, he felt his phone buzzing in his pocket. He looked at the screen and saw it was his father calling. He punched the green button. "Hi, dad," he said.

"Sam, it's me," Bruno Laska said.

"Yeah, dad. I know. What's up?"

"A lawyer called the house. She was looking for you."

"A lawyer?"

"Yeah, a Rebecca somebody. I wrote it down, hang on."

"You can give me the name later, dad. What'd she want?"

"She wouldn't tell me. But she wants you to call her back. I got her number, it's a Chicago area code."

"You could have just given her my number."

"I didn't want to do that until I checked with you. I thought you might not want her to know. What's this about, Sam?"

"I won't know until I talk to her but I can guess."

"That thing you got fired for?"

"I retired, dad."

"Tomato, toe-mah-toe."

"Always nice talking to you, dad. Give me her name and number."

3

DESILVA

DeSilva and Hauser shielded their faces from flying dirt and debris as the helicopters set down on the highway. Agents, their shirt sleeves rolled up, jumped from the bellies of the copters holding their baseball caps to their heads and began conferencing with each other while bending in to hear one another as the rotors slowly wound down. There was pointing and waving and plenty of nodding. Others, dressed in khaki pants and dark blue polos jumped from the second chopper and began unloading assorted bins and tool boxes. They stacked them in neat piles near the side of the road until the tools they held were needed. It was a practiced dance DeSilva knew they had done plenty of times before.

DeSilva picked out the man in charge. He was the first off the lead copter and the man everyone seemed to defer to. He was also the only one wearing a suitcoat.

"Come on," DeSilva said to Hauser. "Time to join the party."

They marched the fifty or so yards down the hot asphalt to the helicopters. DeSilva walked up to the man in the suit. She waited as he dismissed the agent he was talking to. When he finished she introduced herself. "I'm Lieutenant Kathleen DeSilva. DeSoto County Sheriff's Department," she said sticking out her hand.

The suit glanced at her then yelled back to the agent, "And keep the marshals out of the scene until I give the okay." The agent turned back, gave a thumbs up and kept walking.

The suit turned to DeSilva. "Lieutenant...what was the name?" he said.

"DeSilva," she answered. "And this is Sgt. Hauser." She kept her hand out.

The suit ignored Hauser and the offer of a handshake from DeSilva. "Lieutenant, I need you and your people to back out of my scene. Stand by and we'll get to you when we can." He began to turn away.

"Hang on," DeSilva said dropping her hand. "This isn't your scene."

The suit spun around. "What?"

"Not until I know who the fuck you are and you confirm the victims are federal agents. Until then, you can stay the hell away from our scene."

The suit took a step toward DeSilva.

"That got your attention," DeSilva said. "Look, I get it. This *is* yours. The big yellow 'FBI' on the side of the helos are hard to miss. And you're anxious to get to work. You've got the man-power and techs with all the latest scientific gadgets and the full weight and budget of the Justice Department behind you. And we're just a small under-staffed county sheriff's department. But you're not gonna treat us like a bunch of third-rate Barney Fifes."

The suit stared at DeSilva. He took off his Ray-Ban Aviators and said, "Okay, Lieutenant. I apologize if I offended you and your people. I was in a hurry to catch up. You can understand why. Correct?"

"Yes. But who better to catch you up than the first responders?"

"You're right, I apologize again. Let me start over." He pulled out a black leather wallet from inside his jacket and handed it to DeSilva. "Assistant Special Agent in Charge Ronald Gleason, Federal Bureau of Investigation."

She flipped it open, inspected his badge and ID card and closed it up. She handed it back. "And you'll confirm that the two victims are federal marshals?" she said.

"Yes, transporting a prisoner from your jail to our offices in Fort Myers."

"It's your scene, Gleason. My people will be standing by to offer any assistance we can. The highway is roadblocked in both directions so traffic won't be a concern. Deputy Burns discovered the victims and is available to be interviewed when you're ready for him. An APB was dispatched state-wide with the name and description of the escapee, but don't expect to have any luck."

"Why not?"

DeSilva turned to Hauser. "Sergeant, why don't you and the deputies go cool off in your cars? And maybe send one of them for a case of water. They'll be here awhile." She turned back to Gleason. "Come with me," she said and headed off to the black Crown Victoria.

Gleason didn't move. "Hold on," he called after her.

DeSilva kept walking. "Hurry up," she said. "You're gonna want to hear this."

Gleason trotted after her. "Wait a minute. The evidence techs are going to be setting up to process the scene."

DeSilva kept walking. "Don't you do a walk through first? Get a lay of the land?" She pulled a pair of latex gloves from her pocket and held them out for Gleason. "Glove up," she said.

Gleason fell into step next to her. He stared at the gloves. "Don't worry," DeSilva said. "It's just a precaution. We're not going to touch anything." She pulled out a second set of gloves and blew into each one before snapping them on. She caught Gleason watching her. "They go on easier if you do that first," she said.

Gleason followed DeSilva's lead and puffed into each glove. He still struggled to get them on. "Sorry," DeSilva said. "They're smalls. My size."

"The walk through," Gleason said, "the techs do it. They'll let us know what they find."

"You don't check out the scene?"

"Not typically."

"What, you're not allowed? It's against protocol?"

"I'm the ASAC, of course I'm allowed. But we have the best Evidence Response Technicians in the world and we trust them. There's no reason for me to risk contaminating the scene."

"All fine and good, but you can't learn anything for yourself that way," DeSilva said. We'll be careful."

They reached the Crown Vic and DeSilva led Gleason to the open driver's side window. "Okay, first notice the window is open. The only window open. And the car's running," she said. "The A/C is blowing."

Gleason nodded.

"Now, look here," she said. "Look inside." Gleason paused then slowly stooped down. DeSilva noticed his hesitation. "You okay?" she asked.

"Get on with it," he said.

"Okay. Look there." She nodded at the bodies. "All the wounds are on the left side of the body. Their weapons are still holstered."

Gleason stood upright. "They were shot by someone standing outside this window. That's obvious. You brought me here for that?" He looked down to the ground.

"Hard-packed gravel," DeSilva said. "No footprints, no tire tracks."

"Is that it?"

"No shell casings either. They policed their brass."

"Or used a revolver," Gleason said.

"Valid point but unlikely."

"Why?"

"I'll get to that," she said. She squared herself to Gleason and moved a step closer. She lowered her voice. "When I discovered they were marshals on a transport I asked myself why they stopped. They know never to stop. Right? But they did. They pulled over onto the shoulder, rolled down the window and waited in the car to talk to whoever it was walking up to them. They were so unconcerned they didn't even think about drawing their weapons. What could make them do that?" Before Gleason could say anything DeSilva answered her own question. "A cop," she said. "They were pulled over by a police officer. Or a deputy. Someone they'd feel completely safe and confident stopping for. They knew they'd just flash their badges and be on their way."

The expression on Gleason's face didn't change. He snapped off his gloves and wiped a hand across his mouth. "And that's why you think the APB won't do us any good," he said.

"The prisoner was driven away in a patrol car. What cop would ever think of stopping another officer?"

"And the brass?" Gleason asked. "If a semi-auto was used, why would they pick it up?"

"It's easier to change out a barrel than a firing pin. Swap out the barrel, toss the first one. Takes less than five minutes. The slugs won't match to the new barrel. Get rid of the brass and there's nothing for the lab to make a match to. There's no way to match anything to a service weapon."

"Anything else?" Gleason asked.

"Yeah." DeSilva pulled the writ from her pocket and handed it to Gleason. "I took this out of the visor of the victims' car."

Gleason scanned the paper. DeSilva saw the muscles in his face tighten up. She cut him off before he could say anything. "Exigent circumstances. When I saw what it was, I thought it was more important to get an APB out on an escaped prisoner. I needed to read the entire writ to do that."

Gleason cringed a little then said, "I understand. And nothing else was touched?"

"Not a thing."

Gleason gave a nod of his head. He looked around. The Evidence Response techs were buzzing around the scene setting up cameras, pulling out rulers and tape measures, and rifling through their bins for whatever else they needed.

"Let's back out and let them work," he said. "I've got calls to make."

"Yeah," DeSilva said. "Me too."

LASKA

L aska headed east on Main Street with the to-go box on the passenger's seat next to him. He crossed Bayfront Drive and entered the parking lot fronting the marina on Sarasota Bay and Bayfront Park. He found a spot close to the park's entrance and pulled in. Grabbing the Styrofoam box, he walked into the park.

The park, jutting out into the bay, was a favorite spot of his. Banyan trees shaded the path along the perimeter of the park, and its leaves overshadowed a small playground in the center. There was always a soft breeze off the bay that kept you cool on even the hottest of days. If that wasn't enough, you could always get a cold beer at O'Leary's Tiki Hut near the entrance.

Laska walked past O'Leary's and followed the path clockwise, checking out the shoreline and every bench he passed. He eventually came to a spot on the path farthest from the entrance. There, on a shaded bench, was Captain Bob.

Captain Bob was stretched out on the bench. Asleep to the casual observer. His tee shirt was torn and tattered. His pants matched the dirty shirt. A weathered ball cap covered his face and a pair of pink flip-flops hung off his bare feet.

Laska met Captain Bob a few years earlier. Actually, Laska found him. Laska, as a favor, was looking into the death of a friend's nephew. The kid was discovered, apparently overdosed, in a car in the park's parking lot. While checking out the scene for himself, Laska found Captain Bob lounging in a dinghy on the shore of the bay. Bob turned out to be a witness that helped to prove the overdose was actually a murder. Bob helped make the case.

"How are you, Bob?"

Captain Bob peeked out from under his hat. "I'm alive. But I ain't buying no green bananas."

Laska smiled. It was one of those gems his grandfather used to say. "Why don't you sit up? I brought you some dinner."

"More of that Puerto Rican food?" he said as he slowly brought himself upright. Laska thought he could hear every bone in the old man's body creak and groan. "It's Jamaican. Rice and beans and some kind of chicken. Here you go." He handed the box to Bob.

Captain Bob opened it, sniffed his food and closed the box. He set it on the bench next to him. "Thank your woman, kid."

"I will. You need anything else? And don't say cigarettes. I'm done enabling your bad habit."

Captain Bob shook his head. "I'm okay, I guess."

"I'm gonna leave you to your food then. Make sure you eat it all. You're getting too thin. And maybe you should stay at the shelter tonight."

"They steal my stuff there."

"All you have are the clothes on your back. They'd be doing you a favor."

Captain Bob smiled and winked at Laska. It was his way of saying goodbye. Laska sighed and said, "Alright, Bob. If you need anything you know where I live. Right?"

"Don't worry about me, kid. I'll be okay."

Laska nodded, but he still worried about Bob. He was in his seventies and the street life had taken its toll. He turned, followed the path back to his car, pulled out of the lot, and made the drive to Marley's condo.

The trip took less than fifteen minutes. Laska and Marley lived close to the park just east of Sarasota Memorial Hospital in a one-bedroom unit on the second floor of an L-shaped building. It reminded Laska of the motel where they'd find the body in a 60's crime movie.

Marley was working as a morgue assistant for

the county's medical examiner's office when they met. She finally had enough and opened her own restaurant on Main Street. A Jamaican-slash-Caribbean place she named 'One Love'.

It was Marley who asked Laska out for their first date. She was out of his league and he had no clue she'd be interested in him. They hit it off, fell in love, and Laska moved in nearly a year ago. However, he still kept his old mailing address of his father's place on Siesta Key.

He parked on the street and cut across a small weedy square that was once probably grass to the open stairway on the short end of the 'L'. When he got inside, Laska plopped down on the couch and pulled his phone out. He might as well get it over with, he thought. He punched in the lawyer's number and waited.

"Conway, Turrow and McCann," the woman's voice said. "How may I direct your call?"

Laska introduced himself. He asked for the name his father gave him, Rebecca Stafford, and hoped Bruno got it right. He waited again, and after a few short clicks and a buzz, a voice came on.

"Rebecca Stafford," she said.

"Hi, this is Sam Laska. I'm returning your call."

"Hi, Mr. Laska. Thanks for calling back. Let me ask, that was your father I talked to earlier?"

"Yeah, why? Did he give you a hard time?"

"Not at all. It was just – I thought I could hear his

heart pounding over the phone when I told him who I was."

"Yeah, he's a little excitable. He was probably just worried about me."

"You live with him? On Siesta Key, I think it is?"

Laska heard a rustle of papers on Stafford's end. "No, not any more. Listen, before we continue, what's this about? No offense, but I need to know who you represent and what we're talking about here."

"Of course. Let me explain. Our firm has been retained by the city of Chicago to represent you in the case of Kevin King. You should have already been served the summons and received a copy of the complaint."

"I haven't."

"No big deal at this point. They probably have your old address too."

Laska said nothing and let that hang in the air until Stafford spoke again.

"Do you remember the plaintiff Kevin King?"

"Oh yeah. I sure do," Laska said.

The entire incident with Kevin King flashed through Laska's mind. King was suspected of being one of several shooters in a triple homicide in a night club. It was a gang shoot-out. Two opposing factions wound up at the same place and someone started shooting. King was arrested on the scene and transported to the Area HQ. The transport crew locked him in an interview room, unsupervised, and told him the crime lab was called to administer a gunshot residue test on his hands. When Laska returned and entered the room King was washing his hands in his own urine. Laska grabbed him to prevent further destruction of evidence. King spun around and peed on Laska's pants and shoes. Instinctively, Laska lashed out and struck King who fell back into the cement block wall of the room. He wound up with a concussion and almost died.

"The city retained you? I thought the city's Corporation Counsel's office handled these cases."

"The city does this all the time now. They job out these cases to more experienced firms. We have quite a few cases we're handling for the city now. Trust me, this is much better for you."

"I guess."

"We only represent you. That means our only interest is doing the best for you alone."

"I'm assuming the city was named in the lawsuit also. You don't represent them?"

"The city was named along with the police department, the Superintendent and everyone who was in your chain of command. That's common. And no, another firm was retained to represent them. That's both good and bad."

"What do you mean?"

"The good, as I said, is that my firm's only

interest is you. You are our sole focus. We will put every effort into protecting your interests."

"And the bad?"

"The city will try to separate themselves from you. They'll attempt to show you acted outside the rules and regulations and therefore they're not responsible. But the plaintiff's attorneys don't want that because the city has the deeper pockets."

"They sure do. If King is looking for a payday from me, he's gonna be disappointed."

"King's attorneys will ask for a list of your assets, but that's down the road. And when they do, we'll object. Don't worry about that for now."

"Oh, I'm not worried. I have maybe eight hundred dollars in my checking account, I don't own a house or condo, my car is four years old, and I haven't gotten the oil changed in about eight months. On top of that, I won't start collecting on a very small pension for a few more years."

Laska heard Rebecca Stafford chuckle. "Well, we'll do our best to protect that pension. You said you don't live on Siesta Key any longer?"

"No, I live with a friend. On the mainland. You're gonna need the address. And my email too." Laska recited the information for Stafford and listened to her 'uh-huhs' as he paused to let her catch up while she wrote.

After she had his contact info, Stafford recited her email address for Laska then said, "Are you planning to visit Chicago anytime in the near future? Do you ever get back here?"

"I haven't been back since I moved to Florida and I haven't been planning any trips. Not that I'm opposed, though."

"We need to get together soon and discuss the case. And when the time comes for depositions, we'll need to prep you. I think it would be best if we do it here. We can fly you up and put you in a hotel. It'll be on the city's dime. The trip costs will be included when we bill them."

"That's fine. I'm flexible these days so I'm available pretty much anytime you need me."

"Good," Stafford said. "I think we're done for now unless you have any questions."

"Just one. What do you think my chances are?"

"I don't like making any guesses. Or promises. Let's just say we have a lot of work to do."

"That bad, huh?"

"We're not holding a great hand. But we do have one ace."

5

DESILVA

DeSilva sat in her car outside the crime scene and punched the off button on her phone. She talked to her captain and the Sheriff, updating both. She told her captain of her suspicion that the shooter may be a police officer but her captain told her to hold back on telling the Sheriff. Her captain wanted more evidence before bringing it to him.

She had one more call to make. The detention captain at the county jail. She dialed his direct line and waited. It only took one ring.

"Captain Haskins," the head of the Detention Bureau answered.

"Captain, it's Lieutenant DeSilva. We have a situation." DeSilva filled in the captain explaining every detail she could - but leaving out her suspicions.

"Crap," Haskins said. "Thank God it wasn't our

people. What's the plan? Do you need any help with a search for the prisoner?"

"No, Cap. It's all on the feds. And they haven't said so yet, but I think they want minimal involvement from us."

"Why is that?"

"I'm not sure," she lied. "Maybe they want the marshals to take him."

"I'm sure the marshals want him too. Real bad."

"Yeah. Anyway, I need a couple of things from you."

"How can we help?"

"I need Nichols' cell searched. Thoroughly. And I need to know anyone and everyone of your people who have had any kind of contact with Nichols. Even casual."

"No problem. Do you want copies of the video feed too?"

"That'd be great. And can you include a printout of the personnel assignments so I can put a name to the faces when I review the video?"

"We can do that. Anything else?"

"What about a cellmate or anyone on his tier?"

"Nichols was in isolation. No cellmate, no contact with any other prisoner. Ex-cops don't do well with the general population."

"Yeah, I should have remembered that."

"That it?"

"How about a list of every visitor he's had since his detention?"

"That's easy, hang on."

DeSilva heard the click-clack of a computer keyboard between raspy wheezes. Haskins was a heavy smoker. DeSilva swore she could smell the cigarette she knew was hanging off his lip through the phone.

Captain Haskins came back on. "Only one visitor. His lawyer. Name of Jasper Dunlop. Sometimes several times a week."

"No one else? No wife or friends?" DeSilva said. She knew Nichols was married and had a young daughter.

"Nope, that's it. You want a print out?"

"I'll come by and pick it up."

"I can have one of my people drop it off at your office."

"No, I'll pick it up. Later today. And the videos if they're ready."

DeSilva finished up her conversation with the captain and sat in her car thinking. She believed that the only logical possibility was that the two marshals were pulled over by a patrol car. There were only two options. Only two agencies. Her own Sheriff's Department or the Arcadia Police Department. Though possible, an Arcadia patrol car was unlikely. This section of Highway 17 was well out of the city's limits by at least ten miles. That wouldn't stop a dirty cop, but there was a risk involved in a city patrol being seen out this way. That left her department and that conclusion spooked her. One dirty cop, Jesse Nichols, was bad enough. To think a malignancy of corruption ran through her department made her shudder.

She stepped from her car and studied the action around the scene. The FBI's evidence response techs had finished photographing and measuring the scene. They had all the doors of the car open and were carefully examining the bodies of the two marshals. Despite the job they had to do, DeSilva saw a reverence and respect as they moved around and slowly and meticulously searched for and then collected evidence.

Her own people were gathered across the road. She was happy to see there was none of the usual chatter and joking when a group of cops were thrown together while waiting to be told what to do. They stood, solemnly, and watched the techs at work. She was proud of them.

Beyond her troops several vans crammed with equipment arrived from Fort Myers. Crates and boxes had been unloaded, and close to the helicopters in the middle of the highway, two open-sided tents had been set up. The type you'd see beach-goers set up for a bit of shade. The FBI were grouped under the closest tent while the marshals had taken over the second. Both were being used as mini-command posts with folding chairs and tables cluttered with laptops and clipboards. There was a small satellite dish staked to the ground and a gas-powered portable generator between the two tents.

DeSilva headed toward the marshals. One by one they stopped whatever they were doing – tapping on keyboards, pouring over maps, talking on phones - and watched her approach. One of the men, tall and burley with his hair cut high and tight, set down a clipboard and stepped toward her. He waited for her - hands clasped behind his back, feet spread apart - like a soldier standing at ease.

She stopped an arm's length in front of him. She looked up. He was at least a full head taller than her.

"Lieutenant Kathleen DeSilva," she said. "I'm very sorry for your loss. You have the sheriff's office and my personal condolences. "

"Thank you, Lieutenant," the marshal said.

"I've been fortunate to never have suffered the loss of...of... "

"Brothers-in-arms," the marshal said.

"Yes. I'm truly sorry. I promise that we will do whatever we can to help."

"I'm sure you will. Is there anything else, Lieutenant? I'm busy."

DeSilva stood staring at the man. His face was like a blank page offering no outward indication of what he was thinking or feeling. Except, DeSilva knew better.

"Yes, there is. You don't trust us. You don't trust any of us. You knew as soon as you saw the scene."

"Knew what?"

"Why they stopped. Why they pulled over. You didn't need for it to be spoon fed to you like I had to do for the ASAC over there." She threw a thumb over her shoulder towards the FBI's tent. "And because of that, you don't trust us and I'm not asking you to."

"What are you asking?"

"For the chance to prove we can be trusted," she said. "Or at least that I can be."

"And how would you do that?"

"I'll share everything I know. Everything I learn. With no expectation of reciprocity."

"No expectations whatsoever?"

"None. I want to catch these fuckers almost as much as you."

High-and-Tight kept his eyes locked on DeSilva for what seemed like an eternity. He finally spoke. "I accept your offer," he said.

DeSilva gave him a single nod of her head. "Okay then. What can I tell you first?"

"Follow me." The marshal turned and walked under the canopy. He pulled a folding chair from a table and set it in the center. "Have a seat," he said to DeSilva. Then to everyone else, "This is Lieutenant DeSilva. She's offered to help us. She'll provide background information and answer any questions.

No one is to share anything with her without clearing it with me first. Understood?" None of the men spoke. They weren't expected to.

DeSilva felt a flush rising from her neck. She was presumed guilty by association. She steeled herself. This is what she offered and she was going to honor her commitment. She'd tolerate the abuse. For now.

She looked at every face standing around her. "Who's first?" she said.

High-and-Tight spoke up. "What was Nichols doing in your jail? What was he charged with?"

"The FBI didn't tell you?" she said.

"No." He offered no explanation.

"Okay, here's the short version. Nichols was working on the side with a harvesting company. Owned and operated by a family, the Cordeles. No one in the Sheriff's department knew . At least as far as we could tell.

"He ran interference for the Cordele family and protected them. Gave them inside information when they needed it. The Cordeles were involved in human trafficking and indentured servitude. Modern day slavery. They'd buy illegals from a group of coyotes in Texas and use them as their pickers. Their harvesters. They kept them under lock and key. If any one of them tried to run off, if they gave them any kind of problem, they wound up dead.

"Immigration and the state police took over the

bulk of the investigation after we busted the operation. They couldn't hook up Nichols with any federal
charges or any of the murders so he was charged by
our department with conspiracy, official misconduct,
bribery and any other felony we could hang on
him."

"How long ago was this?" High-and-Tight asked.

"Going on three months, give or take."

"He was in custody that whole time?"

"Yeah, bond was denied by the judge. He came
down on him hard. Said Nichols violated the public
trust and broke the oath he swore as a deputy
sheriff."

"Court appearances?"

"A preliminary hearing and a bunch of motion
hearings. His lawyer keeps filing motions and
delaying."

The marshal wiped a film of sweat from his brow
with the back of his hand. The shade of the canopy
helped but not by much. He looked over his shoulders, first one and then the other, at the group
behind him. "Anyone else?" he said.

A marshal in the back of the group stepped up.
He was younger than High-and-Tight but just as tall
and fit. "What was his job? What did Nichols do in
your department?" he said.

"He was a detective for the past three years,"
DeSilva said. "I was his lieutenant."

High-and-Tight hitched his chair closer. He

leaned in, resting his forearms on his knees, and stared at DeSilva. "And you never suspected a thing."

DeSilva stared back into his grey eyes. "I trusted him. He never gave me a reason not to trust him. Until the end." She looked past him at the gathered marshals and then back again to High-and-Tight. "Do you trust your people?"

"With my life."

"Until you find out you can't," DeSilva said, "and then it's too late." She looked at the faces of the other marshals and then back to High-and-Tight. "Anything else?" she asked. "You need his address? I assume you'll be knocking on his door soon."

"We've got it." He nodded over to one of the laptops on a folding table nearby. "We've already got a search warrant approved," High-and-Tight said. "He won't be there but maybe we'll find something to point us in the right direction."

"Yeah, good luck with that."

6

DESILVA

"Why was Nichols being transferred to Fort Myers?" DeSilva asked.

High-and-Tight sat back. "You just said, not fifteen minutes ago, that you didn't expect any answers from us."

"I did say that. But I didn't say I wasn't going to try."

High-and-Tight sat silent. DeSilva saw his gears grinding.

Finally, he said, "You need to ask the FBI."

DeSilva nodded and stood. "I've got a lot of paperwork to do. We can talk more later," she said. She pulled her cell phone from her pocket. "How about we trade numbers? You can call me anytime. And if I find out anything I'll call you."

High-and-Tight stood and pulled out his phone. He turned to the group of marshals and told them to get back to work. He turned back to DeSilva. "What's your number?" he said.

After they swapped cell numbers DeSilva said, "What's your name, marshal?" Before he could answer, she added, "And please don't tell me it's Marshall."

High-and-Tight gave a small smile. "No, it's not Marshall. It's McCarthy. Mike McCarthy."

"Okay, Marshal Mike McCarthy. I'm sure we'll be in touch soon."

"It's not 'marshal'," McCarthy said.

"You said that."

"I mean, we're deputy marshals. There's only one United States Marshal. Just like there's only one DeSoto County Sheriff. The rest of us are deputies. My people back there are all detectives. I'm the Detective Supervisor."

"Alright," DeSilva said. "I get it." She looked over to the black Crown Vic. "What were...what are their names?"

"John Miller and Daniel Wilkerson. Security Officers. Prisoner Operations Division."

"Did they have families?"

"Yeah, they both had a wife and a couple of kids."

DeSilva lowered her head then looked back up to McCarthy. "I'm really sorry," she said. She turned and walked to the FBI's tent.

She stood on the perimeter and watched the activity underneath the canopy. It was more controlled and oddly quiet compared to that of the marshals. The marshals' were more determined and purposeful. Almost frenzied. The FBI's Special Agents stood or sat and talked in small groups. They looked like they were waiting for someone to tell them what to do.

DeSilva scanned the faces of the agents. She was looking for the ASAC. She stepped under the canopy and asked the agent closest to her. He looked annoyed at being interrupted but pointed her to the helicopters. She took the short hike over and found Gleason standing outside the first helicopter. He was on the phone. Gleason saw her approach and held up a finger, asking her to wait. She stopped out of earshot.

When he finished, Gleason tossed the phone into the helo and stepped closer. "What can I do for you, Lieutenant?"

"Weird looking phone. Satellite?" she said.

"Yeah, a secure line. How can I help you?"

"I wanted to touch base with you. I'm heading out. I've got a lot to do. My people will be staying though. We should exchange cell numbers."

"Good idea," Gleason said.

When they finished, DeSilva said, "When you're ready, the sergeant will order a transport for the bodies."

"Not necessary. We'll get our own transport.

We'll be taking the bodies to the Lee County morgue."

"Our ME isn't going to like that. State law says--"

"We'll let him know and get all the authorization he needs. We're flying in a team of pathologists from Quantico. They'll do the autopsies."

DeSilva gave a shrug. "Not my circus," she said.

"Huh?"

"Nothing, just something a friend says."

Gleason cocked his head and frowned. "Is there anything else?"

"Yeah, there is. Why was Nichols being transferred to your office?"

Gleason stared at her through his aviators. "I can't discuss that with you."

"How about I guess? If I'm right all you have to do is nod."

"Lieutenant, I can't –"

DeSilva held up her hands. "Okay, no problem. You just answered my question anyway."

"Did I?"

"Yeah, you did. By not trusting that you could tell me."

"Okay then, tell me what you think."

"INS already declined federal charges on Nichols. As far as I know, he wasn't the subject of any other federal investigation. So, the only reason you'd be pulling him out of jail is because you wanted to talk to him. Far away from this county. He had his lawyer reach out to you, didn't he? He wanted you to intervene. To make a deal. He let on he had information you'd be interested in."

"Really?"

"Yeah, that's what I think."

"And what information do you think he wanted to share?"

"The only thing that would make you salivate. Systemic corruption in the Sheriff's office."

Gleason brought a hand up to his mouth. Stroking a mustache and beard he didn't have. "Again, I can't comment."

"That's okay. You don't have to. The important thing for now is to find that piece of shit Nichols." She turned to walk away but stopped after only a few steps. She stood there as it dawned on her. She turned back, her eyes wide despite the sun. "Wait," she said. "You think that maybe Nichols didn't escape."

Gleason stood mute and folded his arms across his chest.

DeSilva took a step closer. "You're thinking he really did have information. That he wanted to turn on some big criminal operation in our office. Someone found out and set out to stop him from talking. You think that maybe this was a kidnapping and execution."

Gleason shrugged.

"No," she said. "You're wrong. They would have

done him here. Left his body in the car with the deputy marshals. There'd be no reason to take him. Too big of a risk. And if they did, they wouldn't have uncuffed him. You saw the set of cuffs in the back seat. Face it, Gleason. He set up this escape. He played you. But don't feel bad. You're not alone. He did it to us too."

DeSilva left Gleason with that and marched over to her people. Sergeant Hauser was leaning up against his cruiser sipping a bottle of water. A small group of the deputies were standing with him. A few of the others were sitting in their cars cooling off.

"Can I get a bottle of water?" she said to Hauser.

Sergeant Hauser turned to Deputy Burns. "Grab a bottle for the Lieutenant, will ya?"

Burns walked over to the trunk of his cruiser, popped it open and pulled a bottle out.

DeSilva looked at Hauser. "You sent Burns for the water? What if the feds needed him?"

"He volunteered. I figured it'd be okay," Hauser answered. "It didn't take him long. Besides, I thought he needed a break. He looked pretty shook up. Finding the bodies and all."

"I guess it was okay," she said.

Burns walked up and handed the bottle to DeSilva. "Thanks," she said to him. "You okay, deputy?"

"Yes, ma'am," Burns said.

"Good. When the feds talk to you, Sergeant

Hauser will be there with you." She looked over to Hauser who gave her a nod. She looked back to Burns. "Just answer their questions. Tell them what you saw, okay?"

"Yes, ma'am."

DeSilva looked back to Hauser. "I'm heading back to my office. I've gotta update the Sheriff. You got this?"

"I've got it," he said.

DeSilva nodded Hauser away from Burns and the others. "Watch out for that ASAC Gleason," she said. "He doesn't trust us, and I don't trust him yet."

"No problem, L-T," Hauser said.

"Otherwise, full cooperation. Call me if you need anything." She left Hauser and headed to her car.

7

LASKA

After finishing up with his lawyer, Laska dialed his father. He'd better let him know what was going on, he thought. He listened to the phone ring until it went to voicemail. He left a message asking Bruno to call him back and punched the red disconnect button. As soon as he did his phone began buzzing. Without checking the screen, he thumbed the green button.

"Hey, dad?" he said.

"No, it's me." It was Marley.

"Oh, hi. I didn't check the ID. I thought it was Bruno calling me back."

"You called him today? That's good. You two don't talk enough."

"Actually, we already talked once. I'll tell you about it when you get home. What's up?"

"I'm checking to see if you were home. I'm going

to take a break before the dinner rush and come home for a few hours."

She didn't sound angry and that was good, he thought. He screwed up telling her uncle about his proposal and hoped she didn't take it too hard. "Great. I'll see you in a little while then," he said.

"You want me to bring anything home?"

"I am a little hungry."

"You didn't eat the chicken I gave you?"

"I stopped at Bayfront Park on the way home."

"And gave it to Bob again?"

"Yeah, I did."

"You know what happens when you keep feeding the ducks, right?"

"Yeah, they don't learn to fend for themselves."

He heard her giggle.

"Okay," she said, "I'll bring something. See you soon."

Laska disconnected and redialed Bruno. His father answered this time.

"Sam, that you?"

"Yeah, dad. I wanted to let you know –"

"Sam, a guy came by looking for you right after we talked."

"Who?"

"He said he was a sheriff's deputy. He showed me a badge and ID."

"Okay, I think I know what that's about. What did he say?"

"He wanted to talk to you. I told him you weren't home. I didn't give him your address and just played like you still lived here. Was that okay?"

"You could have given it to him. I think –"

Bruno cut him off again. "He gave me an envelope for you. Made me sign for it."

"Dad, let me finish. It's okay. I talked to the lawyer that called the house earlier. It's about that Chicago thing. The city hired her firm to represent me. She said I'd be getting served a summons. That's probably what's in the envelope."

"And they can just leave it with me? Don't they have to serve you?"

"You basically told the deputy I live there. Your address is still on my driver's license. I'm pretty sure the deputy knows what he's doing, so yeah, I'm sure he was good leaving it with you. I think he was sure I'd get it."

"Okay. But I'm not on the hook for anything, right?"

"No, you're fine. I'll come by later and pick it up."

"I can drop it off. I'm not doing anything."

"That's alright. I'll pick it up."

"No, I'll come over. It's no problem. Bye, Sam."

Bruno disconnected before Laska could protest any longer. Laska slipped his phone into his pocket and went to the kitchen to start a pot of coffee. He stood by the coffee machine watching its magic and took in the rich aroma. As the machine wound down dripping the last few drops into the carafe, he heard a key slipping into the front door's lock. He pulled two cups out of a cabinet and set them on the counter. He called out to Marley as he heard her walk through the door.

"You want a cup of coffee? I just made a pot."

"No thanks," she said as she entered the kitchen. "What I really want is a nap." She tossed another to-go box on the counter and said, "Here you go."

Laska pushed the box aside. "How about I join you?"

Marley smiled and leaned a hip against the counter. "Sure, but only if you want to sleep."

He put on an exaggerated frown. "Dang, I guess I'll just eat my lunch then," he said. "Just as well. We wouldn't have had a lot of time anyway. Bruno's on his way over."

"Really? Why?"

"Long story short. A sheriff's deputy dropped off an envelope for me over there. I think it's a summons. He's bringing it over."

Marley pushed off the counter and crossed her arms. "A summons? For what?"

"Remember I told you the story about why I retired?"

Marley let out a laugh. "Yeah, the guy that peed on you."

"Well, it looks like he finally got around to filing a lawsuit. Which is a perfect segue."

"To what?"

"I'm sorry I told Nosmo about proposing."

"It's no big deal, I guess."

"You're not angry?"

"No, I just put that on for my uncle's benefit. I wanted him to know he's to stay out of our business. He and Aunt Vicky would've found out sooner or later, though." She gave a little half smile and arched her eyebrows. "But you should have checked with me before saying anything."

"You're right. I'm sorry." He moved in and put his arms around her. "So, you haven't made up your mind yet?"

She pecked him on the lips. "No. And how is this a segue?"

Laska broke the embrace and took a half step back. "We probably shouldn't get married."

Marley's back went straight as a yardstick. She stood there, hands on her hips and eyes wide. "You're taking it back? You're un-proposing?"

"Yeah, for now. If I'm getting sued, we shouldn't be married. I don't have anything for them to take. You do. You have a business, a healthy bank account and this condo. If we're married they could go after all of that."

Marley relaxed. She bit her lip and stood there thinking. "I don't like it," she said.

"What? Why?"

"I liked that I was in control. That it was my deci-sion to make."

"You liked me dangling on the hook."

"Yeah." Marley smiled at him.

"Okay." Laska got down on a knee and took her hand. "Then I'm asking you again. Will you marry me? But with one condition."

Marley looked down on him. "What condition?"

"You keep me dangling. You don't answer me until this lawsuit is done with. Until it's all over."

"Ha! Okay, you win. I won't even consider giving you an answer until you're in the clear. In fact, I won't even consider considering it until then."

"Good. Are you happy now? You're back in the driver's seat."

"Yes," she said. "Now get up off the floor. I'm going for a nap." She patted her tiny baby bump. "This one really takes it out of me." She gave him a kiss. "Can you wake me in an hour or so?"

Laska stood. "Sure, go ahead. I'll eat my lunch and try to keep Bruno quiet when he gets here."

Marley kissed him again and headed to their bedroom closing the door behind her.

Laska poured himself a cup of coffee, grabbed a fork and took his lunch to the dining room table. He popped open the Styrofoam container. The perfume of spices – ginger, allspice, thyme and nutmeg – intertwined with garlic and lime filled the room. He stared at the jerk chicken sitting on a bed of coconut rice and exhaled deeply. Marley's recipes were great, and her kitchen staff had them down perfectly. But it seemed like that's all he'd been eating lately. He thought about a burger and fries from Knick's over on Osprey Avenue.

He shrugged and jabbed the fork into the chicken. As he stuck the first bite in his mouth, he was interrupted by a rapid knocking at the door. Saved by Bruno, he thought.

Holding a large manila envelope in his hand, Sam's father tried to rush into the room as Laska opened the door. Sam stopped him with a hand to the chest.

Sam held a finger to his lips. "Dad, Marley's sleeping. Let's go get lunch and a beer."

Bruno stepped back. "Is she alright? She feeling okay?"

Sam stepped out and closed the door behind him. "Yeah, she's just really beat. Let's go somewhere and let her get some rest."

"Yeah, okay. Here," he handed the envelope to Sam. "Open it. Let's see what it is."

"I'm pretty sure I know," Sam said. "I'll look it over at the restaurant. Come on, you drive."

Fifteen minutes later they sat at a table in Knick's. With their orders in, beers in front of them, the manila envelope on the table between them, Bruno pushed it closer to Sam.

"Come on. Open it," he said.

"Alright already. Jeez, you're like a kid." Sam took the thick package and ran a finger under the sealed flap. He pulled out a stack of paper. The pages were divided into two smaller stacks. Each paperclipped in the corner. Sam quickly scanned both.

"Okay, the first one here is the summons," he said. He read the header out loud for his father. "'United States District Court, Northern District of Illinois. Kevin King versus Sam Laska, et al.'" He looked up at Bruno. "That's him, the guy I hit. Kevin King."

"Then it's what you thought it was?" Bruno said.

"Yeah." Sam kept reading. "'You are hereby summoned and required to serve upon plaintiff's attorney, blah-blah-blah, an answer to the complaint which is herewith served upon you.'" He flipped through the remaining pages. "The rest looks like details of the complaint. You know, the stuff they said I did wrong. And then a lot of technical stuff."

"What's the blah-blah-blah?" Bruno said.

Sam looked up from the summons. "Huh?"

"You said 'blah-blah-blah'. What's that?"

"Oh, sorry. It's the name of the attorney and his firm."

"What's the name?"

"Darren Jordan. From the firm of Jordan and Jordan."

Bruno frowned. "I never heard of them. You?"

Sam took a slug of his beer. "Yeah, I have."

8

LASKA

"Who are they?" Bruno said.

"Lowlifes," Sam said, "bottom feeders. Two brothers who started out as ambulance chasers. Now they make their living by suing coppers and police departments. In most cases they settle out of court for a quick payday. With bigger cases, they file motion after motion, delaying and delaying. They get their shills in the media to put the case out in front of the public - you know how they love to hate the police - then they let it cook and wait for the city to make a massive offer."

"Are they any good? I mean, in court? Do they ever take a case to trial?

"A few times. And, yeah, they've generally won those cases. But those are the slam dunks with an orgy of evidence. Most times, like I said, they just delay until the city gets tired of paying for their own lawyers and makes an offer. And they will. Even when they know the officer didn't do wrong."

"Why would the city do that?"

"Money, dad. It's cheaper in the long run for the city to make it go away."

"What about your case? What do you think the city will do?"

"It's one of those slam dunks for Jordan and Jordan. The city will try to settle on their end and leave me flapping in the wind."

The waitress brought their burgers and slid the plates in front of Bruno and Sam. Sam shoved the stack of papers back into the envelope and dug in. Bruno edged his chair closer to the table and ignored his food. "What are you going to do, son?"

Sam chewed a mouthful of his juicy burger and swallowed. He wiped his lips with a napkin and looked at his father. "The lawyer I talked to didn't seem very optimistic. But the good thing is I don't have anything for them to take."

"What about your pension?"

"They could go after it." Sam took another bite of his burger and chased it with a sip of beer. "But I'm getting by without it now, so it won't hurt too badly if it happens." He picked up a fat French fry and dipped it in catsup.

Bruno sat back in his chair. "You don't sound very worried," he said.

Sam dropped the fry back onto his plate and

looked at Bruno. "What good is worrying about it? Whatever is going to happen is going to happen. And I'll move on after that. Besides, I've got bigger things to worry about."

Bruno held up his hands in surrender. "Hey, I'm sorry. You're right." He looked down at his plate.

Sam took in a breath and blew it out slowly. "No, dad. I'm sorry. I shouldn't have snapped at you."

"Forget it, Sam. Let's eat." Bruno picked up his burger. "How 'bout we change the subject."

"Good idea."

They finished their lunch and Bruno picked up the check. Sam protested, but not very long or hard. In Bruno's car, on the way to Marley's condo, Bruno asked about the second group of papers.

"If you don't mind me bringing it up," he added.

"I don't mind." Sam opened the envelope and pulled out the papers. "It's a demand for what they call 'Interrogatives'. A list of questions they want me to answer."

"What kind of questions?"

Sam explained as he flipped through the pages. "Stuff like, who else was in the interview room? Or was anyone outside the room who might have heard something? Do I have any copies of reports or notes on the case? Oh, and they want a list of my assets."

Bruno tried to hide a smile but Sam caught it. Sam laughed. "They're gonna be disappointed, huh?" Sam said.

After Bruno dropped him off at his building, Sam bounded up the staircase. He slipped into the condo trying to be as quiet as possible and found Marley in the bedroom. She was still asleep. Sam kicked off his shoes and laid down next to her, spooning her, with his head buried in the nape of her neck.

"You smell like onions and grease," she whispered.

"I thought you were sleeping. Did I wake you?"

She rolled over carefully, so as not to lose his embrace. Their faces just inches apart. "Yeah, but that's okay. How long have I been out?"

"A little over an hour."

Marley began to move away. Sam drew her back. "Stay a little longer," he said.

She smiled and said, "Okay," and closed her eyes. She nuzzled closer. "You went out?"

"Yeah, Bruno came over. I didn't want our talking to bother you. He bought me lunch."

"Uh-huh," she said. "You're gonna eat that chicken for dinner." She wasn't expecting an argument.

"You bet," he said.

They lay there quiet for a time. When he sensed Marley was getting restless -ready to get out of bed - he said, "I've gotta to go to Chicago for this lawsuit."

She opened her eyes. "When?"

"Soon. I talked to a lawyer the city hired to defend me. All she said was 'soon'."

Marley pushed herself up onto one elbow. Her eyes were wide, her eyebrows arched above them. "Can I go?"

Sam propped himself up on an elbow mirroring her pose. "You want to go with me?"

She bounced up onto her knees and looked down at him. "I've never been to Chicago. I've never even been out of Florida. What do you think?"

"I guess we can make a vacation out of it. But there's gonna be some days I'll be tied up with the lawyer. You'll be on your own."

"I think I'll live."

Sam smiled. "Well then, I think we're going to Chicago."

She pumped a fist. "Yes!"

"I'll call the lawyer. See when she wants me. Is there a time that's best for you?"

"I can go anytime."

"What about the restaurant? Do you think Josie can handle it?"

"She's my partner, right? She can handle it."

Marley jumped out of bed and trotted to the bathroom. "I'm going to need some new clothes," she said.

9

JESSE NICHOLS

Nichols walked around the small single-wide trailer, room to room and back again. He plopped down on the musty recliner in the corner of the living room and clicked through the channels on the TV. No news yet. He tossed the remote and stood up. He walked to the window and peeked out, using a single finger to lift a slat of the closed blinds. He scanned the landscape from right to left, trying to figure out exactly where he was. Somewhere on a part of the Peace River he guessed. He squinted against the daylight. The closest neighbor, as best he could tell, was across the river that ran left to right fifty or so yards in front of the trailer.

He went back to the recliner and sat. He got up. He walked through each room of the trailer again. Twice. He didn't like waiting here. His instinct was to keep moving. But he couldn't. Not without his bag. Or a car. He picked up the remote and stood in front of the television clicking through it looking for news. Still nothing.

He walked into a bedroom and peeked through the curtains. Nothing as far as the eye could see. Barely any trees. Only the dirt and gravel road that brought them here from the highway. He turned to leave the room but stopped when he caught his reflection in a mirror over a chest of drawers.

It was the grey and white striped jail-issue jump-suit that got his attention. He opened the closet door and rummaged through the clothes. He checked the sizes on all the pants. Nothing would fit. *How small was this guy anyway*? he thought. He checked the drawers in the bureau and found sweatpants and tee shirts. They'd be tight but good enough. He picked out grey sweatpants and a black shirt with a silk-screened trout on the chest. He peeled off the jump-suit and changed.

He looked at his shoes. Black canvas slip-ons. More jail issued crap. He looked over the assortment of boots and sneakers in the closet. Again, way too small. He'd have to stick with the slip-ons for now.

He checked himself out in the mirror again. He stared at his bent and deformed nose. A reminder of the cheap shot Laska gave him. He'll remember to return the favor when the time came.

He ran a hand through his hair. It hadn't been

cut since his arrest. And then through his beard. He'd been letting that grow as well. He looked himself up and down and turned away. He felt like a backwoods Flor-idiot. *Perfect*, he thought. He wouldn't stand out at all.

He went back to the living room and the television. Still nothing. *What were they waiting for?* He went to the window and peeked out again. He unconsciously patted the sweatpants for pockets that weren't there. He wanted a telephone. He wanted to call that prick and see what was taking him so long.

He walked through every room again checking for a hardline. There was none. All he could do was wait.

He needed his bag.

10

DESILVA

The phone in her pocket began buzzing as DeSilva pushed through the heavy glass doors into the DeSoto County Sheriff's building. She checked the number on the caller ID. The Sheriff's private line. She put the phone back in her pocket and headed straight for his office.

She walked through an open door into the outer anteroom. Seated at a desk facing her was the Sheriff's aide, Deputy Don Whimple. His desk sat between the Sheriff's private office and everyone else.

Whimple's duties, besides being a spy for the Sheriff, included answering the phone, typing and filing, and running interference. He made sure no one saw the Sheriff unless he wanted them to.

Whimple looked up from his crossword puzzle. "Lt. DeSilva, what can I do for you?"

She breezed past him towards the door. "Nothing."

"Hey, you can't go in there." Whimple stood and tried to get between her and the door. He was too late.

"Shut up, Donny," she said as she opened the door and closed it in his face.

Sheriff Clay Wilson was seated behind a wide oak desk. He was tall and lean, maybe 170 pounds. But only if he had rolls of quarters in his pockets. He was leaning back in his chair, legs crossed and hands behind his head. He would have looked relaxed except for the pinched brow and clenched jaw.

DeSilva's captain, Bill O'Connor, sat across the desk from Wilson, his back to the door. He strained against his belly twisting around to see who came into the room.

Wilson uncrossed his legs and sat forward, resting his forearms on the desk. "You didn't answer your phone," he said.

"I was just down the hall on my way to see you," DeSilva said.

Wilson grunted and waved a hand at the chair next to the captain. DeSilva sat.

"Where're we at in all this?" Wilson asked. And before DeSilva could answer he added, "Those two radio stations called. The one here in town and," he looked over to Captain O'Connor, "what's the other one?"

O'Connor said, "WZSP, the Nocatee station."

"Yeah," Wilson said to DeSilva. "They wanna know why we got Highway 17 roadblocked."

DeSilva moved forward to the edge of her seat. "The FBI are still working the scene. They said they'll be taking the bodies to Fort Myers for the post mortems. They're flying in a team of pathologists. They'll be done when they're done, I guess. I'll keep in touch and open up the highway when we can.

"The marshals are concentrating on Nichols as far as I can tell. They're not thinking about anything else." She exhaled deeply and sat back. "This is the feds' show, boss."

"What about the media?" Wilson said. "If it's the Fed's show shouldn't we sic the news people on them?"

"Yeah," DeSilva said. "I say we don't give the media anything. We just refer them to the FBI office in Fort Myers. I've got the ASAC's telephone number. I'll give him a heads up."

Wilson sat back in his chair looking satisfied. "Good. We've got no exposure on this. They lost Nichols and it's up to them to find him."

"Two men were murdered, sir," DeSilva said.

"Of course, of course," Wilson said. He sat forward trying to look concerned. "It's terrible. And we'll give them any assistance they need. I just meant...". He paused in mid-sentence searching for a way out.

DeSilva let him hang for a beat then said, "I know what you meant, sir. But we do still have a problem."

Wilson cocked his head and looked his next question at her.

DeSilva turned to Captain O'Connor. He didn't move. When it was obvious he wasn't going to help she turned back to Wilson and said, "Nichols obviously had help. The two deputy marshals had pulled over and were shot while seated in their car. The shooter was outside their car on the driver's side."

Wilson stared at her. His face expressionless as he tried to piece together what she meant.

"Their weapons were still holstered," she said.

Still nothing. She was walking him through it and he still didn't get it. DeSilva didn't know how good of a politician he was but, as far as police work went, he had a room temperature IQ.

She took a deep breath. "The only possible explanation at this time is that they were shot by a police officer or a deputy. Some kind of LE officer. Those two marshals wouldn't stop for anything else."

DeSilva saw his eyes go wide. He jumped out of his chair.

"What?" He looked at O'Connor. "Did you know this?"

DeSilva jumped in. "I didn't tell Captain O'Connor yet," she lied. "The feds and I just figured this out. I came straight here to tell you."

He pointed a thin finger at her. "You're telling me we've got a murderer in our ranks?"

"It's possible," she said.

"You should have said something as soon as you walked in the room," Wilson said.

"Yes, sir," she said, not really sorry.

"Two federal officers murdered by deputy sheriff? First Nichols and now this?"

DeSilva saw panic in his eyes.

"That's only one possibility," she said. "It could have been a city police officer. And then again, maybe we're completely wrong and the marshals stopped for some other reason. I don't think we should get ahead of ourselves here."

That seemed to help. Wilson came out from around his desk and started pacing the room. He was thinking, evaluating. Re-evaluating.

He turned to her. "Who else knows about this?"

"Only the feds. The FBI and the marshals," she said.

"Our people on the scene?"

"Not unless they put it together themselves."

Wilson grunted. "Unlikely," he said. "Alright then. We keep this between us. It doesn't leave the room." He looked at O'Connor. "We need to stay ahead of the feds on this. I'll be damned if they're gonna be marching in here with warrants and subpoenas. If it's one of ours, we're gonna be the ones to nail him. Serve him up on a silver platter. Now, how do we attack this?"

O'Connor turned to DeSilva for help. She had to stop herself from rolling her eyes.

"We start with the obvious," DeSilva said, "and pull up the GPS history on all our cars."

"Good," Wilson said. "Get right on that."

"I can't," DeSilva said. "My access is limited to detective cars only. You're the only one with access to every car."

Wilson walked behind his desk and looked down at his computer's monitor. "How do I do that?"

DeSilva joined him behind his desk. She gave the mouse a jiggle to wake up the machine and took a step back. Wilson bent over the keyboard and tapped in his password. The monitor's screen morphed into a plain blue screen littered with icons.

"Now, double-click on the GPS app," she said.

Wilson did and the screen came alive with a map of the county. Tiny blue icons, each with a distinct number, dotted the map. Most of the icons stood alone scattered around the county. Some were slowly moving down a road or street, some were stationary. There were also two clusters of stationary dots. The first at their location, the sheriff's office, and the second on Highway 17 between Nocatee and Fort Ogden.

"Explain what I'm looking at, Lieutenant," Wilson said.

"This is the active screen. We're seeing every car in real time. Here," she took over the mouse and zoomed in on Highway 17, "those are our cars at the scene." She zoomed out and in again on their location. "And here's the station. Those are all the cars here."

"That's the parking lot? It picks up the signal even when a car is off?"

"Yeah, the GPS is hardwired to the battery. It's always active."

"Can it be disabled?"

"Someone would have to cut the wires," she said. "But the units have a battery backup built in. When the wire is cut or the car's battery dies, the unit sends a signal. We'd be able to tell if that happened."

"Where do we check for that?"

"Here," she moved the cursor and clicked on a button at the top of the screen labeled 'ADMIN'. After several more menu choices and clicks she said, "Nothing. No dead units, they're all active."

"Good," Wilson said. "Now what?"

"We check the history of every car. But we have to check each car one at a time. If we pulled up the history of all the cars at once, all the streets and roads on the map would be flooded with those little blue dots. Even with limiting the history to the last eight hours, we'd be looking at a bowl of blue spaghetti."

"How long is it going to take?"

"Hours, maybe longer," she said.

Wilson took a step away from his desk. "It would take me a week. You know this program, Lieutenant. You do it."

"Yes sir," she said. "Do you want me work on it here or upstairs?"

"I have a choice?"

"I can assign myself a temporary password with full administrative rights. That way I can work on my own computer."

"Do it," he said.

Five minutes later she was climbing the stairs to her office. Captain O'Connor walked next to her.

"Thanks for covering for me in there," O'Connor said. "I don't need his grief."

She looked at him like a disappointed mother. "Like I do? Tell me, Bill. Are you ever gonna grow a pair?"

With Marley back at her restaurant for the dinner rush, Laska spent the rest of his afternoon reading over the summons and interrogatives. He made notes in the margins and kept a list of questions for his lawyer on the back of an envelope he fished out of the garbage can under the sink.

He checked the time on his phone. He figured it was probably too late to call Rebecca Stafford. He settled for shooting her an email. He stared at his phone and decided against using the phone's mail app. His fumbling fingers would produce more typos than in a millennial's text message.

He moved from the living room to the dining room table and Marley's laptop. It came alive as he opened it and navigated to his email account. He stared at the blinking cursor for a few seconds before hunting and pecking out the letter:

Ms. Stafford, I wanted to let you know I received the summons as well as a Demand for Interrogatives. The summons and interrogatives both state I'm required to reply by a specific date. Am I responsible, or will you be taking care of these? Also, do you have a firmer idea of when you might be needing me in Chicago? As I said when we talked, I'm ready anytime. In fact, the sooner the better. Can we settle on a date? Thanks for your attention. – Sam Laska

He read it over, corrected a single spelling error, and clicked the 'Send' button. He left the laptop open, walked into the kitchen, and put on a pot of coffee. His stomach growled. Coffee wouldn't fix that. He spied the chicken he was supposed to eat for lunch sitting on the counter. He took the box and set it next to the laptop. He'd sip his coffee and pick at the cold chicken while checking out things on the internet for he and Marley to do while in Chicago.

He poked around online for twenty minutes or so nibbling on his dinner, going through an entire pot of coffee while intermittently checking his email. He found plenty to do in Chicago. This was the time of year most Chicagoans tried to squeeze out the last bits of summer fun before the cold weather moved in. There were street art fairs, food and wine festivals, and outdoor concerts. Not to mention it was the best time of year to catch a Cubs or Bears game or just walk Michigan Avenue and window shop.

There were a few can't-miss things to do and see. He'd have to show Marley the Water Tower, Oak Street beach, Buckingham Fountain, and have a drink at the bar on the 95th floor of the John Hancock building. Catching the view from the top of the Sears Tower – he couldn't bring himself to call it by its new name, Willis Tower – was mandatory too.

He pushed away from the computer and took his cup and the remains of his dinner into the kitchen. He went back to the laptop to close it up but checked his inbox one last time. Rebecca Stafford had written him back.

MR. LASKA, Please call me Rebecca. I got your email. Don't worry about responses to the summons and interrogatives. I'll handle those. But we'll have to conference before I can do that. I'll also need you to sign a certification letter attesting to the validity of your answers. If you're up for it, I can make arrangements to fly you up here in a day or so. We could meet Thursday and Friday. I'm also attaching a pdf of the file (police reports, state-

ments, notes, and hospital records) for you to review before we meet. Let me know on the travel arrangements. – Rebecca

HE SAT DOWN and typed a reply.

REBECCA, meeting later this week sounds good. I'll write you back tomorrow to confirm. – Sam

LASKA CLICKED THE 'SEND' button then reopened Stafford's reply. He scrolled down to the bottom and opened the attachment. A stack of pages opened. On the screen were all the reports on the original incident - the triple homicide at the nightclub. It looked like everything was there: the Detective Division's follow-up reports, his report on the injury to Kevin King, a Use of Force report, the IADs investigative file, and the hospital's file for King. He flipped through the pages, only quickly scanning them.

He closed up the file and clicked on the button to download it to the laptop's hard drive. He'd read it carefully later. Right now, though, he wanted to talk to Marley.

He left the condo and made the short drive to the restaurant. He found a parking spot around the corner, walked to the door, and pushed through it into a crowd of people waiting for tables. Jostling his way to the packed bar, he squeezed into a chair between two couples he hoped weren't with each other. The bartender saw him and came straight over.

"How you doin' Sam? Get you something?"

"No thanks Bobby. I came to see Marley. She around?"

"I haven't seen her in a while," Bobby said. "She's probably helping out in the kitchen." Bobby picked up a phone from under the bar. "Want me to call and see?"

"Don't bother. I'll walk back there." Laska got out of the stool and gave the bartender a nod. "Thanks, Bobby," he said, and made his way through the crowd to the dining room.

He zig-zagged around the tables filled with people eating, talking and drinking, and headed to the kitchen. The din of the clinking glasses, flatware scraping on the china and the conversations drowned out the reggae music pumping through the dining room. When he got to the kitchen door he peeked through its small window to make sure he didn't knock over some hustling waitress. The coast was clear. He pushed through the swinging door and stepped into the steamy galley.

The room was bustling with activity. Cooks ran

between the stove and prep tables tossing food and sauces into pans. Sous chefs with food stained chef's jackets stood at stainless steel counters prepping ingredients. Two dishwashers were at the sinks scraping and rinsing platters and plates and loading them into an industrial-sized dishwasher. Waitresses grabbed full plates off warming tables, balancing them like circus jugglers, and ran back into the dining room. In the middle of it all stood Marley, directing them like a traffic cop. She noticed him and came over.

"Hi, honey," she said. "We're slammed tonight. I don't have time to hang with you."

"That's okay. I just needed to talk to you for a minute. Did you call Josie yet?"

"Not yet. I'll..."

"Coming through." A waitress with her arms full slipped between them and out the door into the dining room.

"Let's move out of the way," Marley said and pulled him off to the side. "I didn't have time to call her yet. But I promise I will."

"Make it soon, okay? I emailed my lawyer. I think we'll be leaving for Chicago in a day or two."

She smiled. "Really?"

"Yeah," he said and looked around the kitchen. "Will this place be okay without you for a week?"

"You bet. My people are the best."

"Okay, then. I'm gonna go home and search for a nice hotel."

Marley gave him a peck on the lips. "Bye, hon. I'll see you in a few hours."

Laska moved to the door. "Don't forget to call Josie," he said.

"Don't nag," she shot back.

12

DESILVA

The phone on DeSilva's desk rang. If it was the sheriff again, she wasn't going to answer it. She checked the caller ID display. It was an inter-office number, but not Wilson's. She answered it in a voice that said 'you're bothering me'.

"DeSilva."

"Lieutenant, it's Captain Haskins over at the jail."

Dammit, she thought. She forgot to pick up the visitor's print-out and the videos.

"Cap, I'm sorry. I forgot to stop by."

"No problem. I figured you were busy. I'm on my way home, so I can drop that stuff off."

"That'd be great. Thanks, Cap." She expected him to hang up but he didn't. She listened to the dead air.

Finally, he spoke again. "So, how's it going? The investigation, I mean."

What's he getting at, she wondered. "Um, like I told you earlier, the feds are in charge and we're just assisting," she said. "And, being feds, they're not telling us much."

"Yeah, I was just wondering," Haskins said. "I heard one of the FBI guys give an interview on the radio. He announced a reward for info."

"I called the feds earlier and let them know we were gonna forward all press inquiries to them. If you get any calls, you should do the same." She had also told ASAC Gleason and Deputy Marshal McCarthy about her GPS history search. But Haskins didn't need to know that.

"I'll tell my people. You know, the reward is for fifty thousand dollars."

"Doesn't surprise me. They want Nichols and whoever helped him really bad." She listened to more dead air before Haskins spoke again.

"Okay then, I'll be by in a few minutes with that stuff."

DeSilva heard the line go dead. She hung up and stared at the phone. She dismissed it with a shake of her head and went back to work. She had nearly finished checking the GPS location history of every car when Haskins' call interrupted her. She had found nothing yet. She began banging away on the computer keyboard again until Haskins showed up.

He walked into her office without knocking and tossed a manila folder on her desk. "Here you go," he said. "A printout of Nichols' visitor list, a couple of DVDs, and the camera feed from the hallway by his cell. The camera is motion activated, so you'll only see recordings of when somebody is in the hall."

"And inside his cell?"

"Nothing. No cameras pointed into the cell. The county attorney said it's a Fourth Amendment violation."

She opened the folder, quickly checked the contents, and closed it back up. "Thanks, Cap," she said.

Haskins plopped down in a chair in front of her desk. "We did a search of his cell too. Like you asked."

"Did they find anything?"

"Nothing. No contraband. But there could have been."

DeSilva leaned forward, her arms folded on the desk. "What do you mean?"

"They found a tear in the mattress. More like a seam was ripped open. He could have been hiding something in there."

"But they didn't find anything?"

"No, they pulled it apart. There was nothing in there."

"Any idea how long the tear has been there?"

"No idea. We do searches of the cells every so

often, but we don't have a set schedule. We only record a search if we find something."

"So, you can't say when or even if his cell was ever searched?"

"Oh, I think it probably was. I just can't say when."

What the fuck! DeSilva thought, but instead said, "Thanks, Cap. You've been a big help. I'll get this stuff to the FBI."

"No problem," Haskins said as he got up and walked to the door. He stopped just short and turned back. "Fifty thousand dollars," he said. He winked at her and walked out.

DeSilva sighed and shook her head. She picked up the manila envelope, put it to the side, and went back to work on the GPS program. An hour later she was done. She stared at the screen and the data in front of her. Nothing. Not a single car had been on Highway 17 until Burns discovered the bodies of the two deputy marshals while on routine patrol.

Her eyes were locked on the screen. She went over the data. The only car was Burns at 9:18 a.m. The history proved it wasn't one of DeSoto County's cars that stopped the marshals. She should be relieved. But something bothered her. Something she couldn't put her finger on.

She continued to stare at the screen, the gears in her head grinding away. She picked up the phone on her desk and dialed the jail. She needed the time Nichols was handed over to the deputy marshals.

After DeSilva was bounced around a few times, she was connected to the Inmate Discharge desk and learned that Deputy U.S. Marshals Miller and Wilkerson signed into the jail at 8:05 a.m. and signed out leaving with Jesse Nichols at 8:32 a.m.

She scratched out a quick timeline on her desk blotter. Miller and Wilkerson took custody of Nichols at 8:32. Give them 5 to 10 minutes to get to their car and secure Nichols in the back seat. Then another 20 minutes to drive to the point they pulled onto the shoulder of Highway 17. That makes the time 9:02 a.m. at the latest. Burns arrived 16 minutes later.

That's 16 minutes to walk up, kill the two marshals, get Nichols out of the back seat and drive away. Sixteen minutes. *I'll bet Burns doesn't realize how close he came to driving up on a double homicide in progress*, she thought.

She looked down at the timeline scribbled on her blotter. She picked up the phone and called dispatch.

"Communications Division," said the voice.

"This is Lieutenant DeSilva over in CID," she said. "I need the time the double homicide on Highway 17 was called in this morning."

"Sure L-T, hang on a sec," said the voice. DeSilva heard muffled voices in the background and then silence. When the voice came back on he said, "We got the timestamp reading 9:26 a.m."

"You're sure?" DeSilva said. "9:26?"

"Yes ma'am. Positive. Car 124 called it in at 9:26."

"Thanks, I'm gonna need a hold on the recording of that call."

"Yes ma'am. Got it. Anything else?"

"No, thanks," she said and hung up.

She looked at her timeline again and then the phone. She thought about calling the sheriff's office. *Fuck him*, she thought and pulled out her cellphone. She punched in the saved number and waited,

"Hello, lieutenant," Deputy Marshal Michael McCarthy answered. Caller ID had clued him in.

"McCarthy, where are you?" she said.

"Getting ready to leave the scene. We're all done here."

"Are you going back to Fort Myers?"

"No, well, some of us are. The rest are sticking around. We have a mobile command center coming in. We were hoping to park it in your lot."

"I don't think the sheriff would be opposed, but you'd better ask him."

"Yeah, I'll do that. You got something for me?"

"I've finished the GPS search on all our cars, and I've worked out a timeline."

"Yeah?"

DeSilva paused, then said, "How soon can you be in my office?"

"Bad news?"

"I don't know," she said.

"I'll leave now."

"You know where we're at?"

"I've got Google," he said.

"Second floor," DeSilva said. "I'll be waiting."

13

DESILVA AND MCCARTHY

McCarthy gave a courtesy rap on the door frame before walking into DeSilva's office. He closed the door behind him. DeSilva was sitting behind her desk with her eyes locked on the LCD screen of the computer and swiveled around when he came in. "You got here fast," she said.

"I've got a heavy foot. Or so my wife says." He plopped down in the chair across from her and leaned forward, his forearms resting on his legs. "So, what've you got?"

"What I've got could be something," she said. "Or it could be nothing." She twirled her chair to face the computer again. "Come around this side."

McCarthy did as he was told and stood next to her looking down at the screen. DeSilva pulled up the GPS history of Deputy Burns and pointed at the screen. "Burns was the only car out on Highway 17 today. He arrived at 9:18." She showed him the timeline she scribbled on her blotter. "Miller and Wilkerson left the jail at 8:32. I figure about 30 minutes to get Nichols secured in their car and drive out to that spot. It would make that about 9:02 when they were pulled over. That means about 16 minutes to...to-"

McCarthy helped her finish the sentence. "Murder Miller and Wilkerson."

"Yeah," she said in a voice barely audible. She exhaled deeply and continued. "Sixteen minutes to murder them, get Nichols out of the back seat, and drive him out of there without being seen."

McCarthy pointed a finger at the screen. "And according to the GPS on Burns' car, he came from the direction of Arcadia."

"Yeah," DeSilva said. "Which means they made their getaway in the opposite direction, or they would have been spotted."

"If Burns was paying attention."

"I think he would have remembered any other law enforcement vehicle on that stretch of road. Obviously, according to the GPS, one of ours wasn't there. And an Arcadia PD car would stick out because that's outside the city limits."

"Okay," McCarthy said. "Then they fled southwest on 17. Seems logical. And sixteen minutes sounds like enough time. It's cutting it close, but it's not like they could plan on Burns coming along."

"That's what I thought."

McCarthy walked back around the desk. "Then why am I here?"

DeSilva made a face like she was about to chew on broken glass. "I checked the time Burns called it in. 9:26. It took him eight minutes."

"Eight minutes?"

'Yeah, eight minutes to walk up to the car, see two dead bodies, and call it in to dispatch."

McCarthy plopped down in his chair. "That's a fucking eternity."

"And that's my 'something'." DeSilva hitched her chair closer to the desk and leaned in. "What if my timeline is wrong? What if it took Miller and Wilkerson longer to get Nichols into the car or they stopped for gas or something? What if they weren't pulled over until 9:18?"

"You think Burns killed Miller and Wilkerson and sprung Nichols?"

"I don't think anything yet. I'm just asking a question. And I'm trying to figure out why there's an eight-minute gap between Burns arriving and calling it in."

McCarthy opened his mouth but was interrupted by his ringing cell phone. "I need to get this," he said to DeSilva as he unhooked the phone from his belt. Without waiting for DeSilva to answer, he punched a button on the screen and brought it up to his ear. "McCarthy," he said.

DeSilva sat and eavesdropped on McCarthy's end of the conversation. It was short. After listening to the voice on the other end for only seconds he said, "Okay, go ahead. I'll be there in a few." He punched another button on the screen and reattached the phone to his belt.

McCarthy folded his arms across his chest. "You obviously didn't talk to Burns yet. Did you talk to your sheriff about this?"

"No. He'd have us drag Burns in here in handcuffs before we had all the facts. I need a lot more before I'm gonna accuse anyone of murder. Especially a cop."

"You're right," he said. He stood and pulled a set of keys from his pocket. "You up for a ride?"

"Where to?"

"We're executing the search warrant on Nichols' house."

DeSilva pushed away from her desk. "Lead the way."

McCARTHY PULLED out of the lot, made a couple of quick turns, and headed westbound on Hickory Street, the navigation system of the car directing him. They sat quiet for the first few minutes until McCarthy said, "What's your deal, DeSilva?"

"My deal?"

"Yeah. Tell me about yourself."

"You trying to be my friend?"

"No, nothing like that. Just making conversation."

"I'm sure." She shifted over in her seat and stared out her side window. "Okay," she said, "what the hell." She turned back to McCarthy. "I was an orphan. I was adopted by a man and grew up on a farm not far from here. That life wasn't for me, so when I turned eighteen, I left. I put myself through college and, after I graduated, I applied for the sheriff's department. And here I am."

"This man that adopted you, he was the same one Nichols worked for, right? The one that ran the harvesting business dealing in human trafficking? You busted him and Nichols."

DeSilva gave him a look that would whither an orange grove. "And another of his adopted daughters," she said. "My step-sister."

"And you shot your step-brother. Killed him."

"He was trying to kill someone."

"Yeah, I know." McCarthy said.

"You're a real asshole, McCarthy."

"So my wife says." The navigation system began spouting directions. McCarthy followed along and made the turns.

"Was that some kind of test?" DeSilva asked, her words covered in frost.

"No. Well, maybe. I guess I wanted you to know."

"Know what? I already assumed you had the file."

"That I trust you."

DeSilva shifted in her seat and watched out the front window as McCarthy pulled to the curb near Nichols' house. "I don't think I care anymore," she said.

Government vehicles, double parked and facing every which way, crowded the street. A team of marshals wearing tactical gear and helmets were already loading a battering ram and other entry equipment into a black van. FBI agents, including ASAC Gleason, and deputy marshals milled about on the lawn and sidewalk in front of Nichols' home.

McCarthy and DeSilva exited the SUV. McCarthy asked her to hang back a minute while he talked to Gleason. DeSilva leaned back against the SUV and listened to the tick of the hot engine as it cooled. She watched as McCarthy and Gleason talked and tried to read their lips, but they turned their backs to her. All she could see was a lot of pointing at the house and nodding and shaking of their heads.

McCarthy looked back and called her over with a wave of his hand.

"He okay with me being here?" she said walking up.

"It doesn't matter. You're with me. Let's go inside," he said.

They walked across the lawn, matted with dead grass and crammed with weeds, and into the house. DeSilva looked over the door as they passed through. "Forced entry, huh?" she said to McCarthy.

"Yeah," McCarthy said. "No one home according to Gleason."

"Nichols has a wife and daughter," she said.

McCarthy shrugged and walked into the living room. DeSilva followed and stood next to him. It was a small place and not to DeSilva's style with a pair of plaid recliners parked in front of a TV too big for the room. The rest was furnished in early Target with mismatched lamps and cheap prints of fruit and horses on the walls.

"Okay if I look around?" she said to McCarthy.

"Go ahead. It looks like the search team is finished," he said.

She walked from room to room, going first to the dining room, then through the kitchen, and finishing with the two small bedrooms. She took her time and paid close attention to the closets and dresser drawers and under the vanity in the bathroom. When she wandered back to the living room, McCarthy was still there - standing in nearly the same spot she had left him staring at the phone in his hand.

"That answers the question about his wife and daughter," she said.

McCarthy clipped his phone to his belt and turned his head to her. "How so?" he said.

"Judging from the thick layer of dust on everything, they left a while ago and haven't been back. Probably left around the time Nichols was arrested."

"Yeah?"

"Yeah, and her clothes are gone. The daughter's too. The only thing in the drawers and closets are men's clothes. There's a pile of dirty dishes in the sink too. But the kicker is the note she left."

McCarthy's eyes widened. "The search team missed a note?"

"I don't think so," she said and smiled. "It's on the bathroom mirror in lipstick. It says, 'Rot in hell, asshole'."

"I guess that means she won't be able to help us find him. If we can even find her."

"Yeah," she said. She looked around the room again then at her watch. "We done here? I should get back. I've gotta tell the sheriff about Burns."

"Yeah, about that," he said. "While you were poking around, I texted my guys. You were right about miscalculating your timeline."

"What do you mean?"

"Our cars have GPS too. Miller and Wilkerson stopped at 8:59."

"That's three minutes earlier than I figured. That means Burns didn't get there until 21 minutes later. It couldn't have been him." She felt a cool, calm wave of relief come over her.

"No, it couldn't have been him."

DeSilva stood thinking. She took a step closer to McCarthy. "Wait, so you just now thought to check their GPS?" she said.

"No, that was one of the first things we did. I just double-checked it when you were walking around."

The calm feeling of relief evaporated. DeSilva felt a hot flush rising from her neck up to her face. She took another step. "You knew back in my office and you left me hanging all this time?"

McCarthy held up his hands like he was warding off her approach. "Hey, I was about to tell you when I got the call that they were ready to execute the search warrant."

She gave him a look like she was wondering where she was going to bury him later and said, "You could have said something in the car instead of running your little game on me."

McCarthy shrugged.

"You're a real dick," she said. McCarthy opened his mouth but she beat him to it. "I know, so your wife keeps telling you." She spun around and headed to the door.

14

JESSE NICHOLS

"Where the fuck you been?" Nichols said to the guy walking through the door.

The guy scanned the room and finally picked up the figure in the corner of the room. "Why are you standing in the dark?" He clicked on a wall switch and a lamp in the corner lit up.

"I didn't know if it was safe," Nichols said.

"It's safe. There's no one near enough to worry about."

"Okay, now I know." He took a step closer. "What took you so long?"

The guy tossed the small black leather satchel he was carrying at Nichols' feet. "I had to go back to work, didn't I? I had to get the phone, right? And then you wanted me to get this. Well, there it is."

Nichols picked up the bag and dropped himself

onto the sofa. He set the bag on his lap and unzipped it. He dug through it, checking the contents making sure everything was still there.

He looked up at the guy. "What about the pistol? Did you get it from Jasper?"

"Oh, yeah." The guy lifted his shirt and pulled out a pistol. A Glock model 17. "Here ya go." He tossed it to Nichols.

Nichols snatched the weapon in midair. "Fucker. There's one in the chamber. You're lucky it didn't go off."

The guy laughed. "No, you are." He stepped over to a chair and stood there watching Nichols. "That's your bug out bag, huh?" he said.

"An insurance policy," Nichols said, placing the pistol in the bag.

"Yeah, turned out to be a good idea." The guy pulled a cellphone from his pocket. "Here," he said and tossed it to Nichols. "Your burner."

Nichols caught it on the fly. "No problem getting it?"

"In the mattress right where you said it was. It was easier than getting your bag."

"What do you mean?"

The guy plopped down onto the recliner and dropped his car keys on an end table. "The G was at your house doing a search. I had to wait until they cleared out. Oh, and that lieutenant was there with them. DeSilva."

"Fucking dyke," Nichols muttered.

The guy continued. "It was dark by the time I snuck in. Couldn't see shit in the dark. I was lucky I found the bathroom."

Nichols smiled. "And they didn't find my bag."

"Nope," the guy said. "A false bottom in the vanity. Pretty slick. Your wife left you a note too."

"Yeah?"

"On the bathroom mirror. Said you should rot in hell."

"Dirty bitch," Nichols said and went back to digging around in his bag.

The guy watched him pushing things around inside. "Where'd you get those IDs?" he asked.

Nichols stopped and eyeballed the guy. "You looked in my bag?"

The guy snorted. "You really think I wouldn't?"

Nichols pulled out a wad of cash from his bag. He snapped off the rubber band that bound it together and started flipping through the bills.

"It's all there. But go ahead, count it. And when you're done, you can pay me what you owe me."

Nichols stopped counting and looked up but said nothing.

"That's the deal, right?" the guy said.

"Right," Nichols said and went back to tallying the cash.

The guy watched Nichols finish up his count and begin separating the bills into their denominations.

"You've got a driver's license and a passport. Your picture with a different name. How'd you get those? They look really good."

Nichols answered without looking up. "The Cordeles. They had to make all the illegals look legit for the state inspectors. Everyone had to have an ID. When I decided I might need a way out at some point, I had Addie Cordele make 'em up for me."

"But the blank cards, where'd they get..."

"Addie had a lot of friends. She had a way of getting anything she wanted. Why?"

"I dunno, maybe I should get some."

"Yeah," Nichols said. "But not from the Cordeles anymore." He finished separating the bills and left them on the sofa. He looked over to the guy. "Hey, where's your pistol?"

"It's in my car. In the glove box. Why?"

"Just wondering," Nichols said. He walked over to the window and peeked out at the guy's car parked out front. He turned and glanced over to the guy and the car keys on the side table and pulled his burner from his pocket.

The guy looked a question at Nichols.

"I'm gonna call Jasper," Nichols said.

"You think that's a good idea?"

"You didn't talk to him, did you?"

"No."

"Okay then. He's gonna want to know everything

is cool." He dialed and waited for Jasper Dunlop to answer.

"Whatever," the guy said. He grabbed the remote and clicked on the television. The pale blue glow of the old tube TV filled the room. He flipped through the channels until he found a news broadcast and turned up the volume.

Nichols' connection went through. "What?" he said into the phone. "I can't hear you. Hang on a minute." Nichols covered the phone with his hand and yelled over the TV at the guy. "Are you fucking deaf?"

The guy kept his eyes on the television and dismissed Nichols with a flick of his hand.

"Asshole," Nichols muttered and walked out of the room. He stopped in the kitchen. "Jasper?" he said into the phone.

"Yeah, Jesse. Everything good?"

"So far."

"Where are you?"

"Some trailer near the Peace River. The guy said it's his fishing cabin."

"When are you going to move?"

"The plan was to take his boat down the river to Charlotte Harbor at dawn."

"Smart. Less risk than driving. So, you'll meet the boat tomorrow?"

"No."

"No? What are you talking about?"

"I'm not going to the Caymans. Not yet."

"Jesse..."

"I've got unfinished business. Where'd my wife take my daughter?"

"I don't know. I asked around. As far as I can tell, she didn't let anyone know where they were going."

"Look for them."

"I'll keep trying, Jesse. But you can't risk hanging around..."

"I want something else, too. I need you to get me that address."

"We talked about this already. Don't do it, Jesse. It's not worth it. Just get out of the country and start over again. This is a second chance for you."

"Don't tell me what to do, Jasper. Give me his address. And the girlfriend's too."

Jasper Dunlop sighed and made sure Nichols heard it. "Okay," he said. "Laska's address is in the investigative file but not the girlfriend's. I'll have to get back to you on that. Hang on."

It took only a minute for Dunlop to find Laska's address. "You got a pencil?" he said.

Nichols looked around and found a pen and pocket-sized spiral notebook in the kitchen junk drawer. "Go ahead," he said.

Nichols scribbled the address down and tore the paper from the notebook.

"This is a bad idea, Jesse," Dunlop said. "How are you gonna get there anyway?"

"The guy's car."

"Is he okay with that? Did you ask him?

"He won't care."

"Damn it, Jesse. You're going to get caught."

"You better hope I don't. Call me when you find the girlfriend. You remember her name?"

"Gabrielle Jones, right?"

"Yeah, but she goes by Marley."

Nichols ended the call and walked to the bathroom. He grabbed a towel and headed back to the living room. He went straight to his bag.

The guy was still in his chair, his eyes glued to the TV. He glanced at Nichols then back to the TV and said, "We made the top story on the news. The FBI announced a fifty-thousand-dollar reward."

Nichols ignored him. He pulled the Glock 17 from the bag and wrapped the towel around his hand and the gun. He walked over to the guy.

"What's with the towel?" the guy said.

Nichols fired two muffled shots into his chest and finished with one to the head. "Walls are thin," he said.

15

LASKA

L aska was up before Marley. And the sun. He wandered into the kitchen and put on a pot of coffee. While he waited for it to brew he sat down in front of Marley's laptop and pecked out a quick email to Rebecca Stafford.

He let her know he'd be leaving for Chicago in the next day or two and didn't need an airline reservation. He was going to drive. He hit the 'send' button and closed up the laptop.

He spent his time waiting for Marley to wake up, sipping coffee, and watching television. He found an old western, "High Noon", and watched it with the closed captioning on.

It was almost eleven when Marley got out of bed. She wandered into the kitchen where Laska was putting on a second pot of coffee.

"Good morning, hon. You look great," he said.

She gave him a sleepy smile. "I look like crap. But thanks for pretending."

"I'm not making it up. You'd even look great in a plastic garbage bag."

"That'd be a real fashion statement."

He walked over and gave her a peck on the lips. "It could catch on. White plastic during the summer. Black for evening wear."

"You can never go wrong with a little black plastic garbage bag, huh?"

"Sure," he smiled. "You want a cup of coffee?" He opened a cabinet and took out a cup.

"No, I think I'd rather have a cup of tea."

"Go sit, I'll make it. And how about some breakfast?"

"I don't think so. Maybe later." She settled onto a barstool at the small kitchen peninsula.

"You sure? You might not be hungry but little Bruno could be."

"Gawd! Don't call him that."

"Sorry, you're right. It could be a girl. What's the feminine version of Bruno? Bruna?"

"I'm warning you, Sam."

"Okay, okay." He put a kettle of water on and opened the fridge. "How about some eggs? Scrambled? You could order them some other way, but they'll just turn out scrambled."

"You win. I'll eat something. How about oatmeal?"

"You need protein. Scrambled it is."

"Okay, chef. Whatever you say." She sat, arms folded on the counter, and watched Sam move around the kitchen making her tea and eggs. She tried not to butt in when he burned the first batch of eggs and had to start over.

He caught her trying to cover a smile with her hand as he set her breakfast in front of her. She picked up her fork and pushed the eggs around on the plate. "They look a little...crispy," she said.

"Sorry, I'm still learning. You want me to try again?"

She pushed the plate off to the side. "Tell you what, give me ten, and we'll go out for breakfast."

"I'm good with that," he said. Marley headed back to the bedroom while Sam scraped the eggs into the garbage. After piling the dishes and frying pan in the sink, he went back to the laptop to check his email.

Rebecca Stafford had written him back.

Mr. LASKA, *Driving to Chicago? Are you afraid to fly? (LOL!). Make sure to save your gas receipts. I'll submit them and see if we can get you reimbursed. What about a hotel room once you get here? Should I make the arrangements? Let me know. I'm sure we'll talk again before you get here. Drive safe. – Rebecca*

. . .

HE READ it over again and was about to type out a reply when Marley called out letting him know she was ready. He closed up the laptop and met her at the front door. Fifteen minutes later, they sat in a booth at the Oasis Café on Osprey Avenue just south of Siesta Drive.

Sam's face contorted in mock disgust as Marley ordered a yogurt parfait with berries and granola. He ordered wheat bread lightly toasted and two sides of bacon.

"Don't give me that look, buster," she said. "And you'd better start eating healthier yourself. You don't want to have a heart attack before you ever meet your child."

Sam tried to blow her off with a shrug and a frown.

"You don't think it can happen?" she said.

"I had a physical last year. The doc said I'm the picture of health."

"That was a year ago, Sam." She glanced down at his stomach. "You're starting to put on weight."

He smiled. "Look at us," he said. "We're already going at it like an old married couple."

She smiled back. "Don't start."

"You're right," he said as the waitress returned with their food.

Before the girl left them, Sam began constructing a bacon-packed sandwich. Marley waited for the girl to leave before dipping her spoon into the sundae glass full of yogurt and fruit.

After chewing up his first mouthful, Sam said, "Did you talk to Josie about filling in for you?"

"Yes, I did," she said.

"Good, because I'd like to leave tomorrow."

Marley stopped, a spoonful of yogurt and granola midway to her mouth. "Really?

"Yeah, is that okay?"

"Did you make reservations with an airline already?"

"No, I thought we'd drive." He took another bite of his sandwich.

"Drive? How far is it? How long will it take?"

Sam held up a 'wait-a-minute' finger while he chewed. He swallowed and said, "Twelve hundred miles or so. It'll take about twenty hours if we keep the stops for gas and food short."

"You want to drive all night?"

"No, we'll stop somewhere overnight. Get a motel room. Maybe somewhere in the Smoky Mountains. That's about the halfway point." He watched her eat the spoonful of yogurt and granola and then another. "What do you think?" he said.

She continued to munch on her breakfast as she thought about it. "I've only seen pictures of mountains. Yeah, I think it can be fun. That would be cool. But why don't you want to fly? I've never been on an airplane. I was kind of looking forward to it."

"Well, for one, it'll be cheaper. Getting a flight on short notice is expensive. The city would be billed for my flight, but we'd have to pay for yours. For two, I thought since you've never really been anywhere, this would give you a chance to see a lot more of the country. Except for Indiana, it's a beautiful drive."

Marley wiped her mouth with a napkin and smiled at him. "Are you afraid to fly, Sam?"

"What? No, that's silly."

She pushed the empty bowl aside and leaned in. Her eyes sparkled as she teased him. "You're turning fifty shades of red."

"No. No, I'm not." He held up a spoon and tried to catch his own reflection.

Marley slapped her hands down on the table and grinned. "You're afraid," she said. "You're afraid to fly." The noise startled an old couple in the booth across from them.

Sam jerked forward and whispered. "Shh, keep it down." He looked around the café. "I swear, I'm not afraid of flying."

Marley sat back. "No?"

"No." He looked around again. "What I'm afraid of is plummeting thirty-five thousand feet, crashing into the ground and bursting into a ball of flames."

Marley sat back and smiled. Sam smiled back and said, "Don't look so smug."

"Smug? Not me. I'm just...satisfied," she said.

"The very definition," he said. "Listen, you've

never flown. You don't know what it's like. You have to sit there doing nothing. Waiting to fall out of the sky. You have no control at all."

"Sam, there are hundreds if not thousands of flights every day all over the world. I'm sure it's completely safe. I've even read it's safer than driving."

Sam repeated, "You just sit there waiting to fall out of the sky. Waiting to die."

Marley knew she wasn't going to win. "So," she said, "what's wrong with Indiana?"

16

DESILVA

DeSilva woke up alone. She heard her wife Bobbie rattling around in the kitchen. After a quick trip to the bathroom she joined her.

"Hey, sleepy-head," Bobbie said. "Want a cup of coffee?"

"Please," she said as she yawned. She pulled a chair out for herself and plopped down at the table.

Bobbie filled a cup and set it in front of DeSilva. She gently brushed a wisp of DeSilva's hair off her forehead and tucked it behind an ear. "Tough day yesterday, huh?" she said as she sat down across from her.

"Yeah. You saw the news?"

"Yes. It's horrible. Those poor men. Did they have families?

DeSilva took a sip of coffee. "Yes." She looked at her wife. "Both did."

"I'm so sorry," Bobbie said and took her wife's hand.

"Me too." She looked into Bobbie's eyes and gave her hand a squeeze.

Bobbie pulled her hand away. "I know that look. You're going into work today."

"I have to."

"It's your day off. It's *our* day off. That hardly ever happens anymore. We were going to hang out, maybe grab dinner and a movie. I was looking forward to it."

"So was I. But I have to go in."

"I thought the news said the FBI was in charge. It's their investigation."

"It is. But --"

Bobbie stood, her hands on her hips. "But you can't let it go. You have to stick your nose in. You have to do what you always do."

"It's not like that, Bobbie. I have things to do. Things the FBI and marshals need from us. Things that only the sheriff's department can do."

"And no one else there can do them?"

DeSilva looked up at her wife. "No, they can't."

DeSilva pulled into the parking lot of the sheriff's

department. It was overflowing with cruisers and personal vehicles. She had to circle the building twice before finding a spot because two over-sized RVs parked in the back of the lot hoarding half the parking spots. The sheriff had obviously given his permission to the feds. She wedged her car into a tight spot between two cruisers and squeezed out her door. She started toward the white RV marked with 'U.S. Marshal's Service' in big blue lettering. Halfway across the lot she thought of her last conversation with McCarthy. *Screw it*, she thought. If he needed something, he could come to her. She did an about-face and headed into her building.

As she breezed past the front desk, one of the deputies called out to her. The sheriff wanted her in his office ASAP.

"Bad mood?" she asked.

"He sounded pretty happy to me," was the answer.

She slipped past the stairs that led to the second floor and her office, walked down the narrow hallway and into the sheriff's outer office. Deputy Whimple was sitting at his desk and jumped out of his seat when he saw her. He hurried over and stood in front of the door to the sheriff's private office. He stood there chest out and thumbs hooked on his gun belt.

"Can I help you, Lieutenant?"

DeSilva walked up and stood toe-to-toe with him. "Out of my way, Donny. The sheriff wants me."

"Is it an urgent matter?"

She inched closer, her nose almost touching his. "What he wants me for is none of your business. Now get out of my way before I rip your balls off and make you swallow them whole."

"I'm supposed to announce you. And anyway, he's with someone," he said.

She feinted a punch to his crotch and he instinctively flinched, reaching down to protect himself. She elbowed him away and went through the door.

Sheriff Wilson was seated behind his desk. Across from him was Deputy Marshal Mike McCarthy. The sheriff looked over to DeSilva. "Lieutenant, come on in. Take a seat." He pointed to the chair next to McCarthy.

Don Whimple followed DeSilva in. "Sir, Lieutenant DeSilva pushed past me. And..."

"Shut the fuck up, Donny. Get out and close the door behind you," Wilson said.

Whimple skulked away and DeSilva grabbed the chair next to McCarthy. Sending a message, she pulled it further away from him, gave him her best scowl, and sat. McCarthy returned the favor by giving her his best 'I know something you don't' smile.

The smile confused her, but she turned her

attention to the sheriff. "What did you need, boss?" she said to Wilson.

"Not a lot," he said. "We're in the clear thanks to your work, right?"

"As far as one of our deputies being directly involved? Yes, I believe so. Deputy McCarthy confirmed that also." She made sure to keep her eyes on Wilson and ignore McCarthy. "But there's still work to do."

"What's that?" Wilson said.

"Obviously, Nichols had help. So he must have had a way to plan or coordinate with them. I've got video from Captain Haskins over at the jail to review. I want to see if Nichols had any lengthy contact with a guard or anyone else. We need to double check with the Arcadia PD. Then there's Nichols' lawyer, Jasper Dunlop. We need to talk--"

"Wait a minute. Back up," Wilson said. He rolled his chair closer to his desk and leaned in towards DeSilva. "Are you saying one of our jail guards might be in on this?"

"I don't know. But it's an avenue we need to pursue," she said.

"So I'm not in the clear?"

"None of our deputies were involved, sir."

"But the county jail is still my responsibility. Those guards are sworn members of the sheriff's department."

"Yes sir. I know. But..."

"When will you know?" Wilson said.

"I was on my way to review the tapes when I was told you wanted to see me."

He waved a hand as if he were pushing her words out of the way. "How long will it take?"

"I don't know. There's a lot of video to review."

"Then it's good you'll have help."

"Sir?" DeSilva said.

"You're being detailed to the U.S. Marshal's office. You'll be under the supervision of Deputy McCarthy."

DeSilva looked from Wilson to McCarthy and back again to Wilson. "Why...when did you decide--"

McCarthy interrupted her. "It's at my request," he said. "Sheriff Wilson was gracious enough to honor it."

DeSilva ignored McCarthy and kept her eyes on Wilson. She moved to the edge of her seat. "I thought we wanted to keep our investigation in house. Independent of the FBI and marshal's office."

"I did," Wilson said. "But the deputy here convinced me it would be best to work together. Join forces, as it were."

"That way," McCarthy said, "it will be the sheriff's office that is seen as bringing the investigation to a successful conclusion. With our assistance, of course." He shifted in his seat to face DeSilva. "The marshal's office doesn't care who gets the credit. We just want Nichols and his accomplices captured."

DeSilva finally turned to face McCarthy. Her face told him exactly what she was thinking.

Wilson stood. "I think we're done here. Can you excuse us, Deputy McCarthy?" he said. "I'd like to speak with my lieutenant."

"Absolutely," McCarthy said as he stood. He shook the sheriff's hand, nodded to DeSilva and left the office.

Wilson leaned back in his chair and folded his hands behind his head. DeSilva sat back and waited.

"This is good for us, Lieutenant," he said. "We've got no downside here. Even more so if a jail employee is involved. When Nichols and whoever helped him gets caught, we look good. We'll be crucial in bringing the perps to justice. If Nichols' accomplice is a sheriff's department employee, we cleaned our own house. All good headlines."

"And if they're never caught, the feds are to blame. It's their fuck up," DeSilva said.

"See," he said smiling. "You get it."

DeSilva folded her arms across her chest. "You know, the feds have an ulterior motive too."

"And what would that be?"

"I don't know yet. Maybe the old 'keep your enemies close' move. Maybe for us to be the goat if everything goes to shit. Whatever their reason is, it's for their benefit and not ours."

Wilson brought his arms down and rested them on his desk. "You'll need to stay on your toes. Watch your back." He lowered his voice. "And keep me in the loop. I want to know everything they do. Understand?"

"Yes sir," she said.

"Alright, Lieutenant. You're dismissed."

DeSilva rose and left the room. Wilson smiled to himself. If everything worked out, he and the department would be heroes. And if it went to shit, he would still be in the clear. He had himself a scapegoat.

17

DESILVA AND MCCARTHY

DeSilva walked through the sheriff's outer office. She ignored the stink-eye Whimple was giving her from his seat behind his desk and headed into the hallway. McCarthy was waiting for her there. She breezed past him.

"DeSilva," he said as he started after her.

She picked up the pace, hit the stairwell and took the stairs two at a time.

McCarthy hurried to catch up. "Hey," he called after her. "Hang on."

She stopped on the landing between the floors and spun around. "What kind of game are you playing, McCarthy?"

He stepped onto the landing. "I'm not playing a game. I asked for you because I want your help."

"For what? You're the United States Marshal's

Office. You and the FBI have unlimited resources. Unlimited manpower. What do you need us for?"

"I don't want the DeSoto County Sheriff's Department's help. I want your help."

"Okay, why?"

"You're good. You know your stuff."

"Don't patronize me. It's not gonna work. I'll say it again, why me? Why not all of the sheriff's office. Why not any of my people?"

McCarthy leaned back against the railing and crossed his arms. "Three reasons. First, you know Nichols. You worked with him. You probably know how he thinks.

"Second, you know the area. None of our people, including me, are from around here. Most of us aren't even from Florida. You have more contacts and relationships than any of us. I suspect people around here trust you.

"And third, you know how to conduct an investigation. You know what steps to take, what's important and what's not. And you want to catch Nichols almost as much as we do. Maybe more." He uncrossed his arms, took a step towards her, and put his hands in his pockets. "And you want to catch whoever helped him before we do."

"Why would I care who makes the arrest?" she said.

"Because your sheriff does. He's a politician and doesn't want to be embarrassed."

"You think I give a shit about him?"

"No, but you don't want to be his scapegoat either. That's what he's setting you up for if this goes south. You understand that, right?"

"Of course. Like you said, he's a fucking politician. They take all of the credit and none of the blame. But if it wasn't for you requesting that I be assigned to you, I wouldn't be in this position. And that makes me think you want me for the same reason."

"I don't. I swear." He held a hand over his heart and the other up in the air.

"Put your hand down," she said and put her hands on her hips. "Alright. I don't have a choice here. I'm assigned to you, and I'll give you my best. But," she pointed a finger at him, "you lie to me or hide something from me again and you get nothing from me. I'll park my ass in a chair and play solitaire all day. Got it?"

"I got it," he said.

"And I don't work for you. I work with you. Equal footing. Right?"

"Right."

"Okay then," she said. "What about my people, my detectives?"

"You can use them to do your legwork or for housekeeping issues. But I've gotta insist they stay out of the loop."

"I can live with that," she said. "Come on." She

climbed the remaining steps to the second floor and headed to her office.

McCarthy fell into step next to her. "It looks like you've got a plan already," he said. "What's up?"

"No plan, but a few things to follow up on. What about you?"

DeSilva moved behind her desk but didn't sit. McCarthy followed her into her office and plopped down in a chair. "I was going to pay a visit to Nichols' lawyer. Thought you might like to come along," he said.

"I would. But I've got to handle a few things first."

"Like what? Maybe my people can do it."

"First, we have to check with the Arcadia P.D. and ask them for the GPS history on their cars."

"Easy enough for us to do."

"Okay, good. Next, I was going to review these DVDs." She pulled the pair of disks from a drawer and held them up. "These are copies of the video feed from outside Nichols' jail cell. I wanted to see if he had any extended contact or conversations with any jail personnel."

"Important but time consuming. Again, my people can do that. We've got a good setup in the mobile HQ."

"Alright. I gotta tell you, I don't mind jobbing that one out to you." She started digging through the manila envelope Captain Haskins delivered to her.

"Dammit," she said as she pulled the papers from the envelope and flipped through them.

"Something wrong?" McCarthy said.

"Yeah, the captain over at the jail was supposed to give me a printout of the personnel assignments so I could match the video's timestamp to the names of the guards who were working." She dropped the papers on her desk. "I guess he forgot. I should go get them."

McCarthy stood. "I'll go with you. Then we can head over to the lawyer."

"Sounds good. Here." She handed the DVDs to McCarthy. "You want to drop these off at your command post and get them started on it?"

"Sure, let's go."

They left the building and made the short trek across the parking lot to the RV marked with the marshal's logo. It sat side-by-side to the FBI's RV in the back of the lot.

DeSilva glanced over at it. "What's the FBI doing?" she said. "Are you coordinating with them on all this?"

"Not really," McCarthy said. "They do their thing, and we do ours. If something big breaks, we're supposed to let each other know. But..." he shrugged the rest of his answer.

"So, what are they doing? Are they running a parallel investigation? Are we wasting our time doing things they already did?"

"Not likely. They're following the FBI playbook. They offered the reward, and now they're manning telephones waiting for tips to come in."

"Are they getting any?"

"Oh yeah. Every kook wants you to think they know something when you dangle fifty-thousand dollars in front of them."

"That's it? That's all they're doing? Following up on phone tips?"

"For now. They're waiting for the analysis reports on the evidence collected from the scene too."

"That's not going to help them find Nichols." She shook her head in disbelief.

"I hear ya," he said. He pulled a set of keys from his pocket and unlocked the door of the RV. He climbed in and beckoned DeSilva to follow him.

They stood at the front of the long, narrow vehicle. DeSilva had never been in a mobile command center before. Her head swiveled back and forth and front to back.

Deputy marshals sat back-to-back along each side at built-in desks crammed with computers, telephones, and other electronic equipment she had never seen before. Overhead above each workstation were shelves lined with binders and manuals, as well as doors and drawers that held who knows what. Along the back wall was a tall, built-in cabinet with a heavy steel bar across the front and a very serious lock protecting its contents. The weapons locker, she guessed.

"Wait here," McCarthy said. He walked down the center aisle to the back of the room tapping several of the seated deputies on the shoulder as he went.

Each of those deputies instantly rose and joined him in the back. They stood attentively in a small circle around McCarthy. He handed the disks to one of the deputies and spoke to each of them, one at a time. Within moments, he rejoined DeSilva.

"Okay," he said. "Assignments delivered and understood. We're good to go."

"Without a single question?" DeSilva said as they left the command center.

"They're all ex-military," he said. "They don't question much." He handed a set of keys to DeSilva. "You know the way, you drive."

DeSilva took the keys and followed him to a black Chevy Suburban with full dark tint on every window. She looked at the SUV and back to McCarthy. "I hope my feet reach the pedals," she joked.

Minutes later they pulled into the jail's guest parking lot. A few more minutes had them walking through the door to the office of Captain Haskins. He looked up from his desk as they were ushered in by an aide. "Lieutenant, how goes the investigation?" he said. "And you are?" He stood and stuck out his hand which McCarthy shook.

DeSilva made a quick introduction of McCarthy and said, "It's going slow. And that's why we're here. You forgot to include a printout of your personnel assignments. You know, so we can compare the videos to the personnel working."

Haskins took a drag on the cigarette stuck to the corner of his lips. Smoke floated out his mouth and nose as he spoke. "Dang, sorry about that." He looked at the door and yelled, "Charles, get in here."

His aide Charles came through the door. "What's up, boss?" he said.

Haskins stubbed out his cigarette in an ashtray already overflowing with butts. "Run off a copy of the guard's schedule for Jesse Nichols' cell. Going back to the first day he was here. Make it quick, okay?"

"You got it, boss," Charles said and started out the door. He stopped short, turned back and said, "Oh, and no luck on Castillo."

"Nothing?" Haskins said. "You tried his home?"

"Yeah, we sent a car out. They said they knocked. No answer."

"Dammit. Well, keep trying."

"Yes sir," Charles said and closed the door behind him.

Haskins turned back to DeSilva and McCarthy. "So, nobody claimed the reward yet huh?" he said.

"Not for lack of trying," McCarthy said. He threw

a thumb back towards the door. "Is there some problem? Your aide mentioned 'Castillo'?"

Haskins pulled another cigarette from a pack on his desk and stuck it in his mouth. "Nothing important. Just another no-show."

"A no-show?" DeSilva said. "You mean a guard?"

"Yeah. Didn't show up for work this morning. It happens now and again."

"I take it he didn't call in sick or anything like that," McCarthy said.

"Nothing. No call," Haskins said picking up his lighter.

DeSilva and McCarthy looked at each other then back to Haskins. DeSilva said, "Was he ever assigned to Nichols?"

"I don't know. Probably though. We rotate the work assignments pretty often." Haskins raised his lighter to the cigarette glued to his lips. He stopped halfway, the flame hanging in the air as he stared past his guests to a horizon only he could see. He looked back to DeSilva. "Do you think...?"

McCarthy cut him off. "We don't think anything yet. But we can't ignore the possibility. Can you pull his personnel file for us?"

Haskins pulled the unlit cigarette from his mouth. "Charles," he howled.

18

LASKA

S am and Marley spent the rest of the morning prepping for their road trip. Marley had her list: clothes shopping, a mani-pedi, and a call to her uncle and aunt to let them know they were going to Chicago. Sam was headed to Bruno's place to pick up a couple of suitcases, and after, to get an oil change.

After dropping Marley off at her old pickup truck, he took the north bridge to Siesta Key. He followed Siesta Drive to Higel Avenue and finally to Midnight Pass Road. He pulled into a bayside complex of small villas and followed the twisting road. He jogged around dog walkers and strolling seniors and finally pulled up to his father's house.

He didn't notice the silver Ford Explorer covered in road dust parked a few doors down from his father's place as he drove past it. Nor did he notice the man slumped down in the driver's seat trying to make himself look inconspicuous. He had no reason to. There was no shortage of cars belonging to vacationers and residents around the complex.

As he pulled up to Bruno's villa, he saw a car he didn't recognize in the carport. He parked on the street and walked to the front door. He used his key to let himself in and called out to his father.

When Bruno didn't answer, he figured his father and whatever guest he had were at the pool or the clubhouse. He started towards the closed door of his father's bedroom where Bruno kept his suitcases. As he reached for the knob the door opened. Just wide enough for Bruno to stick his head out.

"Sam," Bruno said, "what are you doing here?"

Sam took a step back. Bruno's beet-red face stared back at him through wide eyes. Tiny beads of sweat dotted his forehead. "Are you okay, dad?" Sam said.

Bruno peeked back into his bedroom then back again to Sam. "I'm fine. At least I was. What are you doing here?" A soft giggle came from somewhere behind Bruno.

Sam smiled as he caught on. "Jeez, I'm sorry. I came to borrow a couple of suitcases. I called out but you didn't answer so I thought you were by the pool or something. I'll come back later." He turned to leave his father to his business.

"Hang on, Sam," Bruno said. "Wait in the living

room." He ducked back into his bedroom and closed the door.

Sam gave his father a thumbs-up without turning around. In the living room he grabbed the remote and clicked on the television and turned up the volume. He didn't want to hear anything.

Within minutes, Bruno came out of his bedroom, closing the door behind him. He had wrapped himself in a terrycloth robe and plodded up to Sam pulling two suitcases behind him. "You gotta call before you come over, Sam," he said setting the bags next to his son.

Still smiling, Sam said, "You're absolutely right, dad. I'm sorry." He nudged his father with an elbow. "So, who is she?"

"Ummm...," was all Bruno could manage as he glanced back at the bedroom door.

"It's not Josie," Sam said. "That's not her car outside." Josie, Marley's partner in the restaurant, had been on-again-off-again dating Bruno for several years. She was a stunning sixty-something with a dancer's legs and more money than God. Sam could never figure out what she saw in Bruno.

"And don't you say anything to her," Bruno shot back. "Or to Marley."

"I won't, dad. Don't worry."

"It's not like me and Josie are exclusive or anything. And anyway, this is just a one-time thing."

"I promise I'll keep it to myself." Sam chuckled.

"You know, I was a little worried when I saw you. Your face was all red and sweaty and your eyes were dilated. I thought you were sick or something."

"Naw, it's just those damn little blue pills. They really do a number on my blood pressure. You know how it is."

"I can't say that I do," Sam said laughing.

Bruno wagged a finger at him. "You will, kid. You will." Bruno shrugged and smiled. "Hey, ya gotta do what ya gotta do. Right?"

"I guess so," Sam said picking up the bags. "And thanks for these."

"No problem. Where're you going?"

"Chicago. We're leaving in the morning."

"To meet the lawyer? Marley's going too? Were you gonna tell me?"

"That's half the reason I came over. And I don't know how long we'll be gone. At least a week I think."

"What time is your flight? I could pick you up. Take you to the airport."

"Thanks, but we're driving."

Bruno cocked his head to the side and looked up at his son. "Still afraid of flying, eh?"

Sam gave his father a shrug. "I just thought Marley would like a road trip. See some nice scenery along the way. That's all."

"Yeah, I'll bet," Bruno said.

"Anyway," Sam said taking a step towards the

door, "I'll call you and let you know when we'll be back. Oh, and one more thing." He set the bags down and dug into his pocket. He pulled out a key and handed it to his father. "Can you check on the condo once in a while?"

"Sure," Bruno said taking the key. "No problem."

Sam and Bruno said their goodbyes, and Sam, with suitcases loaded in the trunk, headed off to find a quickie oil change place. Again, he didn't notice the silver Explorer that pulled out behind him and followed a few cars behind until he pulled into a Jiffy Lube on Tamiami Trail.

It was just after two in the afternoon when he got back to the condo. Marley was already there setting out piles of clothes on the bed. Sam set a suitcase next to one of the piles.

"Here you go," he said while unzipping it. "Fill her up."

Marley stood with her arms crossed and a hip cocked to one side. She looked down at the suitcase and said, "I don't think it's big enough. I won't fit all this stuff in one bag."

Laska looked at her like she had just told him they were having triplets. "You're taking all these clothes? We're only going for a week."

She looked at him. That's all she had to do.

"Okay, he said. I don't need much room. You can use half of my case." He tossed the second suitcase on the bed. "Let me pack what I need, then you can top it off."

Marley smiled. "Thanks. I hope it'll be enough."

Laska tossed the clothes he thought he'd need into the bag. They barely took a third of the case. "Think this will be enough room for you?" he asked.

"I'll make it work," Marley said.

"Good. I'm gonna call my lawyer now and see about a hotel room."

"Don't bother," she said as she continued packing. "I already made a reservation. I found a beautiful place on one of those travel websites."

Laska stopped halfway out the bedroom door. "What? Why? The lawyer said she'd do it. They're supposed to pay for the room."

"I know, but I wanted to stay someplace nice." She looked at Sam. "Do you really think they'd pick a good hotel? No, they'll pick the cheapest place they can find. This is my first vacation, and I want something nice."

She read the expression on Sam's face. "It's my treat, honey," she said.

"You know how I feel about that," Sam said. "I don't want you spending your money. If you want to stay in a nicer place, then I should pay. But you know I can't afford it."

Marley set down the dress she held and walked over to Sam.

"Sweetie, I do know how you feel. It wasn't that

long ago I didn't have much either. If it wasn't for Josie putting up the money for the restaurant, I'd still be working in the morgue and living check-to-check. But she was there for me, and things turned around.

"You've had a bad run lately, but I know you're gonna turn it around. And until you do, I'm here for you. We're in this together, Sam. What's mine is yours, and what's yours is mine."

"But I don't have anything."

"You have everything I want, honey," she said and kissed him. "Let me do this."

Sam wrapped his arms around her. "Okay, fine. But now I'm feeling..."

"Emasculated?" Marley said breaking the embrace.

"Yeah, that's the perfect word."

Marley's lips curled into a coy smile. She began unbuttoning her blouse. "I think there's something I can do about that."

Sam smiled back. "Now I feel like a gigolo."

Marley flopped back on the bed and began kicking the piles of clothes to the floor. She said, "So come on over here and do your job. Be my gigolo."

19

JESSE NICHOLS

Nichols woke up in the silver Explorer. He followed Laska from Siesta Key and watched him pull into the Jiffy Lube. He parked in a strip mall across the road from the Jiffy Lube to keep an eye on Laska and fell asleep. He missed him leaving. Laska was gone. After driving the backroads to Sarasota most of the night, he hadn't slept. He made a mistake by telling himself he'd only rest his eyes for a few minutes. He pounded a fist on the steering wheel.

He tried to think. He assumed Laska didn't live at the address on Siesta Key now. Or he wasn't staying there very often. That meant he was probably staying with the Jones girl. Which is where Nichols was hoping Laska would lead him. That's where Nichols wanted to take Laska. With the girlfriend.

He would make Laska watch as he tortured her.

Cutting her, burning her. Maybe even raping her. Then he'd kill her slowly. He'd strangle her. And he'd laugh as Laska pleaded and begged as he choked the life out of her. And Laska would know what it was like to have everything taken from him.

It was Laska's fault. Everything went to shit after he showed up in Arcadia. If he hadn't stuck his nose where it didn't belong, Nichols thought, nothing would have changed. He'd still be a detective. He'd still have a home, and his daughter, and his wife. Not that she was any prize. And almost best of all, he'd still have Addie Cordele.

He had plans with Addie. When her old man died, the ranch and harvesting business would go to Addie and her brother Mickey. And Mickey would have an accident.

But there was no way of knowing where Laska was going next. He was probably heading to his girl-friend's home, but Nichols lost his chance of following him there. It was useless trying to search for him. He'd have to rely on Jasper to get the address.

But there was a problem. Laska left the house on Siesta Key with two suitcases. Laska tossed them into his car too easily for them to be full. That meant he needed them for something else. Probably a trip.

Was he leaving town because of Nichols? Did that fucking dyke DeSilva wire him up? No, that didn't make sense. How could she know he'd make a move on Laska? She couldn't, he decided. She'd think, like everyone else, that he'd do the obvious and try to get out of the country fast.

Laska was taking a trip for another reason. He decided the reason didn't matter. The only thing that mattered was getting to Laska before he left.

Nichols pulled the burner phone from his pocket, switched it on and waited. Once it booted up, he hit the speed dial. He listened to it ring until it went to voicemail. He hung up, powered down the phone, and tossed it on the seat next to him. Fucking Jasper, he thought. He'd have to try again later.

20

DESILVA AND MCCARTHY

DeSilva and McCarthy sat in the black Suburban in the parking lot of the jail. DeSilva, now in the passenger's seat, flipped through a copy of the personnel file Captain Haskins gave her. As she finished each page, she handed it to McCarthy to read.

"Frank Castillo, yada yada, birth date, address and phone number, social security number," McCarthy said reading from the first page. "Pretty generic."

"What'd you expect?" DeSilva said.

"Maybe a background check? A financial history?"

"It's here, on this page," she said handing it to him.

McCarthy scanned it. It was minimal and incomplete information, he thought.

"Nothing jumped out at me," DeSilva said. "Seems pretty clean. Decent grades in high school. Did two years of community college. Unimpressive work history after that. Worked at Publix a couple of years. Then applied and was accepted as a corrections officer a year and a half ago. Good references from a couple teachers and the manager at Publix.

"Maybe we got excited over nothing. Maybe he's just day-off drunk." She handed the third and last page of the file to McCarthy. He scanned it and checked each page again.

"Well," DeSilva said, "what do you think?"

He turned to DeSilva. "There's no family listed here. No next of kin, no relatives."

"And?" she said.

"He's got no ties. Nothing to risk."

"Other than a death sentence."

"You know what I mean," McCarthy said.

"Yeah, but why do it? I mean, what's in it for him?"

"The oldest reason in the book—money. But maybe something else. We won't know until we talk to him. Or dig deeper."

"You want to keep working this before we talk to the lawyer?"

"I think I do. I kind of got a feeling about this," McCarthy said.

"Never ignore a hunch. Where to?"

"My command post."

Ten minutes later, DeSilva stood in the marshal's RV next to McCarthy. He fed Castillo's info to several of the deputies who began tapping away on their laptops. He turned to DeSilva. "It's gonna take a little while, but we'll know everything about Frank Castillo there is to know."

"What do you mean 'everything'?" DeSilva asked.

"Credit report, tax returns, vehicles he owns, firearms he owns, social media accounts, email address, contact list, IP address and browser history on his computer, cell phone number and call history. All kinds of juicy stuff."

"You can get all that? Without a warrant?"

"We'll have an electronic warrant any second." He nodded towards one of the deputies working on a laptop. "There's a federal judge assigned to us specifically for this investigation."

"And now we wait?"

"Yeah," McCarthy said. He checked the silver watch on his wrist. "Wanna go talk to the lawyer?"

"Let's go," she said.

DeSilva and McCarthy flashed their badges to the mousy woman seated behind a desk near the front of the strip mall storefront office of Jasper Dunlop,

Esquire. She had dull hair, dull eyes and dull interest in accommodating them.

"Mr. Dunlop's calendar is full today. Maybe if you come back tomorrow, he'll have time for you," she said. "Maybe."

"You understand who we are, right?" McCarthy said. He pulled a sheet of paper from a back pocket and held it up. "This is a subpoena to appear at the Federal Grand Jury in Fort Myers. If we don't see Mr. Dunlop in the next five minutes, you'll be appearing there tomorrow to explain why you obstructed a federal investigation."

The woman's jaw tightened and her eyes narrowed as she stared at McCarthy. "I'll see if he has time for you," she said as she picked up the telephone and punched a single button.

DeSilva gave McCarthy a nudge with her elbow and whispered. "Did the room just get colder? I don't think she likes you."

McCarthy gave her a wink.

"You're in luck," the woman said hanging up the phone. "Mr. Dunlop will see you. Do you think you can find your own way?" She slowly pointed a thin finger to the only door at the back of the room.

McCarthy gave her a smile and said, "Thanks for your cooperation."

"Try not to get lost," she said.

McCarthy and DeSilva headed to Dunlop's

office. DeSilva leaned into McCarthy as they walked. "Nice bluff," she said.

"It wasn't a bluff," McCarthy said. "We've got a stack of blank subpoenas already signed by a judge." He handed her the paper.

"Damn," she said, looking over the authentic subpoena.

"Nobody fucks with the United States Government," he said.

McCarthy opened the door without knocking. Jasper Dunlop sat behind a desk too big for the room and stood as they walked in.

"Officers, come in. Come in," he said, extending his hand.

McCarthy and DeSilva shook his hand as McCarthy said, "I'm Deputy United States Marshal McCarthy and this is Lieutenant DeSilva from the DeSoto County Sheriff's Department."

"Pleased to meet you, Deputy McCarthy. And I know Lieutenant DeSilva. Well, I know who she is. We've never formally met." Dunlop pointed to a pair of chairs in front of the desk. "Please, have a seat. I've been expecting you."

"You have?" DeSilva said as she and McCarthy parked themselves in the chairs.

"Yes, I have" Dunlop said as he also sat. "Well, not you specifically. But someone from law enforcement. I assume you're here because I represent Jesse Nichols."

"You obviously know about his escape," McCarthy said.

"It's all over the news, deputy. A terrible thing. Two murders, how very tragic. The two men, the news said they were also deputy marshals? You have my condolences."

"Thank you," McCarthy said.

"So," Dunlop said leaning in and folding his hands on the desk, "how can I help you?"

"Have you talked to Nichols since his escape?" DeSilva said.

Dunlop poked his glasses further back on his nose with a single finger. "I'm sure you're aware that any communications between Mr. Nichols and myself are privileged."

McCarthy leaned forward. "And I'm sure you're aware of the crime-fraud exception to that privilege. If you've communicated with him, you're legally bound to tell us. Especially if you have knowledge of where Nichols might be or might be headed. Or, if you know of any co-conspirators, their identities, and their whereabouts."

Dunlop sat back and smiled. He wiped a thin film of perspiration from his upper lip. "Of course, deputy. I was merely reminding you I can't talk about anything else. Now, let me set your mind at ease. I've had no communication with Mr. Nichols since his escape. And if he does contact me, I'll strongly recommend he surrender immediately."

"And you'll call us immediately if he does contact you," McCarthy said.

"Yes, of course I will."

"Good, McCarthy said. "What about his family? He has a wife and daughter."

"What about them?"

"It seems they're gone. Moved out of their house. Do you know where they might be?"

"No, I'm sorry I don't."

"Did Nichols ever mention them to you? Did he say anything about them leaving the area?"

"Attorney client privilege, deputy. I can't talk about that. But I will say Mr. Nichols expressed surprise when he lost contact with his family."

McCarthy sat back. "Alright," he said. He looked over to DeSilva.

DeSilva hitched her chair closer to Dunlop's desk. "Do you know why Nichols was being transferred to the FBI offices in Fort Myers?" she said.

"I'm sure you know that I do, Lieutenant. Mr. Nichols asked me to reach out to the FBI. He told me he had information they would, in all likelihood, be interested in hearing. He was hoping that, if he cooperated, the FBI would intervene on his behalf with the State of Florida."

"And you contacted the FBI?" DeSilva asked.

"Yes, but you know this already, don't you?"

"Were you aware they were going to transfer Nichols to Fort Myers?"

"Yes," Dunlop said. He looked over to McCarthy. "Haven't you talked to the FBI about all of this?"

"Yes, we have," McCarthy said. "but we'd like to hear it from you."

"Why didn't you accompany Nichols to Fort Myers?" DeSilva said.

"There really was no need. Mr. Nichols already waived his Fifth Amendment rights. The FBI wouldn't bother interviewing him until he did. I think I have a copy of his signed waiver if you'd like to see it." Dunlop opened a drawer of his desk.

"That won't be necessary," McCarthy said.

"I did plan on joining my client in Fort Myers as a precaution," Dunlop said as he closed the drawer. "But I had a court appearance that morning. I was getting ready to drive down there when I heard about the escape."

"What information did Nichols want to give to the FBI?" DeSilva said.

Dunlop smiled. "I don't think the FBI would like me discussing that with the sheriff's department, Lieutenant."

"I don't think he had any information. I think he was just scamming them. I think it was part of his escape plan," DeSilva said.

Dunlop continued smiling. "I wouldn't know, Lieutenant. He led me to believe he had valuable information for the FBI. They obviously agreed." He looked over to McCarthy. "Is there anything else?"

"I'm not done yet," DeSilva said. "Why did you take Nichols' case?"

"Everyone deserves representation, Lieutenant."

"But you took it on *pro bono*. Why?"

A cellphone on Dunlop's desk began buzzing and rattling. Dunlop ignored it.

"Aren't you going to answer that?" McCarthy said.

Dunlop glanced at the phone and back to McCarthy. He pushed the phone off to the side of his desk. "It's another client. I'll call him back."

They all sat watching the phone until it went silent. Dunlop turned to DeSilva. "What was your question Lieutenant?"

"Why are you representing Nichols for free?" she said.

"Respectfully, Lieutenant, that's not a concern of the sheriff's office, or," he turned to McCarthy, "the marshal's office. And, frankly, it's not a subject I'll be discussing with you or anyone else." Dunlop stood. "Now, if you have nothing else, I have a full schedule today."

McCarthy looked over to DeSilva to check if she had anything else. He got a shrug from her and turned back to Dunlop. "I think that's it for now," McCarthy said. "Thanks for your time."

"Always happy to help the men and women of law enforcement. And if there's anything else you need, please don't hesitate to call," Dunlop said.

McCarthy and DeSilva both stood and started towards the door. DeSilva stopped midway and turned back to Dunlop. "Oh, one more thing," she said. "Do you know Frank Castillo?"

Dunlop stood motionless behind his desk. His expression frozen. His eyes locked on DeSilva. She counted the seconds in her head until he answered.

"No, I don't believe I do," Dunlop said.

"Okay then," she said. "Thanks again."

They headed out, walked past the mousy woman who ignored them, and climbed into McCarthy's Suburban. As they settled in, McCarthy said, "I liked that Columbo move."

"What?" DeSilva said.

"That Lieutenant. Columbo thing you did, trying to catch him off guard. When you turned around and asked him if he knew Castillo."

"I don't follow."

"It's an old TV show about a detective. You never saw it?"

"Before my time, I guess," she said as she secured her seat belt.

"Not important," McCarthy said. "Well, what do you think?"

"I think he's lying."

"About what?"

"Probably everything, but definitely about Castillo. He's got a tell."

"The hesitation before he answered? He could

have been trying to remember if he ever heard the name."

"It was nine seconds. I counted to myself. But no, not that. His eye twitched. His left eye. I barely caught it, but it was there. He lied about not knowing Castillo. I'd bet on it."

"A twitch could just be a twitch. But if you're right and he's lying about Castillo," McCarthy said, "that means—"

The buzz of his cellphone interrupted him. He looked at the phone's display. "It's my command post," he said.

21

DESILVA AND MCCARTHY

McCarthy and DeSilva stepped up into the marshal's RV. Several deputies, all cookie-cutter ex-military types, were waiting in the front for McCarthy.

"What've you got?" McCarthy said.

The deputies all looked over at DeSilva.

"It's okay," McCarthy said. "The lieutenant is good by me."

The deputy in the middle started. "We've got a lot. It looks like Frank Castillo could be our guy."

"Let's hear it," McCarthy said.

"He's in debt up to his ass. Credit cards topped out, two months late on his rent, one month late on his car payment. He applied for a home equity loan, but the bank denied it. Not a penny in savings and only sixteen dollars in his checking account."

"Yeah, sounds like a pretty good motive for helping Nichols," McCarthy said.

"Wait a minute," DeSilva said. "You said he was late on his rent?"

"Yeah," the deputy answered. "He leases an apartment just outside of Arcadia. He lists it as his home address."

"But you said he was denied for a home equity loan."

"He inherited some land out on a leg of the Peace River. It has a single-wide trailer on it," the deputy said. "The loan was denied because he's behind on the taxes."

"Where on the Peace River?" DeSilva said.

The deputy reached behind him and pulled a map off a desk. He pointed to a circle drawn in ink a mile or so off Highway 17 south of Fort Ogden.

DeSilva looked at McCarthy. "It makes sense. It's a perfect spot. He stops Wilkerson and Miller – they'd stop for a marked county jail car thinking maybe they forgot something – Castillo shoots them, grabs Nichols and drives south to his trailer."

"Yeah, you're right," McCarthy said. "Would he have access to a marked car? Could he leave work without anyone getting suspicious?"

"I think so," DeSilva said. "I can check with Captain Haskins." She pulled out her cellphone.

"Wait, not yet," McCarthy said. Then to the

deputy, "What else? How about a cellphone we can track?"

"He had a cell, but it was turned off by the provider," the deputy said.

"Let me guess, non-payment," McCarthy said.

"Yep. Next?" the deputy turned to the others.

Another deputy looked at a computer printout in his hand. "Vehicles. He drives a 2015 silver Ford Explorer. Florida registration with a vanity plate – HOOKIN. He also owns a boat with a Florida registration. Registration number FL3401ZX."

"What kind of boat?" DeSilva asked.

"A 2001 Bass Tracker, fifteen-footer."

"Is that big enough to get down the river close to the gulf?" McCarthy asked DeSilva.

"Easily," DeSilva said. "But no further. He'd be nuts to take it into the gulf."

McCarthy nodded and wiped a hand across his mouth. "If he's got the money he could charter something from there." He looked back to the first deputy. "Firearms?"

"One that we found. He bought a Smith and Wesson M&P nine millimeter a little after he started working for the county. Serial number is clear."

"Sounds like we're getting close," McCarthy said.

"I saved the best for last," the deputy said. "We've been going through the jail videos and assignment roster. Castillo doesn't show up until about a month ago. After that, it looks like he's regularly assigned to

Nichols' tier. We confirmed it's him by comparing the video to his picture in the personnel file."

"So, they had plenty of contact," DeSilva said.

"Better than that. We've got one clip from about three weeks ago. Castillo definitely passes something to Nichols through the bars. You can tell he was being careful. He tried to shield the pass from the camera, but you can see he hands him something."

"Can you tell what it was?" McCarthy said.

"Not really. The video isn't the best quality. But it was something he was able to palm. Something about the size of a pack of cigarettes."

"Could it have been a cellphone?" DeSilva said.

"Like I said, the video quality is bad but, yeah, it could be."

DeSilva looked at McCarthy. "Passing contraband, any contraband, to a prisoner is a felony. We've got enough for a search warrant."

"Florida has jurisdiction. It can't be a federal warrant," McCarthy said. "It'll have to be the State of Florida. Do you have a friendly judge?"

"Any one of them at the courthouse will be friendly if you get a federal judge to call and grease the wheels."

"Done," McCarthy said. He turned to his deputies. "Type them up. On both his apartment and the trailer on the river. Lieutenant DeSilva will have to be the complainant. I'll call our judge in Fort Myers."

"We don't have enough manpower to hit both places at the same time," one of the deputies said.

McCarthy looked at DeSilva. "I'll talk to the FBI," McCarthy said. "I'll bet they'd want in on this."

"Fine with me," she said. "But send them to Castillo's apartment. I want the trailer."

"Me too," said McCarthy.

DESILVA SAT NEXT to McCarthy in the Suburban. They led a small caravan of the marshal's vehicles down Highway 17. McCarthy followed the GPS map on the dash and pulled off the highway onto SW River Street, a narrow single-lane-in-each-direction paved road. They followed it on a slight northwest track to an unnamed gravel and dirt road. McCarthy steered the Suburban onto the road and stopped. The others pulled behind him in a single line.

DeSilva looked over a satellite map of the area. "We've got about half a mile on this road to get to the trailer," she said. "Once we make that left turn ahead, we'll be exposed. He'll be able to see us coming."

"If he's there," McCarthy said. "We can use some recon."

McCarthy and DeSilva got out of the car. As DeSilva stepped onto the hard-packed dirt road, she sensed the river nearby. She lifted her head and inhaled the earthy freshness of the water. It triggered a memory of the stream on the Cordele's ranch where she grew up. It was one of the few pleasant memories from her childhood.

"DeSilva, back here," McCarthy called out.

She joined him and the rest of his crew at the back of the Suburban.

"Unpack the drone," McCarthy said to his people. "Let's get a look at what we're walking into."

Several deputies unloaded a large case from the rear of another black SUV. DeSilva watched as they opened it and quickly assembled a small device with four helicopter-like propellers. In minutes, it was airborne, controlled by a video game type handset with an attached video screen.

She and McCarthy stood side by side next to the deputy manning the controls watching the video feed from the drone. The drone closed the gap between their vehicles and the trailer in minutes, flying over a landscape thick with scrub palms, trees, weeds, and bushes.

"How high are you flying it?" DeSilva asked the deputy at the controls.

"About 90 feet. See here?" He pointed to the upper left corner of the screen. Overlaying the video feed were the altitude, airspeed, and direction of the drone.

"Cool," was all she could say. And to herself, *unfucking-limited resources.*

When the drone reached the single-wide, the deputy hovered over it. McCarthy told him to circle slowly.

"No vehicles, a boat on the side of the house, no activity outside. No sign anyone is there," McCarthy said. He turned to the others. "Suit up, we're going in." Then to the deputy controlling the drone. "Stay here. Hover and keep watch. If you see any activity, hit us on the radio. If anyone tries to leave, keep on them with the drone."

When the entry team was ready – jumpsuits, helmets with radio headsets, ballistic vests, knee and elbow protection in place – they piled into their vehicles. McCarthy slipped on his own headset and handed one to DeSilva. She gave him a thumbs up after a radio test and they were off.

McCarthy, leading the line of vehicles, sped down the road kicking up rooster tails of dirt and dust. DeSilva braced herself, gripping the armrest and stiff-arming the dashboard, as the Suburban bounced and bucked in the rutted road.

They zipped down the road, walls of dense foliage on either side, until it finally opened into a clearing with a single-wide trailer at its center. The trailer sat on concrete block piers and had a dilapidated wooden porch that was grey from age and the elements. Beyond it, DeSilva glimpsed slivers of light reflecting off the Peace River.

McCarthy sped to the far end of the trailer and

slammed to a stop a safe fifty feet in front of it. The others formed a semi-circle around the building creating a protective barrier for themselves in preparation of a worst-case scenario.

The entry team jumped from their vehicles before they came to a full stop and stormed toward the trailer, weapons in hand. They crashed through the door as others, assigned to containment duty, surrounded the trailer.

DeSilva cracked open her door, but McCarthy stopped her with a hand on her shoulder before she got any further. He covered the microphone of his headset with a hand. "Hang on a sec. Let's let them clear the place," he said.

DeSilva sat back. She listened as her headset came alive and deputies began calling out "Clear!" as they moved from room to room. The radio went silent. Moments later she heard a squelch of static and a final, "We're all clear in here." McCarthy nodded to her and they climbed out of the Suburban. Before her feet hit the ground, she heard another squelch and then, "But we've got a body."

22

LASKA AND DESILVA

DeSilva looked down at the body of Frank Castillo. Despite the gunshot wound to his head, she recognized him from the photo in his personnel jacket. They'd get a positive ID later when they fingerprinted the body at the morgue, but there was no doubt the corpse slumped in the recliner was Castillo.

And he was likely killed by Nichols because there was no doubt Nichols had been in the trailer. The entry team found a DeSoto County Jail jumpsuit in a bedroom with Nichols' inmate number imprinted on it.

DeSilva was chomping at the bit to do more. She had always been patient and methodical, working every investigation step by step. No shortcuts. No cheating. Examine the evidence and build the case. And she insisted the detectives under her command do the same. But now all she wanted to do was drop Castillo in someone else's lap. Nichols was gone, probably in Castillo's car, and every minute that passed meant he was that much farther from them.

She looked over to McCarthy standing in the middle of the living room. He was on his phone with the FBI and had been since shortly after they walked in. She stepped over to him and caught his eye. Her arched eyebrows and cocked head let him know she wanted to talk.

"Hang on a minute," McCarthy said into his phone. He covered the phone with his palm. "What's up?" he asked DeSilva.

"I was going to ask you the same thing," she said.

"Nothing interesting at Castillo's apartment. They already left there. Gleason is calling for a forensics team and our pathologist to meet us here."

"ETA?"

"Unknown. Over an hour I'd bet."

"How about an APB or a BOLO on Castillo's car?"

"We're taking care of it. But he's probably on a boat in the Gulf of Mexico already. I'll bet we find Castillo's Explorer abandoned near some marina."

"Maybe," she said. She pulled a pair of latex gloves from her pocket. "I'm gonna take a look around." McCarthy opened his mouth but she beat him to it. "I won't touch anything." McCarthy gave her a thumbs up and went back to his phone.

She slipped on the gloves as she wandered through the trailer. As she moved from room to room, she thought all that was missing was a singing fish on the wall. The place was old and ill-kept with cheaply paneled walls and spongy floors. It was decorated in early dumpster fire with furniture that looked like it was discovered on the side of the road. There was an odd smell to the place too. And it was more than just Castillo's body. It was musty and fishy with a touch of body odor.

She ended her tour in the kitchen. She found nothing in the rest of the trailer that offered any kind of help. Nothing that gave any clue where Nichols was or where he was going. She leaned against the avocado green range, pissed off they'd be stuck here for hours.

She looked over the countertops covered in dirty dishes and food waste. Her eyes landed on a small notebook. The kind with a spiraled wire holding the top of the papers together. The type you could slip into a breast pocket.

Something about it caught her attention. She tilted her head trying to get the best angle from the light of a nearby window. She saw the faint impressions. Strokes from a pen or pencil made on a missing sheet of paper and transferred to the page beneath. She moved closer.

She bobbed her head, changing the angle of the light and shadows. She could make out numbers and more. It was an address. She bolted upright. She knew the address. She had seen it before.

"McCarthy," she called out as she pulled her phone from her pocket.

MARLEY WAS RIGHT. Laska felt much better about himself. And Marley played her part well. Docile and timid at first, pleading innocence. Then desperate and hungry, urging him on, pulling him tighter to her. Moving with him, faster and faster. Her moans growing louder and louder until they collapsed together spent and contented.

Laska lay on the bed, hands behind his head, while Marley slipped off to the bathroom for a shower. He smiled. He certainly didn't feel inadequate now.

He jumped out of the bed and pulled on his boxers. After straightening the bed linens, he picked up the suitcases and clothes they knocked to the floor. He was still folding and stacking when Marley, wrapped in a towel, came out of the bathroom. She pretended to stumble. He turned to catch her and she fell into his arms.

"Are you okay?" he said.

"It's your fault. I'm exhausted," she said. "I can barely walk."

"Okay," he said, pulling her up onto her feet,

"knock it off. I'm better now."

She stood in front of him and moved her hands to his biceps. "I'm serious," she said. "You're too much man for me." She gave his arms a squeeze. "Wow, have you been working out?"

He rolled his eyes and smiled. "I said knock it off. Your therapy session worked. I'm good now."

"You sure?"

"Yeah, I'm sure."

"You're not going to give me any more grief about the hotel?"

"No, I promise."

She smiled. "Good," she said giving him a gentle push away. "Now get out. I have to get dressed and finish packing."

"Can't I watch?"

"You want to watch me get dressed?"

"Yeah, why not?"

"I kind of get you wanting to watch me undress, but...dressing?"

"Hey, naked is naked."

"I don't know whether to be flattered or creeped out." She began pushing him towards the door. "Now, get out and let me get dressed."

"Okay," he said backing out. "I'm going. But I'm disappointed."

Marley smiled and slowly dropped her towel. She gave him a wink and one last shove and closed the door.

Laska walked to the kitchen and fished a beer from the refrigerator. He looked down at his bare belly and traded the beer for a bottle of water. He hummed a song he didn't know the name of as he sipped his drink.

He took his bottle of water to the dining room and sat in front of Marley's laptop. He shot off a quick email to Rebecca Stafford and let her know he was making his own hotel arrangements. After hitting the send button, he checked the search history on the browser.

Marley had made a reservation at the Peninsula Hotel. One of the more exclusive and expensive hotels in Chicago. He began scrolling through the reservation to find out what she had paid for an entire week when he heard Marley calling out to him from the bedroom. He closed up the laptop and headed to the bedroom. Marley cracked open the door and stuck her head out before he got there.

"Your phone's ringing," she said as she tossed it to him.

Laska picked it out of the air and before she closed the door again he said, "The Peninsula? Really?"

"Hey, you promised no grief," she shot back as she ducked back into the bedroom.

He shook his head. "I think I got played," he muttered to himself as he looked at the phone buzzing in his hand. The screen displayed a number he thought looked familiar but couldn't quite place. He punched the green button and held it to his ear.

"Laska," he said.

"Laska, it's DeSilva."

"Hey, how are you doing? I was wondering when I'd hear from you."

"What? You were?"

"Yeah, I figured the Cordeles would be going to trial soon. When do you need me? Not too soon I hope."

"No, this isn't about the trial. Jesse Nichols escaped."

Laska stood with the phone to his ear. He wasn't sure he heard what he just heard.

"Laska, you still there?"

"Yeah, sorry. What happened?"

DeSilva laid it out for him from start to finish. From the murders of Deputies Wilkerson and Miller to the raid on Frank Castillo's trailer. She explained quickly and Laska sensed the anxiety in her voice. When she finished, Laska said, "You're calling me for a reason."

"He's got your address," she said. "We found a notebook in Castillo's trailer. Someone wrote your address on it."

"What address?"

"Your house on Siesta Key. I think he's coming for you. We're notifying the Sarasota Sheriff's Office and we're going to be heading your way any minute.

But he's got a good head start on us. Maybe as much as a full day." She was talking fast trying to feed him as much information as possible, as quickly as possible.

"Hold on," he said, "Slow down. I'm not there. I don't live there anymore."

"Thank God, where..."

Laska cut her off. "But my father still does. I have to call him and let him know. Can I call you back at this number?"

"Yeah, tell him to hunker down until the sheriff gets there and then hit me back."

Laska disconnected with DeSilva and hit the speed dial for his father. Bruno picked up after only two rings.

"Dad?" Laska said into the phone.

"Yeah, Sam. What's up?"

"Where are you, dad? Are you at home?"

"No, I'm at Captain Curt's having a beer. You wanna meet me for dinner?"

"Dad, you can't go home."

"What are you talking about, Sam? Why?"

"Dad, listen to me," he said and gave his father the quick version. When he finished, he told his father to come to Marley's condo. He hung up and redialed DeSilva. When she answered, he said, "How did he get my address?"

"He had access to the Cordele file before he got arrested," DeSilva said.

"Yeah, but it doesn't sound like he remembered it and wrote it down over there. It sounds like someone got it to him. Maybe he made a call. So, who did he call?

"We're working on it. Where are you now?"

"At home. I'm living with Marley Jones. Does he have her address?"

"I don't know, but it seems unlikely. It wasn't in the file."

"Good. And we don't have a landline so there's no listing he can check."

"Do you rent or own?"

"It's a condo. She owns it. I guess a property tax record search is possible."

"Yeah, so watch your six until we get there. What's your address?"

Laska recited it to her and gave her quick directions from Interstate 75. "But we won't be here. We're driving up to Chicago. We were going to leave in the morning, but now I'm thinking we'll head out this evening."

"Even better," she said. "I gotta go now. We'll keep in touch. I'll keep you in the loop."

"Hey, DeSilva," he said. "Thanks."

"No problem. Like I said, watch your six."

Laska disconnected and stood thinking. He walked over and rapped on the bedroom door. "Marley?" he said through the door. "Hurry up and finish packing. We're leaving tonight."

23

LASKA AND MARLEY JONES

"We're leaving today?" Marley said as she stood in the doorway wearing only a bra and cutoff jeans.

"Yeah," he said walking past her. He headed to his nightstand and opened the top drawer. "That call was from the lieutenant at the DeSoto Sheriff's Office. Jesse Nichols escaped."

Marley followed behind him. "Who?"

"Jesse Nichols. He was a sheriff's detective. He was working with the Cordeles."

"He's the one who investigated my father's murder?"

Sam turned and faced her. "Yes. The same one."

"The one who...lied. The one who covered it up for the Cordeles."

"Yes," he said. "They think he may be coming to Sarasota. Looking for me."

"Why? Why would he come for you?"

"I don't know. Revenge maybe? He probably blames me. I did play a big part in exposing him."

"And he's coming here? To our house?" She slowly wrapped herself in her own arms hugging herself like she was bundling against the cold.

Sam saw the fear in her widening eyes. "No, not here. He doesn't have our address. The only address he has is my dad's place on the key. And I already talked to Bruno. He's on his way here. And sheriff's cars are on the way to his house just in case."

He saw Marley relax just a bit.

"He doesn't know where we live? You're sure?" she said.

"Yeah, but that doesn't mean he can't find out. That's why I want to leave tonight."

"Okay," she said barely above a whisper. "I'm almost done packing."

Sam went to her and put his arms around her. "Hey, it's okay. We're safe. He doesn't know where we are. And if he finds out, we won't be here. I'm going to stay in touch with the lieutenant, and we won't come back until they get him."

"Okay," she said.

He broke the embrace and looked into her eyes. "We're fine. I promise. There's nothing to worry about."

"I believe you." She moved to the bed and sat down. "What about your father?"

"He's gonna be okay. The sheriffs will watch his house. But he shouldn't stay there until they catch Nichols. I was going to tell him to stay here while we're gone, but on second thought he probably shouldn't. Just to be safe." Sam thought for a minute. "What about your aunt and uncle? Can he stay with them?"

"Uncle Nosmo is on vacation, remember? He and my aunt are going on a cruise. What day is it? Thursday? They're leaving day after tomorrow."

"Scratch that idea. What about Josie? He can stay with her."

Marley wrinkled her nose and bit her lower lip. "That might not work."

"Why? Do you know something that I don't?"

"They kind of had a blowout. Bruno proposed but Josie said no."

"You're kidding?"

"No, Josie told me he took it kind of hard. He threw a tantrum and told her he never wanted to see her again."

"When did this happen?"

"A couple of weeks ago."

"And you didn't tell me?"

"I thought you should hear it from Bruno."

Sam sat on the bed next to Marley and stared at the floor. "Yeah, I wonder why he wouldn't tell me?" He stood up. "I guess it doesn't matter. It's not important right now. We'll figure out where he can stay later. We have to finish packing and get moving."

"You're right," she said standing up. "I have to dry my hair first," she said as she headed to the bathroom.

Sam called after her. "Get a shirt on too. Bruno will be here soon." He walked back to his nightstand, dug through some clothes to the bottom of the drawer, and pulled out a plastic case. He opened it and took the pistol in his hand.

It was brand new. Well, new for him. It was a Beretta 9mm he bought from the local gun store. It was on consignment and dirt cheap. He preferred Glock's though, and especially the Glock 17 he carried as a detective in Chicago. He lost that weapon a few months back on the Cordeles' property and it almost got him killed. He wanted another, but couldn't pass up the deal on the Beretta.

This Beretta, a model 92FS, was the civilian version of the sidearm the military currently carried. If it was good enough for them, it was more than good enough for him.

He checked the weapon and magazines, placed it back in the padded box, and stored it safely under a pile of clothes in his suitcase. He'd bring it to Chicago. *Hope the fight never comes to you, but be ready for it if it does*, he thought.

Marley finished up in the bathroom and Sam jumped in the shower. After throwing on a pair of jeans and a tee shirt, he plodded into the bedroom. The suitcases, closed and zippered, sat on the bed. He grabbed them and headed to the front door.

As he walked out of the bedroom, he saw Marley in the kitchen tending to the coffee maker. She looked over to him, rolled her eyes, and waggled her head towards the living room.

Laska headed that way, bringing the bags with him, and found his father sitting in a chair staring out the window. When Bruno saw him, he jumped out of his chair.

"Sam," he said, "what's going on? Did you hear anything else?"

"No, dad. Nothing else. Just what I told you. Sarasota sheriff's deputies are supposed to be watching your place and our place." He set down the suitcases and walked to the window. "Although I don't see any around yet."

"What are we supposed to do then?"

"Well, we hang tough until we know more. I'll make a call and see what's going on, but I don't see much changing until they capture Nichols. What we do have to do is find you a place to stay until then."

"I can't go home?"

"It'd probably be best if you didn't."

"And I can't stay here?"

"You probably shouldn't. The lieutenant from DeSoto County doesn't think Nichols has this address, but it's possible he does or can get it. We shouldn't chance it." He turned to face Bruno. "What about Josie? Can you stay with her?"

Bruno stuck his hands in his pockets. His head bobbed around like it was on a spring. He looked everywhere except at his son. "I don't think that'll work. We kind of had a fight."

"Anything you want to talk about?"

"No, I don't think so. Maybe later."

"Okay, maybe later. Do you have any place else you can stay?"

"I could probably stay with Jimmy and his wife. They're my neighbors. Their place is a few doors down from me."

"Give them a call. And I'll call and see what's going on with the sheriffs."

Bruno finished his call first and waited for Sam. When Sam finally disconnected, he slipped his phone back into his pocket and turned to his father. "Can you stay with your neighbors, dad?"

"Yeah, they said it's no problem."

"Good. Here's the deal. There's a Sarasota County sheriff's deputy sitting outside your villa. He'll walk you through while you pick up any clothes you need. After, they'll keep a car there 24/7 until they catch Nichols. I wish I could tell you when that'll be, but there's no way of knowing."

"That's okay. What about here? What about you and Marley?"

"We're leaving, so they're not gonna put a car here."

"Alright, I should get going then."

"I'll call you when we get to Chicago or if I hear anything else."

Sam walked Bruno to his car and watched until he was safely on his way. When he got back inside, Marley was sitting in the living room. A cup of hot coffee sat on the table in front of her.

"Can you throw your coffee into a travel mug?" Sam asked. "I'd like to get going."

"It's not mine. Your father asked me to make him a cup. I don't think he really wanted it. I think he was giving me busy work to avoid being in the same room with me."

"Yeah, sorry about that."

"Don't apologize. You didn't do anything." She stood up with the cup. "Do you think he'll ever be able to talk to me?"

"I don't know, Marley," he said. "I wish I did."

She exhaled deeply and changed the subject. "I heard you made another call," she said.

"Yeah, to the DeSoto County lieutenant."

"Is there any news?"

"Not much. The U.S. Marshals are sending a couple of cars. They'll work with the local sheriff and police looking for Nichols. But the lieutenant isn't coming for a while. She's on an active crime scene."

"Then, nothing's changed."

"No," he said. He looked over at the suitcases. "We should get going."

"Okay, but I need to call my uncle and let him know what's going on."

"Why worry him? Let them enjoy their vacation. Just let them know we're going to Chicago and leave it at that."

"I guess you're right. Okay then, I'll hurry and we can get out of here."

Over the next thirty minutes Sam loaded the car and tried to get Marley moving. Finally, after numerous 'don't rush me's' and 'I think I'm forgetting somethings' they locked up the condo, settled into Sam's car, and were on the way to Chicago.

24

DESILVA AND MCCARTHY

DeSilva punched the off button on her phone. She walked over to McCarthy in the living room. He was watching the FBI's evidence techs work on Frank Castillo's body. They buzzed around the body wrapping up the scene photos and measurements and were getting ready to examine the body closely for evidence.

"I still think we should've sent a car to the girl-friend's condo," she said.

"A waste of resources," McCarthy said. "You said yourself, Laska's leaving. Heading where? Chicago, right?"

"We should still be watching it. Nichols doesn't know they won't be there. If he finds out where the condo is, he might show up there." She looked down at Castillo's body. "I should be on my way to Sarasota," she said, more to herself than McCarthy.

"We'll get there. But we can't just leave this". He checked the watch on his wrist. "Our people will be there any time now. The Sarasota Sheriff's Department is on it too. Every LEO in that county is looking for him. If Nichols is really in Sarasota, I'd be willing to bet he'll be in custody before sunset."

"What do you mean *if* he's really in Sarasota? There's no doubt he's there. I found Laska's address in the kitchen. That's not a coincidence."

McCarthy turned to face her. "We'll get there. I promise. We have work to do here first."

DeSilva knew he was right, but it didn't make her feel any better. She shoved her hands into her pockets and resigned herself to the task at hand. She promised herself she'd try not to sulk. She refocused and watched the techs as they moved around Castillo's body searching for evidence. One of the techs began going through Castillo's pockets. McCarthy, also watching the tech, said, "Find a wallet?"

The tech, his voice muffled by the surgical mask over his mouth and nose, answered. "I've got something here." He reached into Castillo's front pants pocket and pulled out a cellphone. He looked it over quickly and deposited it into an evidence bag. "It's a phone. Looks like a burner."

"Let me see that," McCarthy and DeSilva said in unison. The tech handed the clear plastic evidence bag to McCarthy.

"I think we just got lucky," McCarthy said

looking over the phone through the bag. He didn't have to explain why to DeSilva. It made sense that Castillo would need a way to keep in touch with Nichols, other than whispering through jail bars. They already suspected Castillo smuggled a phone to Nichols so it made sense. Burner phones were cheap and anonymous. But they weren't infallible. If Castillo and Nichols were communicating via the burner phones, this phone - Castillo's phone - would have Nichols' number in the call list. And if Nichols still had his, they might be able to track Nichols' phone.

DeSilva stepped closer and peered at the phone. "Yeah, lucky," she said. "In more ways than one. Does this phone look familiar to you?"

"It's a burner. They all kind of look alike."

"The lawyer, Jasper Dunlop. His phone, the one he wouldn't answer while we were there? It looked just like this."

"I'm not sure," McCarthy said as he took a closer look at the phone. "I guess I didn't pay attention."

"It's looking more like Dunlop is in on this."

McCarthy handed the bag and phone back to the tech. "Get this inventoried right away," he said. He turned back to DeSilva. "Let's not get ahead of ourselves."

DeSilva's mouth hung open and her eyes went wide. "What are you talking about?" she said. "That phone is--"

"Yeah, it's great evidence. It's got the potential to lead us to Nichols and maybe even hook up Dunlop."

"Then why did you give it back to him?" she said pointing to the tech. "We've gotta go through it. Now."

"Yeah, we do. But we have to do it right. We have to protect the chain of evidence. It'll get inventoried. Then we'll take it back to the command post and I'll have a mobile CART team meet us there."

"What's a CART team?"

"It's the FBI's Computer Analysis Response Team. They're the best of the best. They do the forensic exam on all digital devices. They'll pull the phone apart, metaphorically speaking, and we'll know everything there is to know."

"They'll come to us? Like the Geek Squad?"

"Ha! Yeah, like the Geek Squad. That's a good one. I'm gonna steal that from you."

"Sure, go ahead," she said rolling her eyes. "How long is this gonna take?"

"I'll call now. They'll be coming from Fort Myers. And then, it'll probably take a couple of hours for any results after they get their hands on the phone."

"I was hoping it'd be faster, but...okay. Make your call."

～

DeSilva sat in her office sipping coffee and staring out the window while she waited. The CART team was working on Castillo's burner, the Evidence Response team was wrapping up the scene at Castillo's trailer, and there was nothing to do until they finished. McCarthy went off to huddle with ASAC Gleason and the FBI, so she decided to use the time to catch up her sheriff.

She was surprised Wilson took the news about Castillo so well. It didn't seem to bother him that Castillo was a county jail employee and that his involvement would reflect on the sheriff's campaign. He seemed distracted as she explained how she and McCarthy began to suspect Castillo. He became a little more interested as she told him about the raid on his trailer and finding the body and Nichols' jailhouse jumpsuit. He got very interested when she described finding Laska's address.

"You think Nichols is going after Laska?" Sheriff Wilson said.

"Yes, I do," she said.

"Why would he do that? Why take the risk?"

"I think he blames Laska for finding him out. And with good reason. If Laska hadn't gotten involved, we might have never discovered that Nichols was dirty."

Wilson rubbed his chin. "You called this guy Laska?" Sheriff Wilson said.

The question confused DeSilva. "Well, yeah, of course," she said.

"Maybe you should have waited."

"Why would we do that?"

"You could have used him to draw Nichols out into the open."

"Use Laska as bait?"

"I wouldn't put it that way, but yeah. Anyway, it's too late now. Anything else?"

Screw this asshole, she thought. He didn't deserve to be in the loop anymore. He didn't deserve to know about the burner phone. The hell with the repercussions. "No," she said. "Wait, yeah. Only one more thing. The FBI and the marshals want to keep this quiet for now. They don't want the media to know. We don't want Nichols to know we found Castillo's body."

"Makes sense," Wilson said. "I'll let Haskins over at the jail know."

DeSilva excused herself and headed out.

Back at her desk, she spun her chair away from the window. She should call her wife. She at least owed her an explanation. She should try to get her to understand. Maybe even apologize even though she didn't have anything to apologize for. As she pulled her cell from her pocket it began buzzing in her hand. It was McCarthy.

"DeSilva," she said into the phone.

"The CART team is wrapping up."

"Anything good."

"Oh yeah."

"I'll be right there," she said.

She hustled down the stairs, across the parking lot, and pounded on the command post's door. One of McCarthy's cookie-cutter deputies opened up and stood aside as she climbed in. He ushered her into the rear of the trailer where McCarthy was conferencing with two CART team techs.

"You ready for this?" McCarthy said as she walked up.

"I can't wait," she said.

McCarthy quickly introduced the two techs then said to them, "I'll give her the rundown. Correct me if I screw anything up." He turned back to DeSilva. "I'll give you the non-technical version. These guys here pulled up the phone number of Castillo's cell. That was easy. Next, they hit the contact list. There were only two numbers. Both sequential phone numbers."

"You mean like only one digit off?"

"Yeah, the last one. And Castillo's phone is only one number off from those two."

"Holy shit."

"Yeah, that means the three numbers were activated one after the other. They bought three burners and had them activated at the same time, from the same place."

"Who are 'they'?"

"I'll get to that. After that, the techs pulled the recent calls. There's probably, what?" He looked over to the tech. "Twenty calls or so?"

The techs nodded in unison.

"All the calls were to or from the other two numbers in the contact list. No calls to any other number. The most recent call, an incoming call," McCarthy said, "was the morning of the murders and escape."

"Finalizing plans."

"Yep, looks like it."

"Okay," DeSilva said, "we can assume Nichols has one of the phones and that last call was from Nichols to Castillo. Who has the third phone?"

"You asked me who 'they' was? Well, these tech geniuses here worked their magic. A credit card in the name of Carol Ann Heyward was used to buy and activate the phones at the Walmart here in town."

"Who's Carol Ann Heyward?"

"You're gonna love this. She works for Jasper Dunlop."

25

JESSE NICHOLS AND JASPER DUNLOP

Nichols pulled open the metal framed glass door and stepped in. The store smelled of stale air, dust, and old books. Straight ahead, beyond the cash registers, were racks of cheap vases, chipped pottery, and knickknacks. Behind that, a wall of shelves filled with old kitchenware, dishes and utensils. He looked left and then right. A sign pointed him to the racks of men's clothes.

He flipped through the rows of pants and shirts and picked out a pair of worn jeans and a polo shirt. He added two plain tee shirts and headed to a bin piled high with shoes. He stood staring at it, wondering if it was worth digging through.

"What size?" The voice came from behind him.

Nichols turned and faced the man. He wore a blue vest over his shirt. His nametag read 'David'.

"What size you lookin' for?" David repeated. "I'll help you go through it."

"Ten and a half," Nichols said.

David began digging through the mass of shoes. "What do you want? Dress? Tennis? Maybe work boots?"

"Whatever we can find." Nichols joined David, checking the sizes before tossing the shoes aside.

"Here you go." David pulled a worn pair of brown leather work shoes from the mountain. "Try them on."

Nichols kicked off the canvas slip-ons and stepped into the shoes. "They'll work," he said. "Thanks for the help." He stooped to pull off the shoes.

"Leave 'em on," David said. "I'll toss these jail-house kicks in the trash."

Nichols stiffened.

"Hey, be cool man. I been there too," David said. "Ain't no big thing." He bent over and grabbed the slip-ons. "What was you in for?"

"Bullshit," Nichols said.

"Yeah, me too." David moved in closer to Nichols and lowered his voice, his eyes flitting around the room. "Hey, if you need, you know, anything else, I can hook you up."

Nichols stepped even closer to David. His eyes narrowed and his jaw clenched. "I ain't no fucking doper. Got it?"

David backed up. "Sure, man. Yeah, I didn't mean nothing by that. I was just trying to, you know, help you out."

Nichols moved in again. Even closer. "Where's the changing room?" he said.

David pointed.

Nichols stood staring at David. David's eyes dropped to the floor as he stepped back again and bumped into a rack of shirts.

Nichols snorted, turned, and headed to the changing rooms. Inside, he peeled off the too small sweat pants and tee shirt and changed into the jeans and shirt he picked out. He left the sweats and tee shirt in the changing room and walked over to the register. He thought about walking out without paying but decided against it. There was no reason to take that chance.

Outside the re-sale shop, sitting in the Ford Explorer, he packed the extra tee shirts he bought into his bugout bag. He grabbed his new ID's and slipped them into the pockets of his jeans along with a good bundle of his cash. He kept the pistols, his Glock and Castillo's Smith & Wesson, and the rest of his cash in the bag and covered them with his new shirts. He grabbed his phone off the seat and booted it up. It was time to try Jasper again.

Dunlop picked up on the first ring. "Jesse," he said, "where are you?"

"Fuck that. Why didn't you answer when I called you earlier?"

"That lieutenant was here, DeSilva. And she was with a fed. A U.S. Marshal. I couldn't pick up in front of them."

"What'd you tell them?"

"I blew them off. Said I didn't know anything. We expected this though, right? We knew they'd come to me."

"Yeah. Did it sound like they knew anything?"

Nichols listened to silence on the other end.

"Jasper," he said, "You're pissing me off. Did it sound like they knew anything?"

"DeSilva asked me...she asked me if I knew Frank Castillo."

"How the fuck do they know about Castillo?"

"I don't know."

"You must have told them something."

"I swear, Jesse. I didn't say anything. She came up with his name out of the blue. I told her I never heard of him."

"Then what?"

"Then they left. They didn't say anything else."

"Shit," Nichols said. He sat with the phone to his ear and tried to think. He had to assume the worst. They knew Castillo was in on the escape. That means they probably knew, or at least would find out about his trailer. And that meant they'd find his body - if they didn't already. But, so what? He knew they'd figure it out sooner or later. What they didn't know is where he was.

"Jesse," Dunlop said. "Where are you? You've gotta get out of the country. Stick to the original plan. Get on a boat and get to the Caymans."

"That was never my plan. Not yet anyway. Did you get the girlfriend's address?"

"Jesse--"

"Did you get it or not?"

"Yeah, but Jesse, it's not a good idea."

"It's the perfect idea. DeSilva and the fucking idiot feds will figure I'm trying to get out of the country. They'll waste days checking the coast and boats for hire. Now give me the address. I'm tired of you wasting my time."

"Alright, but you gotta give me a minute to bring it up on the computer. I found it on the Sarasota County Property Appraiser's site."

"Hurry up," Nichols said. He waited for Dunlop, listening to the clickety-clack of the keyboard on the other end. Seconds later, Dunlop came back on.

"Here it is. You ready?"

"Yeah," Nichols said, "go ahead."

Dunlop recited the address and Nichols repeated it to himself, committing it to memory. Dunlop said, "Jesse, let me say it one more time..."

"Don't bother. And what about my daughter? Did you find where my wife went with her?"

"No, I can't find anything. I need more time. And

information. Do you have any idea at all where she might have gone? Like maybe a relative or friend or something?"

"No, but keep trying. I'm not leaving the country without my daughter."

"You're gonna get caught, Jesse."

"You don't want that, Jasper. Believe me, you don't want that. And you better answer the next time I call, so leave your phone on." Nichols punched the disconnect button and switched off his phone. He fired up the Explorer and pulled out of the parking lot. He didn't notice David standing in the doorway of the resale shop watching him drive away.

26

DESILVA AND MCCARTHY

DeSilva pulled a chair out and sat. "Is this Carol Ann Heyward the receptionist that gave us a hard time?" she said.

"Yeah," McCarthy said. He twisted around and tapped a few keys on the computer behind him. The receptionist's photo popped up on the screen. "We pulled her driver's license photo."

"Yep, that's her," DeSilva said, leaning closer to the screen. "What's our next move?"

"Let's talk about it." He nodded her into the back of the RV and a small room outfitted as an office. He turned to the techs. "Nice work guys. Keep at it. Let me know when you get something new."

DeSilva followed him into the office and took a chair in front of a small desk. Instead of sitting across from her behind the desk, McCarthy plopped down in the chair next to her.

"The techs are gonna keep plugging away. They'll try to get the SIM card serial numbers from all three phones, and they'll track any new calls," he said. "We've also submitted a warrant for a tap on Nichols' phone so we can listen in if there's a call."

"What about tracking Nichols? You can locate him by the phone's signal, right?"

"Only when the phone is turned on. And it's not. The last time it was on was yesterday morning."

"When he was in the jail."

"Yeah. The call to Castillo."

DeSilva leaned in closer. "I thought you people could track a phone even when it's turned off. I mean, if you can't, can't you call the NSA or Homeland Security or whoever and ask for a favor?"

"That's pretty much nonsense. It can't be done," McCarthy said.

"I thought I read about it being done in Iraq and Afghanistan."

"The only way to do it is to plant a trojan horse, a virus. A software workaround that keeps the phone powered on even when it looks like the phone is powered down. We'd have to send an email or text with a file containing the trojan horse to Nichols and he'd have to open it."

"Shit," DeSilva said. "He wouldn't take a text or email from a number he didn't recognize." She perked up. "We could do it from Dunlop's phone."

"And that brings us to the next item on the agenda," he said. "What do we do about Jasper Dunlop?"

DeSilva sat back in her chair and crossed her legs, making herself as comfortable as she could in the hard metal chair. "The way I see it, we have two options. We go in with a search warrant for the phone, and when we have it we arrest him and the receptionist."

"Or?" McCarthy said.

"We do nothing. We wait for phone calls between him and Nichols and use that to locate Nichols."

"I agree," McCarthy said. "But there are risks attached to both. If we arrest Nichols and Heyward, there's a strong chance they lawyer up and say nothing."

"And we have no cooperating co-offender to answer any calls Nichols might make," DeSilva said.

"Exactly. If we answer a call, he'll hang up and ditch the phone. If we don't, he may try to call again or he may not. Either way, it limits our ability to track him."

"But if Dunlop does cooperate, we'll be in control of the phone and can make Dunlop make as many calls as we need until we get Nichols."

"Right. Now, if we do nothing – don't arrest Dunlop and Heyward – we have to rely on luck. We'll just sit and wait twiddling our thumbs until one of them makes a call to the other."

"And we don't know when or even if that will ever happen. For all we know, they're done with each other. There might never be another call," DeSilva said.

McCarthy stood up and shoved his hands into his pockets. "And those are our choices. What do you think?"

DeSilva stood and faced McCarthy. "I think I'd like to grab Dunlop and his asshole receptionist and beat the dog crap out of them. They helped murder two men. Men with families. Oh, and Frank Castillo too. And they set Nichols free endangering my friend Laska and who knows how many other people." She sat down again. "But I can't do that." She inhaled deeply and slowly let it out. "I think the right thing to do is nothing. Don't arrest Dunlop and Heyward. At least for the time being. Let's let it ride and see if Dunlop or Nichols makes a call."

"I agree," McCarthy said. "It's hard playing the waiting game, but I think it's the right thing to do."

McCarthy and DeSilva turned their heads to a soft rap at the door. One of the techs poked his head in. "We've got activity," he said.

They followed the tech to a work station, stood behind him, and watched the screen on his computer. "The phone we think Nichols has was active twice," the tech said. "The first time for less than a minute. It looks like he tried to make a call but it didn't go through. Then the phone shut down. He turned it off. But that was a couple of hours ago."

"What?" McCarthy said. "You missed it?"

"Yeah," the tech said, "it happened right as we were trying to get up to speed. Just bad luck. It won't happen again."

"Can you tell where he was," DeSilva said.

"Yeah," the tech answered. "Here." A map popped up on the computer's screen. A red dot marked the spot.

"Where is that?" McCarthy said.

"Sarasota. Looks like a parking lot on Highway 41, Tamiami Trail. Just north of, what is that?" The tech moved his face closer to the screen. "Just north of Stickney Point Road." The tech sat back but kept his eyes on the screen. "But, like I said, that was a couple hours ago."

"What about the second time?" DeSilva said.

"That was ten minutes ago. He made a call to the second phone. Duration of just over four and a half minutes. Location...here." He pointed to a second red dot on the map. Still on Tamiami Trail, just south of a street named Mecca Drive.

"Is the phone still active?" McCarthy asked.

"No," the tech said.

"And the location of the second phone? The one he called?"

The tech rolled his chair to an adjacent computer. He tapped the keyboard and a second map popped up. "Here," he said. "That one has been powered on since we started the trace. Still is. The location isn't far from here."

"Dunlop's office," DeSilva said.

"You should have started with the second call. We've lost precious minutes. He could be a mile away from there by now," McCarthy growled. He stepped away from the tech's station and began barking orders to his people.

"Get on the radio to our people in Sarasota. The sheriff's office and Sarasota police too. I want a two square mile perimeter around that last location flooded with law enforcement. Make sure everyone has a good description of Castillo's Ford Explorer, but make sure they know he could have ditched that car by now.

"I want a BOLO out to the State Police and Highway Patrol. In fact, all surrounding agencies. I want to know about any traffic cameras and private security cameras in the area, and I want that video now.

"And put eyes on Dunlop and the receptionist. I wanna know where they are every minute. We're not gonna lose those two."

He turned to the CART techs. "Do what you gotta do to expedite that warrant. I want that tap active ASAP. And no more delays if there's another call on Nichols' burner. I want a call as soon as it's powered on."

He turned to DeSilva. "Let's go."

"Where to?" she said following him to the front of the RV.

"We're going to Sarasota," he said.

Five minutes later they were westbound on Highway 72 headed to Sarasota. DeSilva settled into the passenger's seat of the government Chevy Suburban. She tightened her seatbelt as she watched McCarthy take a two-handed death grip on the wheel and the speedometer inch up to ninety miles per hour.

"Ease up," she said. "Let's arrive alive."

"I thought you were in a hurry to get there. You said so standing over Castillo's body."

"I am in a hurry. But I want to get there in this car, not an ambulance. And ten or twenty more minutes won't make a difference."

McCarthy glanced down at his speed and backed off. "Sorry," he said. "You're right. That tech pissed me off wasting all that time." He relaxed a bit more. "I guess it's my fault. I didn't make the urgency clear from the get go. And they're just techs. Geeks."

"I don't think it's your fault. They should've figured that out themselves." DeSilva loosened her belt. "Precious?" she said.

McCarthy's brow crinkled. "What?"

"You told the tech 'we've lost precious minutes.' Precious? Really?"

McCarthy chuckled. "A little dramatic, huh?"

"More like melodramatic. I almost choked trying to keep a straight face. But you made your point."

"Yeah, I guess."

DeSilva settled back and stared out the windshield. The sun was low in the sky. It was going to be a pretty sunset, she thought. Her stomach growled.

"You hungry?" she said.

27

JESSE NICHOLS

The sun had just dipped below the horizon as Nichols pulled up to the pumps on the far side of the Chevron station. He unhooked the nozzle, stuck it into the fuel tank neck, and headed inside. He waited at the counter perusing the candy bars and beef sticks while the clerk sold lottery tickets to the only other customer - an old man wearing cargo shorts cinched up over his belly to his chest, white socks, and sandals.

When the old man waddled away, the clerk, barely glancing in Nichols' direction, mumbled a how-can-I-help-you?

"Thirty bucks on pump six," Nichols said tossing the bills on the counter.

The clerk gathered up the cash. "Anything else?"

"Yeah, you got maps?"

NICHOLS LEFT the Explorer on the top level of the Sarasota Memorial Hospital's parking garage. He tucked it into a dark corner and took the elevator down to street level, the Glock 17 tucked into the front waistband of his second-hand jeans and covered by his untucked shirt. The Jones girl's condo was only a few blocks away according to the map.

He made the walk in just over ten minutes and stood watching the building from across the street. He almost couldn't believe his luck when he first saw the building. He had imagined a big condo building with a doorman at a desk or at least a vestibule with locked doors that required a resident to buzz in a guest. This was nothing more than a two-story building with outdoor walkways that led right to the front door of each apartment.

He was too far to be able to read the apartment numbers, especially in the dark. But he knew by the apartment number Dunlop gave him that it was on the second floor. He would have to get closer. He looked over the building again. More than half of the apartments had a light on. Some with only the pale blue light of a television flickering against curtains in the front window.

He checked up and down the street for potential witnesses, and seeing none, crossed quickly. He climbed the staircase to the second level and moved down the walkway checking the numbers on the doors. His target was only the second door he checked.

He peeked in the window. The apartment was dark. He stood beside the door and listened for any sound inside the apartment. Hearing none, he rapped lightly on the door. Nothing. He knocked again. Still nothing. He grabbed the doorknob and twisted. The door was firmly locked, secured by a deadbolt. He scanned the walkway, turned, and headed back down the staircase.

Walking back to the hospital parking lot, he went over what he knew. Laska picked up suitcases. No one was home at the girlfriend's condo. That's all he knew for sure. The most likely scenario is Laska and the girl went out of town. But maybe not. Maybe only Laska was gone. Maybe the girl's condo was dark because she was working or something and would return. The only way to know for sure would be to either continue watching the condo and wait for Marley Jones to show up, or break in. And Nichols wasn't the patient type.

He got to the Explorer and drove around, sticking to the main streets, until he found a hardware store. He picked out a few basic tools – a small prybar, a hefty flathead screwdriver, a hammer, a pipe wrench, and a small flashlight – and headed back to the hospital's parking lot.

He loaded the tools into his bugout bag and

walked back to Marley Jones' still dark condo. Standing outside the door he examined the lock closely. It was a cheap deadbolt that wouldn't be much of a problem. He wrapped the jaws of the pipe wrench around it and gave it a jerk. The lock split in half and fell to the floor clanking on the cement walkway.

The sound startled Nichols and he stood frozen. His hand went to the grip of the Glock in his waistband as he waited for any activity from the other apartments. Nothing. He scooped up the pieces of the lock, tossed them in his bag, and slipped inside Marley Jones' apartment.

He cursed himself for not having the flashlight ready as he stood in the dark. He fumbled through his bag until he found the flashlight. He switched it on and quickly moved through the apartment to confirm he was alone. He paused in the bedroom when his light fell on stacks of folded clothes piled on the unmade bed. Even more were tossed haphazardly around the room. Most of the drawers of the dresser hung half open and the contents pushed around like a burglar had been searching for something.

Nichols smiled as a thought struck him. *He* was a burglar now. He moved the beam of the flashlight around the room. He had no doubt now. Laska and Jones were gone. And there was no telling where or for how long.

He wandered out of the bedroom and into the kitchen. He popped open the refrigerator flooding the room in light. He stood staring inside. He grabbed a bottle of beer, twisted the cap off, and drank half the bottle in a single pull. Taking a second beer with him, he walked through the kitchen into the dining room leaving the refrigerator's door open.

The glow from the open door spilled enough light into the dining room, so he switched off his flashlight. His eyes fell on the table. And a laptop computer.

Nichols set the two beers next to the laptop, pulled out a chair and sat down. He lifted the clamshell lid and the computer sprung to life. And smack dab in the middle of the screen were two icons, 'Sam's email' and 'Marley's email'. He clicked on Laska's email. No password required. Nichols smiled and knocked back the rest of his first beer and began reading.

Twenty minutes later he closed the laptop and pushed away from the table. He grabbed another beer from the fridge and plopped down on the sofa in the living room. He had a lot to think about. The computer was an orgy of information, and he needed to assess his options.

Laska and the Jones girl were on their way to Chicago. They had a reservation at a hotel there, the Peninsula. But not for a few days yet. So more than likely they were driving. That was good and bad. He knew where they were going and where they were staying. But if he followed them, he'd be on unfamiliar turf. And getting to them in a hotel, an expensive hotel, could be hard. On the plus side, they had no idea he was coming for them. And no one would be looking for him there.

There was something else. Laska was being sued, a Federal lawsuit, and he had an appointment with a lawyer. That was the reason for his Chicago trip. Nichols hadn't read the entire file yet, but maybe there was something in there he could use. He'd have to think more about that after he read the file. But he was tired. It was getting late and he needed to sleep.

He went to the front door and peeked out. There were fewer lights on in the neighboring condos now. Maybe he could catch a few hours of sleep here. He went back and stretched out on the couch. He laid back and stared at the ceiling, his mind racing.

He sat up, laid down, and sat up again. He got another beer and went back to the couch. He grabbed the TV remote and began clicking through the channels. He stopped when he saw his face. His mugshot.

The video flipped, alternating between shots of men in suits and uniforms, police cruisers with their lights flashing, and another shot of Nichols' mugshot. The banner at the bottom of the screen read "*Search for escapee moves to Sarasota*". Nichols jumped to his feet. The rolling banner continued. "*Former DeSoto County detective Jesse Nichols considered armed and extremely dangerous – may be driving a silver Ford Explorer with Florida license plate HOOKIN*".

He threw the remote at the TV. *How the hell do they know?* he thought. *It had to be Jasper. There was no other way.* If they knew he was in Sarasota, they knew why. He had to get out of the apartment. But the Explorer was burned. He'd have to leave it.

He ran through the apartment. He checked the kitchen and the bedroom looking on the countertops and through drawers. He ran to the front door and then to the back. There, on a hook next to the back door, he found it. A set of keys.

The keys were old. Not one of those fancy push button fobs for a late model car, but something older. From the look of the old-style keys, thirty or forty years at least. He hoped they weren't just a keepsake.

He pocketed the keys, shoved the laptop and its charger in his bag, and slipped out the back door.

28

DESILVA AND MCCARTHY

DeSilva and McCarthy were standing bathed in the light from a secondhand store tucked into a corner of a strip mall on the north side of Sarasota. They stood surrounded by two of McCarthy's men and three uniforms from the Sarasota PD and the county sheriff's office who had been waiting for them the better part of an hour.

While McCarthy and DeSilva were barely half way to Sarasota, the uniforms and McCarthy's deputies sped to the mall. They reported no sign of Nichols but a quick canvass of the stores led to David Adebayo who identified Nichols' photograph. One of McCarthy's people gave them the rundown.

Adebayo was a clerk in the store and had helped Nichols pick out clothes and shoes. Having spent time in county jails himself – Adebayo claimed he was on the straight and narrow now - he recognized the canvas slip-ons Nichols wore. Adebayo attempted to strike up a conversation with Nichols and even invited him to a prayer meeting at a local mission, but Nichols became enraged and threatened him. So Adebayo backed off but watched Nichols as he left the store, entered a silver Ford Explorer, made a telephone call from the car, and then drove off southbound on Tamiami Trail.

"It's pretty obvious now," DeSilva said.

"What's obvious?" McCarthy asked.

"Nichols is here for Laska. He's not leaving the country. Not yet at least," DeSilva said.

"Is that your way of saying I told you so?"

DeSilva smiled and shrugged.

"Yeah? Well, if you didn't want to stop for food we could have been here sooner," McCarthy said.

"It was a drive-through burger joint. It took five minutes."

"Hey," one of the county sheriff's deputies said, "I don't mean to interrupt, but when you two are done bickering, do you think you can let the rest of us know what you want us to do with Adebayo? He wants to go home."

"Yeah, sorry," McCarthy said. He looked over to the secondhand store and the small group of people milling about inside. "What time does the store close?" he said.

"Eight o'clock. Half an hour ago," a marshal's

deputy said. "We were holding everyone in case you had more questions."

"Do you think you got everything from them?" DeSilva said.

"Yeah," the deputy said. "No one else really paid any attention to Nichols. Not even the clerk that checked him out. I don't think we'll get anything else that helps us."

"How about Nichols' old clothes? Do we have them?"

"He left them in a changing room. We've got them bagged and in our car now. And we have a description of the clothes he's wearing now."

"Any cameras in the area?" DeSilva asked.

"A few," the Sarasota uniform said. "I checked them out. All dummies or disconnected."

"And Nichols obviously slipped through the perimeter," McCarthy said.

"It wouldn't have been hard for him. We don't have the manpower to lock down every street," the uniform said.

"Great," McCarthy said. "Just great. I guess that's it. We can cut everybody loose. Unless anyone here has anything."

The county deputy spoke up. "Adebayo wants to know if there's a reward."

After Adebayo and the store employees got the wave, McCarthy asked the uniforms to check motel, bar, and restaurant parking lots. He wanted the marina lot checked as well. He sent his people to the Sarasota PD headquarters to check on available video from traffic and red-light cameras and to look at any reports of stolen boats.

When they were alone, DeSilva and McCarthy sat in the Suburban. They had parked under a lamp-post. The sodium vapor lamp cast a sickly orange light through the windows. "Now what?" she said.

"You got any ideas?" he said.

DeSilva took a deep breath and blew it out slowly. "I think Nichols is still in the area. I think he wants Laska bad. We should stay and keep looking. Maybe we get lucky and he makes another call to Dunlop."

"I'm not so sure he's going to stick around. If he came here for Laska, he knows we have cars on the Siesta Key house," McCarthy said.

"And that means he knows that we know he's here."

"So maybe he's not here. Maybe he gave up on Laska. Maybe he just got a change of clothes and left."

"And we'll be chasing our tails if we stay here," DeSilva said.

"There's only one way to know for sure."

"Dunlop," she said.

"I think it's time to get that search warrant," he said.

McCarthy pulled out his phone and dialed his

command post. He set the phone on the console between them and switched on the speaker so DeSilva could listen in.

"Deputy Thompson."

"Thompson, it's McCarthy."

"Yes sir."

"What's the 20 on Jasper Dunlop?"

"He left his office over three hours ago. Went directly home and has been there ever since. Wronski is sitting on the house."

"Did the phone move too?"

"Yes sir. Tracking says it's with him in the house."

"Good. It's time for the search warrant. Get it typed up and submitted and let me know when we've got the judge's signature."

"Yes sir."

"What about the woman, Heyward?"

"She left the office a little before the lawyer, stopped at a liquor store, got some take out, and went home. She's still there."

"What about the phone tap?"

"Approved and active. But there's been no calls in or out. We would have called you."

"Good work. Anything else going on there?"

"Yeah, the FBI's ASAC stopped by. We filled him in. Was that okay?"

"Sure. Did he say anything else?"

"No, but I think he's pissed we didn't let him know about the lawyer and the phones sooner."

"Don't worry about him. I'll deal with the FBI later."

"Yes sir. What's going on there?"

"We missed him. There's no telling where he is now."

"Are you gonna head back now?"

"Yeah, I think so. We should be there for the search warrant."

"We can handle it if you think you should stay in Sarasota. The overnight relief team will be here soon. We'll have the manpower."

"I know, and I know you can handle it. But we're running out of leads here anyway. Everyone hanging in there?"

"You don't have to worry about us. No one wants to quit. We're working for Miller and Wilkerson."

"Good man, we'll see you soon."

"You got it, boss."

He punched the off button and looked at DeSilva. "How about you? Getting tired? It's been a long day. Or do you want to hang around for the search warrant?"

"I'm okay," DeSilva said. "I'll stick around. I've had longer nights. But I'd better call home. I'm in the dog house as it is. Today was supposed to be my day off."

McCarthy fired up the engine. "Okay then, let's hit the road."

29

SAM AND MARLEY

"I get what you said about Indiana now," Marley said.

"Sucks, huh?" Sam said.

"It's just so flat. There's nothing to see. Nothing interesting anyway." She stared out her window at smoke stacks spewing black clouds, shuttered factories, and row upon row of electric transmission towers paralleling the highway. "Yuck, what is this place?" she said.

"The city of Gary, Indiana."

"It's horrible. I hope Chicago doesn't look like this."

"Nope, you're gonna like it. At least I think so." Laska pointed at an overhead road sign that read *Welcome to Chicago.* "Here we go," he said as he maneuvered the car onto the Dan Ryan expressway.

SAM STOOD off to the side, a little embarrassed, as Marley checked in at the front desk. He glanced around the opulent lobby taking in the marble floors, crystal chandeliers set into recessed medallions, twenty-foot high ceilings, and bouquets of flowers in tall vases on nearly every flat surface. And were they pumping in vanilla scent? He felt out of place. Like when he was still on the job off-duty at a party and he was the only cop there. He knew he shouldn't be there. And everyone at the party knew it too. He wished he was at the Best Western.

He looked over to Marley. She was all smiles and chatting away with the desk clerk, a pretty Asian girl about Marley's age. Sam imagined Marley explaining it was her first trip to Chicago and her first time in such a luxurious hotel. And the clerk, excited for her, explaining all the hotel's amenities – restaurants, bars, spa, the and the not-to-be-missed afternoon tea – for her to experience. And then, all the local sights she shouldn't miss. The shopping on Michigan Avenue (everyone calls it the Mag Mile, don't you know), Water Tower Place, the bar on the 95th floor of the Hancock building, and make sure you stop at Garrett's Popcorn and ask for the Garrett's mix. Sam wished he was at the Best Western.

Marley was finishing up. She and the desk clerk

shook hands – he was sure they would have hugged each other if there wasn't forty feet of marble-topped mahogany desk between them – and she strolled over, her hands filled with pamphlets. A bellhop followed behind her.

"Tia up-graded us to a suite," she beamed.

"Tia?"

"The clerk. She was so nice. I promised to get her some popcorn. Don't let me forget. Did you ever hear of Garrett's?"

Why couldn't they stay at the Best Western? he thought.

In their room, the bellhop placed their bags in the closet and gave them a tour of their room and all the amenities and explained how to use the tablet computers scattered around the room that controlled the TV, curtains, sound system and phones. Sam tipped him and realized, by the look on the man's face, it wasn't enough. He handed him another ten and the man left only slightly more satisfied.

"Look at this place," Marley said. "It's beautiful." She moved around the room touching everything as if she couldn't believe it wasn't a dream. She ran to the bathroom with its soaking tub, double sinks, marble countertops and gold-plated fixtures. "Look," she said, "look in here. The bathroom is bigger than our bedroom at home. And this shower, you can fit four people in here." She stood under the rainfall shower head and ran her hands over the ten nozzles poking from the side walls.

"Well, I'm not ready to invite another couple to shower with us, but how about you and me..."

She ran from the bathroom to the window. "Look at the view, Sam. I've never been in a building this big before. Or this high up."

The window looked out over Michigan Avenue to the north with views of the John Hancock building and beyond that, Lake Michigan.

Marley pointed down towards the street. "What's that?" she said.

Sam joined her at the window. "The old Water Tower. It supplied all the water for the city. It used to house a water pump that drew water from the lake. It was built in the late 1800's and was one of the only buildings to survive the Great Chicago Fire. I think it's a museum or art gallery or something now."

"And that building?"

"The John Hancock building."

"That's where the clerk said there's a bar on the top that we can't miss."

"We won't, I promise."

Marley turned to Sam and hugged him. "I'm so happy. It's like all my birthdays and Christmas's rolled into one."

She moved to the middle of the room and did a Mary Tyler Moore twirl and flopped back on the bed.

"Wow," Sam said. "You're a bundle of energy."

Marley sat up, crossed her legs, and smiled at him. "Come on over here and help me burn some of it off."

Sam looked down and sniffed himself. "It was a long day in the car. How about we try out that shower?"

SAM SAT on the edge of the bed wrapped in one of the hotel's plush robes. Marley was still in the bathroom doing her hair or whatever took women forever while they were in there. He grabbed his pants, pulled his phone out and checked the time. It was almost 6:30 p.m.

He dialed Rebecca Stafford. She was still in her office, working on his case she told him.

"I'm sorry," he told her.

"For what?" she said.

"I'm keeping you there late."

"It's not a problem. If it wasn't your case, it would be something else. What can I do for you?"

"Well, I wanted to let you know I'm in town now. We can meet anytime."

"Great, but I didn't expect you for another day or two."

"We decided to leave yesterday."

"Yesterday? You made good time."

"For stopping at every roadside attraction and historical marker, yeah, we did."

"We?"

"Yeah, my friend...my girlfriend. She's never been out of Florida before, so we decided to make a sort of vacation out of the trip."

"Is she going to mind you spending a day working with me? We've got the Interrogatives to go over and as long as you're here, I'd like to go over the case and prep you for a deposition. In fact, as long as you're here, I think I'll contact the plaintiff's attorneys and see if we can get your deposition in before you leave. That way we won't have to bring you back until the trial."

"She knows why we're here. I've already told her I'd need to spend at least a full day with you. And getting the deposition over with sounds good. The sooner the better."

"Great, how about tomorrow morning? Nine o'clock?"

"Sounds good to me."

Laska reconfirmed Stafford's office address and punched the off button on the phone just as Marley came into the room fiddling with an earring. She wore a slim-fitting emerald green satin dress, her tiny baby bump barely noticeable. Her hair and make-up were perfect. Sam thought she looked like a Bond girl.

"How about we go down to the bar for a drink?" she said.

"Did you forget you're pregnant?"

"No, of course not. You can have a drink. I'll have a club soda, and we'll talk about dinner. I'm starving."

"Give me five minutes," he said.

In the elevator, he told her about his morning appointment with his lawyer and asked if she was okay with him leaving her alone.

"Sure, of course. That's why we're here. I'll go exploring on my own. Maybe do a little shopping on the Mag Mile."

Sam smiled at how casually she used the nickname. "Or you could spend the day at the spa here in the hotel. Get a massage or facial or whatever else women do there," he said.

The elevator doors opened.

"Don't worry about me, honey. I won't get lost. I'm gonna be just fine," she said stepping out into the lobby.

30

LASKA AND REBECCA STAFFORD

S am woke to the buzzing of the alarm on his phone. He sat up and switched it off but didn't get out of the big, comfortable bed. He snuggled close to Marley and promised himself he'd only stay five more minutes. He had to admit, he was beginning to enjoy the luxury of the hotel.

After a couple drinks in the bar last night, he and Marley had dinner at an Asian themed restaurant in the hotel. Despite the early autumn Chicago weather, they sat on the outdoor terrace overlooking Michigan Avenue. Marley ordered nearly everything on the menu and gobbled down every bit. She excused herself by saying she was eating for two now.

After dinner, they took a short walk to the Water Tower and sat on a park bench until Marley complained that she was getting chilly. They ended their night making furious love and falling asleep in each other's arms.

Sam caught himself falling asleep again, so he sat up and grudgingly climbed out of bed. He showered, dressed, kissed a sleeping Marley on the cheek and headed out to meet Rebecca Stafford. In the elevator heading to the lobby, he tapped out a text to Marley reminding her of his appointment and that he'd call her later.

Stafford's office was just over a mile south across the river on Michigan near Wacker Drive. He knew there was no parking in the area, so he decided to walk. He set out at an easy pace and thirty minutes later, he was sitting on a sofa in an office lobby waiting for Stafford.

He barely had time to look over the magazines on the end table when she popped her head out of a nearby door.

"Mr. Laska?" she said waving him over. "Come on in."

She held the door for him and directed him to a chair in front of a large oak desk. Extending her hand, she said, "It's nice to finally meet you in person Mr. Laska."

Sam shook her hand and sat as she maneuvered around a stack of white cardboard file boxes, smoothed her grey skirt, and took her chair behind her desk.

"Call me Sam," he said.

"Okay, Sam. And again, call me Rebecca. Did you and your girlfriend have a nice trip? I'm sorry, what's her name?"

"Marley, Marley Jones. Yeah, I guess. It was fun seeing how excited she was to be out of Florida."

"Good. It's nice you have this trip together. I'll try not to keep you away from her too long." She grabbed a pencil and held it to a yellow legal pad. "Can I ask where you're staying?"

"The Peninsula."

Stafford looked up from her legal pad and her eyes widened slightly. "The Peninsula?"

"I know what you're thinking," Sam said. "Marley owns a pretty successful restaurant in Sarasota and does pretty well. She said that as long as we're making a vacation out of this trip, we were going to stay at a nice place."

"Nice place is right." She put the pencil down and leaned forward resting her crossed arms on the desktop. "I don't think we're going to be able to justify a reimbursement for The Peninsula."

"I already explained that to her, and it's okay by the both of us."

"Okay, I'm sorry, but I needed to be up front about that."

"No problem."

"Do you mind if I pry a little and ask about your relationship with your girlfriend?"

"I think I know where you're going with this. I've

asked her to marry me, but we've decided to put it off until this lawsuit is behind me."

"That's exactly where I was going. Good, you understand her money could be in jeopardy if you were to get married before then."

"Yes, and with that...how's it going?"

"Like I told you, we don't hold a great hand."

"But you also said we have an ace."

"Yes, Kevin King is HIV positive. And he knew he was when he...urinated on you."

Laska ran his hands through his hair and leaned forward in his chair. "You're kidding right? Why wasn't I told sooner? Did the city know?"

"No, no one knew. Well, the hospital did. After you...after he urinated on you and you defended yourself, he was hospitalized for his injuries. The hospital ran a series of tests, and they learned he was HIV positive. Test results and all medical procedures are private and protected by HIPAA regulations, so no one other than King and the hospital knew.

"We subpoenaed the hospital records in the course of our information gathering, and that's how we found out. When we saw he was HIV positive, we subpoenaed every record we could find and learned he was diagnosed about a year before your contact with him."

Laska slumped back in his seat. "Holy shit."

"Yeah." Stafford picked up her pencil again. "Have you ever been tested for HIV?"

"No, I mean I've had routine checkups since then and blood tests were part of the exam."

"Routine blood tests don't check for HIV."

"Then, no. I've never been tested for it."

"I can see by your face you're worried. Don't be. For one, the urine of HIV infected people contains little or no virus. Unless, of course, there's blood in the urine. And you didn't get any of his urine on your skin, did you? No open sores or cuts or anything back then?"

"No, I don't think so."

"Good, then there's no way you could have contracted the virus. But just to be safe we're going to set up an appointment for the test. Is that okay with you?"

"Yeah, of course."

Stafford swiveled her chair to the computer display and keyboard to her left and began tapping away. She turned back to Laska. "Okay, Marie out at the front desk will make the appointment. She'll give you the details when you leave. Do you know how to get to Northwestern Memorial?"

"Yeah."

"You'll go right to the HIV clinic in the Arkes Pavilion. They'll be expecting you."

"How long before I get the results?"

"Pretty darn quick. They'll do a quick screen. Maybe twenty minutes to an hour. We have a good relationship with them."

"You do a lot of referrals to the clinic?"

"No, to the hospital in general. We pay quickly and they like that." She leaned forward and put on her best sympathetic face. "Are you okay? Because I'm sure you really have nothing to worry about."

"I'm okay. It was just a bit of a shock."

"I'll bet it was. Are you good to start work? There's a lot I'd like to cover today. If we get it all done, I won't need to bother you again until the deposition. Oh, did I tell you I was able to get it set for early next week?"

"No, but that's fine. I want to get this whole thing behind me as soon as possible. Let's get to work."

Stafford grabbed a thick blue three-ring binder and several manila file folders from the side of her desk. She handed one of the folders to Laska.

"You'll see the top few papers in the folder are our draft answers to the Interrogatives I've prepared," she said. "Let's go over them."

They spent the next hour going over the prepared answers. Nearly every answer began with objections to the form and substance of the question. There were plenty of 'the question is vague, ambiguous, overly broad, and unduly burdensome' and 'beyond the scope of Defendant's knowledge' preceding every answer. Particularly interesting to Sam was the question demanding an estimate of his net worth. The answer Stafford drafted – in legal mumbo jumbo – was basically 'none of your business yet'.

"And when will it be their business?" Laska asked.

"Sometime before trial," was all Stafford offered.

They finished up and after Laska could think of no additions or corrections, he signed the final version and a certification letter attesting his answers were true and correct.

Well, that's done," Stafford said. "Do you want to break for a few minutes?"

"No, let's keep working. But a cup of coffee would be great."

"I could use one too," she said buzzing Marie at the front desk.

Stafford moved on with prepping Laska for the impending deposition, going over every minute of the event and Laska's frame of mind during that time. She posed pointed questions, and he provided detailed answers as articulately as he could.

"What you're saying," Stafford said, "is that when you tried to pull King's hands away from his stream of urine, you did that to prevent him from destroying evidence."

"Yes, and when I pulled on his arm, his body twisted towards me spraying me with his urine."

"And knowing that bodily fluids – blood, saliva, semen, and even urine – can carry and transmit numerous viruses, bacteria, STDs, and all manner of diseases, you knew that this was more than an insulting action on King's part. This was an attack meant to cause you physical harm."

"Absolutely. And to stop the attack, to defend myself, I struck King to back him off."

"With a clenched fist," she said. It wasn't a question.

Laska hesitated.

Stafford began shuffling through a stack of papers. "That's what you said in a report, the TRR I think it was."

"Yeah, the Tactical Response Report. We have to fill one out every time we apply the use of force."

She looked up at Laska. "It's in your report. It would have sounded better to a jury if you just shoved him back. But I think you were justified. We just have to sell it to the jury."

"How do we do that?"

"The HIV thing is big. It will really play well to the jury. They'll hear King had HIV and knew it when he attacked you. I can't imagine anyone not being sympathetic to your position."

"But I didn't know he had it."

"No, but he did. And it can reasonably be assumed he was intending to infect you. In the least, he was criminally negligent in that he knew he was potentially spreading an infectious disease in a room frequented by police officers. Even though you didn't know he was HIV positive, you quickly and correctly understood any exposure to another person's bodily fluids could infect you with all kinds of diseases. You assessed the situation as an attack and reacted appropriately in defending yourself. That's our position."

"I like it, but I don't count."

"Like I said, we have to convince the jury."

They continued on going over King's subsequent injury, Laska radioing for the EMTs, and King's transport to the hospital. But the subject of King's HIV and the possibility, however remote, that Laska was infected hung in his thoughts.

When Stafford finally said they had finished for the day, she reminded him about his appointment at the clinic.

"I'm going straight there, believe me," he said.

"Are you going to tell your girlfriend?"

"Not until I get the results. And if the results come back negative, maybe not at all."

"I don't blame you. So, before you go, do you have any final questions about all this?"

"I do. What happens to the lawsuit if King dies?"

31

DESILVA AND MCCARTHY

DeSilva grabbed at the buzzing phone hoping it was her wife Bobbie.

"It's McCarthy. Did I wake you?"

Disappointed she said, "No, I'm awake."

"You sound...off. You get enough sleep?"

"Yeah, sorry. I'm okay, I guess. I got a few hours. How about you?"

"Me too, only a few hours. In a chair in my office," McCarthy answered.

"At least you got that. So, what's up? Did you interview Dunlop and the girl yet?"

"No, we're gonna wait and let them stew for a bit. And that's why I'm calling. I'd like you to sit in on the interviews."

DeSilva perked up. "Really? Why?"

"Last time you and I talked to Dunlop, I thought

we worked well together. We were in sync, you know? You showed good instincts."

"You're blowing smoke up my ass again."

"No, I mean it. So, how about it?"

DeSilva paused, then figured it'd take her mind off her wife. "Sure, I'm in. Give me an hour and I'll meet you at the command post."

"No, we're doing this in Fort Myers. We're breaking down the mobile command post and moving everything back to our offices. Dunlop and Heyward should be there already."

"It's gonna take me longer than an hour to get there."

"We'll drive together. I'm outside your house now. Take your time getting ready. I don't mind waiting. Oh, and pack a bag. I got you a hotel room near the Federal Building."

THE SEARCH WARRANT - along with arrest warrants for Jasper Dunlop and Carol Ann Heyward - was ready to go by the time McCarthy and DeSilva returned to the command post in Arcadia from Sarasota. McCarthy quickly organized his people, and DeSilva, after a quick talk with her department's midnight watch commander, borrowed several uniformed deputies to assist.

After working out the logistics at the command

post, they executed the warrants simultaneously and took Dunlop and Heyward into custody without incident. McCarthy found the third burner phone on Dunlop's nightstand after he dialed its number from his phone and followed the tinny ring to the bedroom. Dunlop's jaw nearly hit the floor and his knees buckled under the weight of the realization that he'd be spending the rest of his life in prison. If he was lucky enough not to get the death penalty.

Heyward, according to the deputies assigned to her arrest, was defiant. She immediately demanded an attorney and threatened the deputies with lawsuits. She only softened when she begged for a phone call to her sister. She needed a cat sitter.

Regrouping at the command post, they dumped Heyward and Dunlop in the sheriff's department's holding cells and got ready for a long night of paperwork. DeSilva sat alone to the side watching a flurry of activity. She checked the time on her phone. It was four in the morning, and she felt as useless as a knitted condom. She left a note for McCarthy on his desk, slipped out the door, and headed home.

DeSilva walked out her door hauling a full-sized suitcase and a travel bag. As she approached the government Suburban parked out front, its rear hatch popped open courtesy of McCarthy in the driver's seat. She loaded her bags and climbed into the seat next to McCarthy.

"Morning, sleepyhead," McCarthy said as she settled in and latched her seatbelt. "You look like shit. Didn't sleep well?"

DeSilva laid her head back against the headrest and stared straight ahead. "No, I didn't."

McCarthy cranked up the engine and pulled away into the nearly non-existent afternoon traffic. "Maybe you should close your eyes and try to get some rest. I'm gonna need you for those interviews."

"I don't think I can sleep. Maybe you should rethink me sitting in."

McCarthy glanced at her. "Something bothering you? I mean, other than the lack of sleep."

DeSilva shrugged.

"Hey, if you don't want to talk about it that's fine. But you can deep-six any thoughts of me replacing you in the interviews. I really do need you in there. So, get your head on straight."

DeSilva turned her head and watched the tomato plants flying by outside her window. "My wife left me," she said.

"What?"

She turned back to McCarthy. "I said my wife left me. I got home this morning and found a note on the bed. She left me."

McCarthy sat nearly motionless, his eyes on the road ahead.

"Nothing to say, McCarthy? Surprised I have a wife and not a husband? Didn't the file on me mention?"

He looked over at her and then back to the road. "Yeah, it did. I don't care about that. I just don't know how to react. I mean, what do you say to someone who tells you their marriage just went to shit? I only met you two days ago for Christ's sake."

DeSilva turned away and stared out her window again. She sat quietly for a moment then said, "I'm sorry I snapped at you."

"Don't worry about it," he said. "And I'm sorry. You know...about your wife."

"Thanks."

"You...want to talk about it? We've got about an hour to Fort Myers."

"No, not really. Besides, I'm pretty sure you don't want to hear about it."

"Yeah, you're right," he said. He looked over to her and let out a little laugh. "Hoo boy! I dodged a bullet there, huh?"

"Yeah, you did."

They sat, neither speaking, as the miles rolled by. As they drew nearer to Fort Myers and moved out of farm country, DeSilva said, "I could use a cup of coffee. Why don't you pull in when you see someplace?"

"You got it," McCarthy said. "I'll buy."

"And I won't argue."

It was twenty minutes before McCarthy spied a Waffle House and pulled in. They grabbed a booth in a far corner away from the few mid-morning customers. McCarthy ordered eggs and bacon and the obligatory hash browns – smothered and covered. DeSilva passed on a heavy breakfast and stuck with coffee and dry toast.

They sipped their coffee, waiting for their food. McCarthy looked across the table. "I think we should talk," he said putting down his mug.

"I thought you didn't want to talk about my crumbling life," she said.

"I don't. Good God I don't. No, there's something else."

"Good. I don't want to talk about that either. So, what is it?"

"I've requested that you be deputized into the Marshal's Service. You'll stay on with us until we get Nichols. If it takes longer than a year, we'll talk about renewing you then. Basically, you'll have all the same enforcement powers you hold as a State of Florida law enforcement officer. But you'll also have federal enforcement powers. Plus, you'll be able to participate in and monitor electronic surveillance and Title 18 federal criminal offenses."

DeSilva sat back. "Huh, I didn't expect this."

"I'll need you to sign this application form. I took the liberty of filling it out for you." He pulled the folded application from a back pocket and set it in front of her.

DeSilva looked over the multi-page form. "Wow, you've got it all down here. You even checked the 'married' box."

"You still are, right?"

"Yeah, I still am. Technically."

"She might come back, Kathy." It was the first time McCarthy used her first name.

DeSilva looked up at him. "Don't call me that."

"I'm sorry. I didn't mean to get familiar."

"No, it's not that. No one calls me Kathy. It's Kat. All my friends call me Kat."

"We're friends now?"

"Don't push it." She smiled for the first time since she got into the Suburban. "You can call me Kat, but never at work, okay? Never in front of anyone around the office."

"Understood. Now, how about it?" He handed her a pen.

DeSilva took McCarthy's pen and hesitated. "Did you talk to my sheriff?"

"He knows."

"And he's okay with this?"

"We don't know and we don't care. You'll still be an employee of the county. Paid by them but assigned to us - and you won't need to report back to them. In fact, you can't. What you do for us stays confidential."

She nodded, put the pen to the form and signed her name.

McCarthy scooped up the form before she had a change of heart. "I talked to the Assistant Director already. He's gonna try and expedite this." He took a sip of coffee. "This assignment is temporary, but I think you should apply for the Marshal's Service."

"Leave the Sheriff's Department?"

"Yeah. Your talents are wasted there."

"I disagree. There's work that needs to be done in DeSoto county. People that need help. Plus, I've got a lot of time in there. I don't know if I like the idea of starting over somewhere else."

The waitress shuffled over and dealt the plates of food to them. McCarthy grabbed the shaker and salted his food without tasting it first. "Think about it," he said.

32

DESILVA AND MCCARTHY

DeSilva and McCarthy stood in the dark room peering through the one-way mirror. In the adjacent room Jasper Dunlop sat at a table handcuffed to a steel ring bolted to the table's top. His head bowed as if in prayer, chin to his chest. His lower lip trembled and his shirt – government issued jail garb – was damp with sweat.

"He looks ripe for the picking," DeSilva said. She turned to McCarthy. "Are you sure you need me in there? I don't see you having a problem getting anything you need."

"Yeah, you're right. But I still want you with me." He grabbed a thick manila file folder off a table. DeSilva gave him a look and he smiled. "It's a prop. Come on, this is gonna be fun."

DeSilva followed McCarthy and they headed

into the interview room. He and DeSilva sat in two chairs opposite Dunlop. Dunlop didn't look up until McCarthy tossed the file folder onto the desk.

"Good morning Mr. Dunlop," McCarthy said. He checked his watch. "Or I should say good afternoon."

Dunlop looked from McCarthy to DeSilva and back again. He began to open his mouth.

McCarthy held up a hand. "Before you say anything, before you exercise your fifth amendment protections and ask for representation, I want you to know what you're looking at.

"Three counts of first degree murder. And the murders of the two United States' marshals carry the death penalty. Then there's aiding and abetting an escape and lying to a federal officer. And those are just the federal crimes you'll be charged with. Lieutenant DeSilva has a host of state charges she'd like to pile on, but the State of Florida will have to wait. Do you understand what we're talking about here?"

"Yes," Dunlop said.

"A little louder please. Otherwise the microphone won't pick it up." McCarthy turned his head and motioned to a camera and overhead mike.

"Yes," Dunlop said, still weak but louder. "I understand."

"Good," McCarthy said. "You're looking at the death penalty. But it doesn't have to go that way. I can't and won't make any promises, but if you agree to cooperate and to be entirely candid and truthful, the assistant U.S. attorney assures me he'll only ask for life.

"You can spend your time in the law library of a nice federal penitentiary up north helping the other prisoners file motions and writs. You may even be assigned a job in the kitchen, or better yet, the library."

"I'll keep my law license?"

"No, you'll be disbarred." McCarthy turned to DeSilva. "Right?"

"Most definitely," she said.

McCarthy turned back to Dunlop. "You understand our position. Do you want some time to think it over?"

"No," Dunlop said. He drew in a deep breath. "I'll cooperate."

"Good, then let's get started."

McCarthy read Dunlop his Miranda warnings from a waiver form he pulled from the manila folder. He pushed the paper in front of Dunlop and told him to read it aloud and state whether or not he understood each of the warnings. Dunlop did and McCarthy uncuffed him, handed him a pen, and told him to sign at the bottom.

After he and DeSilva signed as witnesses, McCarthy slipped the paper back into the folder. "Let's start at the beginning," he said. "When was your first contact with Jesse Nichols?"

Dunlop began by telling them how Nichols first

approached him when Nichols was still in uniform patrol. It was a minor narcotics case, a drop case. Nichols' report stated he saw a teen peering into parked cars late at night in a residential neighborhood. As Nichols pulled to the curb to conduct a Terry stop, he saw the teen toss a small clear plastic bag. He recovered the bag and found it contained what he suspected was marijuana.

The kid turned out to be the son of a friend to Dunlop, and Dunlop promised his friend he'd do what he could. The deal was that Dunlop would keep the kid's bail as his fee after any verdict. Before the preliminary hearing, Nichols ran into Dunlop in the hallway of the courthouse. He told Dunlop he'd throw the case for half of the bail.

Dunlop told McCarthy and DeSilva he agreed only because the kid was on probation for cannabis possession already and was looking at jail time. It would break his father's heart, so Dunlop made the deal. Nichols screwed up his testimony and the kid walked.

Everything snowballed after that. Nichols kept coming to Dunlop with cases. Throwing them for half of Dunlop's fee. Dunlop eventually turned information he learned from clients over to Nichols who'd use it to make even more arrests he'd throw for Dunlop.

When the sheriff's department promoted Nichols to detective, the cases and the payouts got even bigger. Dunlop got the reputation on the street as a lawyer who couldn't lose and his practice and bank account grew.

"And when Nichols was arrested with the Cordele family, you agreed to represent him," DeSilva said. "Pro bono."

Dunlop looked over to DeSilva. She thought he was about to cry. "I had to. He threatened me. Said he'd give up the whole scheme. I'd get disbarred. Maybe even land in jail."

"He had you by the short hairs," she said. "But you still had a choice, and three people are dead because of the choices you made. And you're still gonna wind up in prison."

"And get disbarred," McCarthy said.

The rest of the interview lasted over two hours with only a short break to get Dunlop a bottle of water and to take a supervised bathroom break.

When they resumed after the break, Dunlop said Nichols told him of his plan to escape at their first attorney/client meeting. He needed Dunlop to contact the FBI and tell them Nichols was willing to exchange information on systemic corruption in the sheriff's department in exchange for them intervening in his case. He also needed burner phones and more importantly, an insider at the jail.

"And you found Frank Castillo," DeSilva said.

"How'd that happen? Were you handling a bankruptcy for him or something?" McCarthy asked.

"Chapter Eleven," Dunlop said. "He was terrible with money and he was desperate."

"So, you hooked Nichols up with Castillo, and got three burners so you could all keep in touch. You had your receptionist buy the phones and you reimbursed her. Isn't that right?" McCarthy said. "Be careful how you answer. This is a test question."

Dunlop's chin dropped to his chest again. "Yes," he said.

"And did she know why you needed her to buy the phones?" DeSilva said.

"Again," McCarthy said, "be careful. It's another test question. She's just down the hall sitting in a room like this."

"Yes," Dunlop said.

McCarthy reached across the table and patted Dunlop's hand. "You're doing good, Jasper." He sat back again. "Let's talk about those phones. How many times did you talk to Nichols since the escape?"

"I think two...no, three times."

"When was the last time?"

Tap, tap, tap

McCarthy and DeSilva both turned to the knock from the other side of the one-way mirror. McCarthy stood and nodded DeSilva to the door. "Hold that thought, Jasper," he said. "We'll be right back."

McCarthy and DeSilva stepped out of the room and into the hall. Waiting for them was the deputy marshal DeSilva recognized as Thompson from McCarthy's team. Before McCarthy had a chance to ask why he called them out of the interview, Thompson said, "They found Castillo's car. It was parked on the upper level of a hospital's parking lot."

"Nichols?" McCarthy said.

"Nowhere around. But that's not all. The girlfriend's apartment was broken into."

DeSilva stepped closer. "Laska's girlfriend? Marley Jones?"

"Yeah," Thompson said. "A neighbor saw the door lock broken as she was leaving her apartment. Our team is on the scene with the local police."

"How far is the hospital from the apartment?" McCarthy said.

"Two blocks," Thompson answered.

"Does it look like Nichols broke into..." McCarthy said.

"Who the fuck else would it be?" DeSilva said. "But how would he know where it is?"

McCarthy looked at DeSilva. In unison they said, "Jasper."

She stuck her hand out. "I need your keys. I'm going to Sarasota."

"What's the point?" McCarthy said. "There's no reason for you to go to Sarasota. Nichols is gone."

"But he's still there. And without a car. We've gotta mobilize more people and throw a net over the entire area."

"She's right, boss," Thompson said. "He's gotta be close."

"Unless he stole another ride. But, yeah. He could still be in the area. We can't take the chance that he's not. Get ahold of the police and sheriff's departments. Have them flood the area. Give them a description of Nichols' new clothes and tell them to pay extra special attention to any reports of suspicious persons calls, break-ins, and stolen vehicles."

Thompson took off down the hall and McCarthy turned back to DeSilva. "There's still no reason for you to go to Sarasota. We've got Dunlop here and he's talking. Let's finish up with him and then make a plan. Who knows? Maybe he'll be able to point us in the right direction."

DeSilva kept her hand out. "You told me I'd work with you. Not for you. Equals. You can stay here with Jasper. I want to go and help in Sarasota."

McCarthy shook his head slowly. He dug into his pocket and pulled out a set of keys. "Here you go," he said handing them to her.

DeSilva took the keys and turned to walk away.

"Wait," McCarthy said. "Give Dunlop just a few minutes. Please."

DeSilva stopped and looked back at him over her shoulder.

"Like you said to me," he said, "another ten or twenty minutes isn't going to make a difference."

DeSilva turned back. "I'll give it ten."

DeSilva and McCarthy sat across from Jasper Dunlop for the second time. He looked even more defeated than when they left him fifteen minutes prior.

"Where were we?" McCarthy said. "Oh, yeah. The phone calls. Did you ever call him? Is there a certain time you have to call?"

"No, I can't call him. He turns his phone off between calls. I have to leave mine on and wait for his call," Dunlop said.

McCarthy sat back. "What about a voicemail? Can you leave...?"

DeSilva cut him off. "Your last phone call from Nichols. When was it? Yesterday, right?"

Dunlop turned to DeSilva. "Yes. I think...in the evening."

"What did you talk about? What did he say?" she said.

"He wanted me to find his daughter. He wanted to know where his wife took her. I told him I couldn't do it. I don't have the resources. He told me, threatened me, that I better do it. He wasn't going to leave the country without her."

"Then his plan is to leave the country?" McCarthy said.

DeSilva cut him off again. "What else did he want? Did he ask you for anything else?"

Dunlop looked from DeSilva to McCarthy.

"Answer her first," McCarthy said.

Dunlop turned to DeSilva. "Yes, he wanted me to get him the address of a girl...a woman."

"What woman?" she said leaning across the table.

"Somebody Jones."

"Gabrielle Jones?" DeSilva said, her voice louder.

Dunlop moved back in his chair, fear creeping over his face. "Yes, I think...I remember now. Gabrielle Jones. That's it."

DeSilva bolted up out of her chair, leaning across the table. "And you found it for him. You gave him the address."

Dunlop cringed and sunk deeper into his chair. McCarthy put a hand on DeSilva's arm.

"Right?" she shouted. "Answer me!"

Dunlop's head dropped. "Yes," he said in a near whisper.

DeSilva pushed her chair aside and hurried out the door.

McCarthy looked at Dunlop. "I'll be back," he said and went after DeSilva.

He caught up to her down the hall falling in step with her as she walked. He could barely keep up with her. "That was some show. You scared the crap out of him. Have you ever played the good cop?"

DeSilva stopped short and poked a finger in his chest. "I wasn't playing good-cop-bad-cop. It was all I could do not to throttle the asshole. He gave up my friend and his girlfriend knowing Nichols was going to kill them."

"Yeah, but they're not dead. They're alive and safe in Chicago. Nichols doesn't know that, and there's no way he can find out."

"Are you sure? Are you willing to bet their lives on it? We had no idea Nichols' plan was to go after Laska. We had no idea he would go to Sarasota until we got lucky and found that note. We weren't smart enough to figure out he'd find Gabrielle Jones' condo. But he did. He was smart enough. And now you're telling me he has no way of knowing they're in Chicago. How do you know?"

"I don't."

"He broke into their apartment. Maybe he found something. Travel plans...whatever. I'm not going to take that chance."

She started back down the hall.

"Hang on a second," McCarthy called out.

DeSilva spun around. "What?"

McCarthy walked over to her and pulled his wallet out. He handed her a card. "Here, a government credit card. Food, gas, and lodging only, okay?"

She took the card and left McCarthy standing in the hall. As she walked, she pulled out her phone and dialed Laska.

33

SAM AND MARLEY

The question surprised Stafford. "What?" she said.

Laska repeated it. "What happens to the lawsuit if King dies? I mean, he's HIV positive. What if it develops into AIDS and he dies? Does the lawsuit just go away?"

"Oh," she said. "You had me worried for a second."

Laska chuckled. "You thought I was going to arrange an accident for him or something?"

"Yes...no, I mean you caught me off guard. No one's ever asked me something like that before."

"I thought it was a reasonable question."

"Yeah, I suppose it is. Although I never considered it."

"Well? Does it go away?"

"The short answer...probably not. His attorneys

don't have standing to continue without him and they would need to find someone who does. A relative. Mother, father, grandparent. That kind of thing. And you can bet they'll probably search high and low for someone to continue with."

"But if they couldn't, the lawsuit goes away?"

"Yes, but I wouldn't get my hopes up if I were you. Let's just proceed with our preparations and the expectation that this will go to trial."

AFTER LEAVING STAFFORD'S OFFICE, Laska headed over to the clinic at Northwestern Memorial. He was in and out in half an hour with good news. The screen was negative. He said a little prayer of thanks on the way out.

On the walk back to the hotel, he called Marley like he promised. Getting no answer, he left a voicemail and let her know he'd be waiting for her in the hotel bar. He needed a drink.

He was deep into his second beer when he felt his phone vibrating in his pocket. Marley calling him back, he thought. But the phone's display told him it was DeSilva.

"What's up?" he answered.

"Where are you?"

"Chicago. We got in late yesterday."

"Are you alone? Is Marley there with you?"

"No. She's out shopping. I'm sitting in the hotel bar waiting for her."

"Good. You might not want her to know about this yet."

"Know about what?"

"I don't know how to say this, so I'll just say it. Nichols found out where you and Marley live. He broke into the condo. At least we're pretty sure it was him. The car he was using was found abandoned two blocks away in the hospital parking lot."

Laska took a long pull on his beer. "How did he find it?"

"His lawyer. We took him into custody yesterday. Short version, he's been in on the escape from the beginning. He supplied Nichols and another guy with burner phones and has been feeding Nichols info as needed.

"We've been trying to track his phone, but he turns it off between calls. The last hit we had showed him on the north end of Sarasota. We think it was on that call that the lawyer gave him your address."

"How bad is the condo? Did he trash it?"

"I don't know. I'm in Fort Myers with the marshals. But I'm leaving there now and heading to Sarasota. I'll let you know as soon as I get there."

"Don't call. Text me and I'll call you back. You're right. I don't want to upset Marley. At least until we know more."

"Alright. I'll talk to you later."

"Yeah. Oh, and thanks."

"No problem, man. You'd do it for me."

Laska punched the red button and pocketed his phone. He took another swallow of his beer. "Shit," he mumbled to himself.

"Hey you."

He heard Marley's voice behind him. He swiveled his stool and saw Marley walking through the door of the bar, her arms laden with bags and boxes. Sam jumped off his stool.

"Here," he said. "Let me take those from you."

She began setting them on the floor and an empty stool. "I need to sit. I'm exhausted." She gave him a kiss, took the chair next to him, and knocked back the last swallow of his beer.

"Hey, what are you doing?"

"One sip isn't going to hurt."

"Okay, but let me get you something else." Sam gave a wave to the bartender and ordered a club soda for Marley and another beer for himself.

Marley looked at him. "You okay?"

"Yeah, just a little tired. It was a long day." He looked over her pile of loot. "You've been busy."

"It was so much fun. I was up and down Michigan Avenue twice. There's so much to see."

"And even more to spend your money on."

"Cool your jets, honey. But that reminds me. I bought you a present."

"Marley, you shouldn't spend your money on me. I don't need anything."

She smiled and gave him a wink. "You're gonna like it."

"We'll see." He turned toward her bags. "Which one is it?"

"The pink bag." She looked around the bar. "But I can't show it to you in here."

He turned back to her. She gave him a little nod and winked again.

"Oh, I get it now."

"That's my brilliant detective."

"Well, let's knock back these drinks and get you upstairs."

"Not so fast buddy. You're gonna have to buy me dinner first. I'm starving. But I need a shower first."

Up in their room Marley surrendered to her fatigue and plopped down on the bed. She said she only needed ten or fifteen minutes so Sam hit the bathroom. He showered and shaved then handed it off to Marley. He dressed, slacks and a nice polo topped by a sport coat, and flipped on the television while he waited.

He ran a hand through his hair. He was starting to feel piled upon. First the lawsuit, Nichols, the HIV scare, and now Marley's condo. He briefly considered telling her about the break-in at the condo – she had a right to know - but he dismissed the notion. They were safe in Chicago. Nichols was on the run, but he'd be in custody soon. Hopefully. And there was no reason to upset her and spoil her vacation. He'd tell her later. Much later.

Marley scampered out of the bathroom wrapped in a towel. She shuffled through her bags and boxes and picked out a few, including the little pink bag – Sam's present. She held it up for Sam to see, smiled, and scooted back to the bathroom.

Thirty minutes later she re-emerged wearing a rose colored backless little number. She slipped on a pair of heels, struck a pose and said, "How do I look?"

"I don't think I've ever seen you more beautiful," he said. *Marley Jones*, he thought. *Bond girl.*

"I do look good, don't I?" she said as she checked herself out in a nearby mirror. She turned back to Sam. "Where are you taking me?"

"I've gotta show you off. I think we'll head over to Rush Street. Maybe Tavern On Rush or Gibson's."

"Is it far?"

"A couple of blocks. Walking distance." He looked down at her shoes. "We'll take a cab."

Sam decided on Tavern On Rush. They had dinner at a quiet table on the second floor with a view of Rush Street below. Marley couldn't stop staring out the floor-to-ceiling windows at the vibrant scene outside. Sam couldn't stop staring at her. They lingered over dessert and espresso talking and planning their next few days in the city, but afterwards, they hurried back to their room.

Inside their suite, Marley pushed Sam onto the bed and told him to wait and watch. She dimmed the lights using one of the tablets and stood at the foot of the bed. "Ready?" she said.

"I can't wait much longer."

Shimmying out of her dress, she let it fall around her ankles. She posed there naked wearing only the smallest, laciest, wisp of a white thong.

"I don't know what you paid for that," he said, "and I don't care." He began peeling off his own clothes.

Marley stepped out of her heels.

"No," he said. "Keep them on."

34

JESSE NICHOLS

Nichols spent his first night in a budget motel near the Florida-Georgia state line. After bailing out the back door of the Jones girl's apartment, he found an old beat up Ford pickup - maybe a 1970-something – parked on the street. The keys he found in the apartment fit. The truck complained a bit but sounded okay once it warmed up. Fifteen minutes later he was northbound on I-75 putting miles between him and Sarasota.

The motel advertised free wi-fi and that aside from the cut-rate price was the reason he picked it. He laid on the bed and opened the stolen laptop and spent the next hour going through Laska's email account and the entire file attachment regarding Laska's lawsuit. He smiled as he finished up and closed the laptop. Too bad for Kevin King, he thought. He'd never collect from Laska. You can't get anything from a dead man.

He got a late start the next day. It was a long time since he laid in a decent bed so he overslept. He gassed up the pickup, loaded up on beef jerky and energy drinks, and promised himself he'd make it to Chicago before he slept again.

A long, hard drive later he made it. Almost. It was nearly midnight, and he was fighting to stay awake behind the wheel when he spied the sign. *Chicago – 46 miles*. He pulled off at the next exit, gassed up again – for the fourth time – and bought a Chicago street map. He downed another energy drink, stretched, and loaded himself into the truck to finish the drive.

Now all he needed was a plan. How was he going to grab Laska and the girl? It shouldn't be too big of a problem to figure out. He had forty-six miles to do it.

35

DESILVA

DeSilva left for Sarasota just after 7:30 pm. As she pulled out of the Federal Building parking lot, she radioed ahead to McCarthy's people and set up a meet with the team sitting on the Jones' apartment.

The drive was torture for her. Not because of traffic or the anxiety she felt over the investigation and the threat to her friends, but because she was alone. Not alone in the government Suburban, not because the seat next to her was unoccupied, but alone with her thoughts.

Though she had many more weighty matters to focus on, she could only think of her wife Bobbie. She should have seen it coming. A separation. Maybe a divorce. They spent less and less time together lately. Both of their careers put demands on their time. And when they were together, when they had the rare day off together, they always seemed to bicker.

The arguments always started over petty matters; a towel left on the floor, who's turn was it to empty the dishwasher, who left the lid off the peanut butter? And those led to increasingly significant grievances. You never say I'm pretty any longer, why don't we talk more, when was the last time we had sex? You've changed.

· DeSilva knew marriages needed constant attention, and she was not putting in the time and effort that she should. But Bobbie wasn't exactly trying either. *Scratch that*, she thought. *I'm not going to fault her*. That kind of thinking is what started their problems.

She wiped her watering eyes. Crying while driving on I-75 at eight-five miles an hour wasn't a good thing. She needed to snap out of it and to look for some hope.

She still loved Bobbie. She was never surer of that. And she hoped Bobbie still loved her. If she did, there was every reason to try and work out their problems. To salvage their life together. To stay together.

She shivered at the thought of starting over. Finding someone to love and who loved you back was tough enough. Damn near impossible for a gay woman in bumfuck backwoods Florida.

It was already after 9:00 pm when she pulled to

the curb behind an identical Chevy Suburban. Two tired looking deputy US marshal's popped out of the Suburban and waited for her on the sidewalk in front of the building where Laska and Jones lived.

She nodded a hello to them as she walked up.

"This way," the taller of the two said.

DeSilva followed their lead across an open courtyard to an exterior staircase.

"Sorry," she said. "I don't know your names."

"Tallon and Bielski," the shorter man said. "He's Bielski and I'm Tallon."

"I'm DeSilva," she said.

"We know," Bielski said.

As they climbed the stairs DeSilva said, "You've seen the apartment already?"

Tallon answered. "Yeah, just walked through it. The police and sheriffs handled the processing."

"Anything missing that you can tell? Any damage?"

They stopped in front of the apartment. Yellow crime scene tape crisscrossed the entry.

"They're gonna need a new TV," Tallon said. Pushing open the door he said, "Can't tell if anything is missing though. It looks like he searched a few drawers. But all in all, the place is in pretty good shape."

As they passed through the door and stood in the living room, Bielski flipped a switch. A dim light poured into the room from a ceiling fixture in the entry hall. He said, "Careful what you touch. There's fingerprint powder everywhere."

DeSilva looked over the room. Tallon was right. They were going to need a new television. Someone – Nichols – had thrown something at the screen. She looked closer at the crushed and cracked glass.

"It was the remote," Tallon said. "It was imbedded in there like a spear. The processing team took it. They said they'll superglue it."

DeSilva nodded. "What else did they collect?"

"Three empty beer bottles they dusted. Good latents off all of them."

"Are they doing a rush on them for us?"

"Yeah, they grumbled a little about overtime for their AFIS tech, but they're doing it. We should know soon. I hope."

She continued her tour around the apartment touching nothing but looking at everything. She ended at the back door. "Did we unlock this door?"

"No, that's how it was. We think he exited that way. Less likely someone would see him," Tallon said.

DeSilva nodded her agreement. She walked back to the living room and stared at the television. "How about this? He breaks in hoping to find them here. They're not, so he figures he'll wait for them to come back from wherever they are. He makes himself at home. He has a couple beers, turns on the TV and relaxes. He sees something on TV that pisses him off

– likely a news story about him – and throws the remote. He figures he's not safe so he beats it out the back door."

"It sounds right, but there's a hole in that theory," Bielski said.

"You're right," DeSilva said. "There is. If he was going to lie in wait for them, why get comfortable with three beers? Why turn on the TV and broadcast that someone was in the apartment?"

"Why bust up the front door lock for them to see as they walk up?" Tallon said.

"Exactly," DeSilva said. "Why do any of that unless he knew they weren't coming back?"

She hung around the apartment talking with Tallon and Bielski double and triple checking and trying to blow holes in their theory. They kept coming back to the same conclusion: Nichols knew Laska and Jones were gone and were not coming back.

At 1:30 in the morning Bielski took a phone call from the sheriff's department confirming Nichols' fingerprints were on the beer bottles and scattered everywhere else around the apartment. After he relayed the message to DeSilva he said, "There's not much else to do around here. Do we need to keep sitting on it?"

"If it were up to me, yeah. At least until we confirm Nichols left the area. But that's on your boss. You want to call him, or should I?"

"Go for it," he said.

"Okay," she said. She glanced at the front door. She pointed to the phone still in Bielski's hand. "Why don't you see if you can find a twenty-four-hour locksmith?"

DeSilva dialed McCarthy.

"McCarthy," he answered.

"It's me," she said. "You still with Dunlop?"

"I ended the interview about a half-hour ago."

"I thought you might have headed home for the night."

"No such luck. I'll be here for the duration. There's a lot of work to do. What's going on in Sarasota?"

"The break-in was definitely Nichols. We just got a fingerprint confirmation. From the looks of it, he broke in knowing they weren't home. We think he either knew going in Laska and Jones weren't coming back, or he figured it out while he was in here." She laid out her theory explaining the easy to see broken lock on the front door, the speared television, and the time Nichols spent in the apartment leisurely drinking three beers.

"Yeah," McCarthy said, "it sure sounds like you're right. Laska's in Chicago now, right?"

"I called him and confirmed. Yeah, he's there."

"Any indication Nichols knows that, or do we think he'll give up on finding him and get the hell out of Dodge?"

"There's nothing lying around the apartment that says they were headed to Chicago unless Nichols found something and took it with him. I'll get in touch with Laska and see if he left anything. An itinerary or something."

"Alright, you're gonna get a room in Sarasota I assume?"

"Yeah, it's too late to drive back. Listen, one more thing. What do you want your people to do? They've been sitting on the apartment, but there's almost no chance Nichols is coming back. And we're ordering up a locksmith to secure the door."

"They can knock off for the night. I'd say we can tell the police and sheriff's deputies they can stand down too. Maybe just keep their cars aware he may still be in the area."

"I'll take care of it. What's going on there with Dunlop?"

"A shitload. I can't shut the guy up. He's down for the night now. We're keeping him close though. Making him sleep in one of the interview rooms. We'll need him to answer his burner if Nichols calls."

"Yeah, that's going to be the only way we'll get a location on Nichols, huh?"

"I'm trying to hurry that up. I had him leave a voicemail for Nichols."

"I hope it works."

"Me too. Get some sleep, Kat. You gonna come back here in the morning?"

"Yeah, I might as well. See you when I see you." DeSilva clicked off and turned to Tallon and Bielski. "You guys are done for the night. I gotta make a few calls and then I'm calling it a night too."

"You want us to wait for the locksmith?" Tallon said. "He's on the way."

"I'll do it," she said. "Go on and get out of here."

Tallon and Bielski thanked her, gave her a see-you-later-wave, and headed for the door.

"Hang on," DeSilva said. "Where are you staying tonight?"

"The Hyatt across from the airport," Bielski said.

"Want to meet me for a drink at the bar?" DeSilva said.

36

SAM AND MARLEY

Sam sat on the sofa in their suite hunting and pecking on his phone's search app. "Did you figure out what you want to do today?" he called out to Marley. She was primping in the bathroom putting the finishing touches on the face and hair she would present to the city of Chicago today.

"I thought we decided on the Art Institute and Millennium Park," she said poking her head out so Sam could hear her.

"The Cubs are home today. Against the Cardinals. They missed the playoffs so there'd be no problem getting tickets."

Marley strolled in adjusting an earring. "You heard me, right? We decided on the Art Institute and Millennium Park last night at dinner. No last minute changes."

Sam continued fiddling with his phone. "They're

playing a night game. We could do the museum and the park and even have time for an early dinner before the game."

"What time is the game?"

"Seven-fifteen. Plenty of time for all that other stuff."

"Sure, okay. I'm in."

Sam kept poking away on the screen of his phone. "Shit, dammit," he said.

Marley sat down next to him. "Problem?"

"I'm trying to buy tickets, but I keep screwing up on this shitty keyboard." He handed her his phone. "You didn't bring your laptop, did you?"

"No, sorry. Never entered my mind." Marley started typing on the screen and said, "Let me see what I can do."

Sam leaned over and watched the screen as she typed. "Get bleacher seats. It's more fun in the bleachers."

"Done," she said. "Two tickets for the right field bleachers. They'll be at 'will call' under your name." She handed his phone to him.

"How the hell do you do that with those fingernails?"

"I've got skills." She gave him a peck on the cheek and stood up. "You ready for another fun day? I can't wait to see the Art Institute. I checked it out online. There's a new Impressionist exhibit and another one on Folk Art."

Sam hoisted himself off the sofa and tried to look enthusiastic. "I can't wait. Out of focus paintings and garage sale trash. Whoopee."

Marley elbowed him. "Let's get moving."

Waiting for the elevator down to the lobby Sam felt a single vibration from the phone in his pocket. That meant a text. He checked the message. It was from DeSilva. *Did you get my last msg? Call me.* He scrolled up a little farther. She had texted him at 2:34 am last night. *Call me.*

Marley nodded to his phone. "What's up?"

"I got a text from Lieutenant DeSilva last night and again just now. She wants me to call her."

"What do you think that's about?"

The elevator signaled its arrival with a soft ding. As the doors opened Sam said, "I don't know. But it can't be too important if she texted and didn't call." He wasn't yet ready to give her any bad news.

Marley watched him pocket his phone. "Aren't you going to call her back?"

"There's no reception in elevators. I'll call later. Like I said, it can't be too important if she only texted."

The bad reception was true, Sam thought. But he knew DeSilva would talk about the break-in at Marley's apartment. That was a conversation he didn't want her to hear.

Outside, they stood in front of the hotel trying to decide on driving, walking, or getting a cab. Sam convinced her it was too far to walk and he didn't want to fight traffic and then search for parking.

"We could Uber," Marley said.

Sam checked out the line of cabs. "Why wait for an Uber? There's plenty of cabs right here."

He nodded to the doorman who waved over the first cab in line. He slipped the doorman a five for doing nearly nothing and they piled into the back seat.

Marley leaned over close to Sam. "You could have saved that tip by ordering an Uber," she whispered so the driver couldn't hear her.

"You could have said something earlier."

"I thought it was obvious, detective."

At the Art Institute Marley had them beeline to the Impressionist exhibit and they lingered there through the Monets, Van Goghs, Manets, and Renoirs.

"These guys must of all had cataracts," Sam said as they passed a series of paintings of what he figured were haystacks in a field.

"Hush," Marley said, "be nice. I think they're beautiful. Just be quiet and enjoy."

After an hour of not-so-quiet suffering from Sam they moved on. At a kiosk in the main hall Marley grabbed a map printed on a pamphlet and tried to figure out how to get to the Folk Art exhibit. Sam leaned over her shoulder.

"Is there a bathroom marked on there?"

"Here." She pointed to a spot on the map.

Sam moved in closer and saw the bathrooms were located near a food court that served adult beverages.

"How about you go on ahead and I'll catch up after I hit the bathroom?" he said.

"I see the food court on the map, Sam. I can see they serve beer and wine."

"Really? I hadn't noticed."

"Knock it off. You're not fooling anyone."

"Okay, but how about it? I'll have a beer, one beer, and catch up to you."

"You're not afraid of losing me?"

"You'll be at the Folk Art exhibit. How hard can it be?"

She punched him on the arm. "That's not the way I meant it." She gave him a you-better-watch-yourself look and headed off down the hallway.

Sam called after her, "You're joking, right?"

She turned her head and smiled, shrugged her shoulders, and kept walking.

Sam knew she was just messing with him. But to be on the safe side, he decided to hurry.

After his visit to the bathroom he looked over to the food court, decided he'd rather be with Marley than have a beer, and headed off to find her. He wound up taking a wrong turn then several more and entered a section displaying modern art. Against all of his manly instincts he figured he'd better ask for directions. He spotted a museum employee and started towards the man but something caught his eye. It was a painting - a painting he had seen before. Maybe in a magazine. Maybe in a movie or a documentary when he couldn't find anything else to watch on TV. He thought he even remembered seeing silly spin-offs on it with cartoon characters or movie stars taking the place of the people in the painting.

He moved in to get a closer look. A little information card next to the painting said it was titled 'Nighthawks' and painted by a guy named Edward Hopper. He stepped back again and stared. It was a simple scene: four people in some diner on some street in some city. The city outside the diner was dark and lonely. The harsh light inside the diner offering a temporary escape from that loneliness.

Three tired looking people hunched around a counter. The men in dark suits and fedoras. The woman, the classic femme fatale, dressed in red. A man in chef's whites was behind the counter looking happy to have some company. It reminded him of a scene from some old black and white movie, a *film noir*. He wondered what happened next? Did someone pull a gun? Did a robber burst in the door? Did nothing at all happen?

Laska's phone began buzzing in his pocket. He knew it was DeSilva even before he answered.

"Before you say anything," he said into the phone, "I'm sorry I didn't call back."

"What the hell, man?" DeSilva said. "Call me means call me."

"I was with Marley. I didn't want her to hear us talking."

"That's why I texted you. You couldn't get away for ten minutes?"

"Are you gonna lecture me, mom?"

"Asshole. Where are you? Can you talk now?"

A young couple nearby gave Laska the stink-eye. He moved away from the exhibits into a hallway. "Yeah, I can talk. We're at an art museum. Marley's off somewhere else."

Laska heard DeSilva exhale heavily. "Bad news," she said. "I think it's possible Nichols knows you're in Chicago."

"How?"

DeSilva ran it down for Laska explaining her theory and the holes in it that made her believe Nichols might have learned about Sam and Marley's trip. "Did you leave anything around? A note or something he could have found?"

You didn't bring your laptop, did you? Laska's own words to Marley echoed in his head.

"You were in the condo, right?" he said.

"Yeah."

"There was a computer, a laptop, on the dining

room table. Did you see it? Is it still there?" A wave of anxiety swept over him.

"No. There was nothing on the table."

"You sure?"

"Fuck yeah, Sam. I'm sure." DeSilva unconsciously sensed and mirrored his concern.

"Marley made our hotel reservations online. Nichols must have seen the search history."

"You didn't password protect the laptop?"

"She took it off when I moved in so I could use the computer too."

"Shit. That's it. He knows you're there."

"Shit is right. And he stole Marley's laptop."

"That's the least of your worries. You've got to leave. Come back to Florida. Go someplace else. Go anyplace else. Just don't leave any bread crumbs for him to follow this time."

"I've got a deposition next week."

"A deposition? For what?"

"I'm getting sued. That's what this trip is all about. It's a long story. I'll fill you in some other time."

"Put it off. Reschedule. I think everyone will understand."

"I've got to think. I need some time. I'll call you back, okay?"

"Yeah, okay. But I don't see what there is to think about. For all you know he's tailing you now."

"Thanks for that," he said. "What about the condo? Was it trashed?"

"No, it's fine. But he did bust up your TV. You're gonna need a new one. And he destroyed the front door lock. We called a locksmith and got that taken care of for you. Where do you want me to leave the key?"

"Can you get it to my dad?"

"Yeah, no problem."

"DeSilva...thanks again."

"Sure. Later, man."

Laska punched the red button on his phone, slipped it back into his pocket, and went in search of Marley. He heard DeSilva's voice in his mind: *He could be tailing you now.* He found the museum employee he saw earlier and got directions. He needed to back-track the way he came from the food court and take a series of lefts and rights to get back on track.

Passing the food court, he saw Marley scanning the tables. He exhaled in relief.

"Hey, I was just on my way to look for you," he said.

"And I came looking for you." She saw something in his face and crinkled her brow. "Are you okay?" Her looked shifted from worry to irked. "How many beers did you have?"

"None, actually." He smiled trying to hide his

concern. "I thought I'd rather be with you so I went to find you but I got lost. How was the folk art?"

Marley shrugged. "Meh," she said. "I think we're done here. How about we go to Millennium Park now?"

"Okay, but when I was lost I somehow wound up in the Modern Art section. We should go back there. There's a really cool painting I want to show you."

37

DESILVA

eSilva finished up a call to McCarthy and tossed her phone on the empty seat next to her. Speeding along I-75 on the way back to Fort Myers, she filled him in on her conversation with Laska. There was no doubt – at least in her mind – that Nichols was on the way to Chicago. Whether he stole another car or found some other way, she knew he was headed there. Thankfully, McCarthy agreed.

He told her that when she and the rest of his people got back to Fort Myers he'd have a plan mapped out. He didn't have the details worked out or authorization yet, but he said they should move their operation to Chicago.

She spent the previous night at the Hyatt. By the time the locksmith finished up and she locked up the apartment, it was nearly three in the morning. The hotel bar had closed sometime earlier and Tallon and Bielski, she assumed, bedded down for the night.

She didn't get into her room until nearly four. After stripping down and laying out her clothes – she would have to wear them again in the morning – she collapsed, exhausted, on the bed and fell asleep.

She woke up to the room's phone ringing on the nightstand next to the bed.

"Yeah?" she said into the handset.

"It's Tallon. You awake?"

"I am now. What time is it?"

"Eight-thirty. We talked to McCarthy. He wants us all back in Fort Myers, and he wants you to call him."

DeSilva did the math in her head. She barely got four hours of sleep.

"Alright, I'll jump in the shower then meet you in the lobby."

"We're in our car already. We were gonna leave now. You want us to wait for you?"

"No, go ahead. Don't wait. I'll meet you in Fort Myers. If you talk to McCarthy again, tell him I'll call when I'm on my way."

∾

DeSilva pulled up to the gate of the Federal Building's parking lot. The man in the guard house directed her to a closed garage. She was to pull into the garage where Deputy Michael McCarthy and his team would be waiting for her.

The garage, which was nothing but a Quonset hut, was a flurry of activity with deputies and agents loading equipment and bags into vans. While parking the Suburban she spied McCarthy and ASAC Gleason from the FBI huddling off to the side. She started towards them.

As she walked up, Gleason glanced her way. He turned back to McCarthy and said, "We'll talk more on the plane." He turned back to her and nodded, "Lieutenant," he said, and walked away towards one of the vans.

When he was out of earshot and she and McCarthy were alone she said, "That was a frosty greeting. What's his problem?"

"Forget about it," McCarthy said. "He's just a little pissy because we have the lead on this. It's a fugitive investigation, and that's our purview."

"He mentioned a plane. We're flying to Chicago?"

"Yeah, we'll be leaving for the airport any minute. I took the liberty of collecting your bags from the hotel. They're already loaded in one of the vans."

"Good, I can use a change of clothes. These are getting a little ripe." She looked back over her shoulder at all the activity. "Can I do anything to help?"

"No, we got this. But I do need you to do something."

"Sure. What do you need?"

"The authorization came through. I'm going to administer the oath of office to you. Raise your right hand."

McCarthy swore her in and handed her a temporary ID card and badge. "We rarely supply badges to special deputies," he said, "but I figured you deserve one. Plus, I want you to get used to carrying one."

"Thanks," she said. "But I haven't even given a single thought to applying yet."

"It's a three-hour plane ride. Maybe you should."

"I was hoping you'd catch me up on your interview with Dunlop then go over your plan for locating Nichols."

"I'll do that," he said. "And speaking of the devil. There's Dunlop now."

DeSilva followed McCarthy's eyes and saw Jasper Dunlop, wearing an orange jumpsuit and shackled from his wrists to his ankles, escorted by Tallon and Bielski to one of the vans. Behind her, McCarthy called out, "Okay everyone. Let's wrap it up and get going."

THE SMALL CARAVAN of cars and SUVs drove onto the tarmac in a secure section of the Fort Myers airport reserved for government use. The deputies and agents piled out and set about loading the gear and equipment into an unmarked Airbus-220. McCarthy grabbed a bag, DeSilva's suitcase, and brought it over to her.

"Here," he said handing it to her. "I thought you might want to change on board. Store it in one of the closets until we're in the air."

She took the bag, thanked him, and nodded over to the cars. "Can I help with anything?"

"No, we'll handle it. Get on board and pick out a seat in the back. I'll join you before takeoff."

McCarthy walked off and DeSilva headed to the boarding steps. She climbed the stairs dragging her suitcase behind her and stepped aboard the plane.

She stopped and looked down the length of the plane's interior. It was smaller than most commercial jets she had been on but outfitted completely different. It was more utilitarian than luxurious, but pretty darn comfortable looking, she thought.

Unlike commercial passenger planes that had endless rows and narrow seats crammed together, this plane had widely spaced rows. The seats, two on either side of the aisle faced identical seats with a table between, much like on a passenger train. On the far end near the tail of the plane she saw a large galley and a door leading to a bathroom. Beyond that was another door which she hoped was the closet McCarthy mentioned.

She moved down the aisle to the galley. She checked the door she thought was a closet and found it was the entrance to another room altogether. This room contained a small conference table and chairs, a credenza holding some kind of electronics, and several television monitors hung from the wall above the credenza. Inside the room and adjacent to the entry door was the closet she was looking for. She stored her suitcase inside and moved back through the galley to the main cabin. She picked a forward-facing seat, so McCarthy could see her as he boarded, and waited.

She sat alone for twenty minutes before everyone boarded and scattered themselves around the cabin. McCarthy joined her, sitting across from her, only minutes before they lifted off. They made small talk until the plane reached cruising altitude and the pilot switched off the seatbelt light.

McCarthy fetched a bottle of water for each of them from the galley. After taking a gulp he sat and said, "Alright, let me get you caught up on Dunlop."

"You said you had him leave a voicemail for Nichols, right?" DeSilva said.

"Yeah, but Dunlop said he doesn't think it will do any good. Nichols will only turn on the phone when he's going to call Dunlop, so it's not really going to speed anything up. But he does expect Nichols to call him at least once more. Nichols wants Dunlop to keep trying to locate his daughter. Nichols told him he won't leave the country without his her."

"And that's why we're bringing Dunlop to Chicago?" DeSilva said.

"Yeah, the FBI and their techs will handle monitoring and tracking any calls. They'll have Dunlop with them."

"What else?"

McCarthy took another slug from his water bottle. "The ballistics report came in on the weapon that was used in the escape. The gun that killed Miller and Wilkerson. They determined the gun's characteristics from the rounds recovered from the bodies. The weapon that fired the rounds was a Smith & Wesson M&P 9 millimeter. The same gun Castillo owned."

"What about the gun that killed Castillo?"

"Different. That was a Glock 17."

"That means Nichols has two guns. The Glock and Castillo's Smith & Wesson."

"Yeah. We figured Castillo had two guns and brought along the Glock for Nichols. We were right about that. Dunlop confirmed it. But that's only part of the story.

"Dunlop says Nichols had him contact a guy. I've got his name somewhere, I'll get it to you later. Anyway, Nichols told Dunlop this guy is holding a gun for him, a Glock. It's special somehow. Nichols wants this gun bad. He tells Dunlop to get the gun from the guy and pass it on to Castillo who'll bring it to Nichols after the escape."

"What's so special about the gun?"

"Dunlop said he doesn't know. He only knows that Nichols demanded Dunlop get the gun."

"Okay," she said. "Dunlop runs down this guy and tells him he wants the gun. Right?"

"Yeah, that's what he said. He was worried the guy would give him a hard time but he didn't. He gave the gun right up. The guy told Dunlop he was happy to be rid of it."

"What do we know about this guy?"

"Like I said, we have his name and we know that he lives somewhere on the outskirts of Arcadia. Dunlop said he had the address written down but he shredded it after he got the gun. I've got people working on locating him."

DeSilva cracked the seal on her bottle of water. "Did Dunlop have anything else to say?"

"Yeah," McCarthy said. "When he met up with Castillo to pass him the gun, he bitched about Nichols having him running an errand like he was a lackey or gofer instead of his lawyer."

DeSilva snorted, water almost coming out of her nose. "Like it's beneath him. Fucking bottom feeder."

"Yeah, but then Castillo told him Nichols gave him an errand too. He wanted Castillo to fetch a bag, he called it a go-bag, from his house. It was under a false bottom of the bathroom vanity."

"Shit, we missed it."

"Maybe, Maybe not. We don't know when Castillo retrieved it."

"Did he say what was in the go-bag?"

"Yeah, he said Nichols had a stash of money and a set of fake IDs. Including a passport."

"Crap. I think I know how he got the IDs."

"How?

"The Cordeles. Remember the file said Nichols was working for them on the side? The reason this whole thing jumped off? Addie Cordele had some political connection and got authentic blank IDs. She'd make forgeries for the illegals they had working for them to fool the state inspectors."

"Who's the political connection?"

"We never found out. Addie wouldn't give him up."

"I'll pass that on. Maybe we can get the FBI or INS working on it."

"I hope they do better than we could."

"We have better resources, but we'll see.

"Anything else from Dunlop?"

"Not really. I think you're all caught up now."

"What about the secretary?"

"Heyward? Fuck her. She lawyered up. She'll be going away for a long time."

"Then what's the plan going forward?"

"I was hoping you had an idea," McCarthy said. "All we've come up with is to wait for Nichols to call."

38

JESSE NICHOLS

Nichols had his plan. A new plan, a better plan. Laska would suffer before he finished him. In more ways than one. In a delicious way. He'd learn what it was like to be in Nichols' shoes.

He checked out the Peninsula hotel and decided there was no way he'd be able to get to Laska and the girlfriend there. He even called, and pretending to be a friend, asked for Laska's room number. They shot him down. The best they'd do is call Laska's room for Nichols. That wouldn't work so he abandoned that angle.

After that, he staked out the hotel waiting for Laska to leave. It was boring work, and he nodded off a few times while he watched and waited. But it paid off eventually. He saw Laska and the girl leave and catch a cab. He followed them to a museum, but by the time he found a place to park the pickup, they were inside someplace. He didn't want to follow them inside and risk being seen. So, he waited outside.

He never saw them again. They must have gone out a different exit. He decided that this way, waiting for an opportunity to get them alone, wasn't going to work.

He went back to his motel. He found one on the north side of the city that morning. It was a dump but it was cheap and centrally located so getting around wasn't a problem. He laid back on the bed and started thinking.

He grabbed Laska's laptop and reread the emails to and from his lawyer. He reread the file on Laska's lawsuit including the police file. The seed of a plan was forming. His new plan. His better plan.

He clicked on Laska's account and composed an email.

39

LASKA AND DESILVA

The jet carrying McCarthy, DeSilva and company was wheels down at 7:23 pm. It was just about the same time Sam and Marley were picking up their Cubs tickets at Wrigley Field's will-call booth.

After leaving the Art Institute Sam and Marley walked through Millennium Park. They checked out the bean, the big mirror-finished metal sculpture officially titled "Cloud Gate", and the Crown Fountain, a fifty-foot tall monolith of LED screens that projected faces of Chicago citizens. They wandered through a large garden and the pavilion and wound up at the beginning of the BP pedestrian bridge - a winding span designed by Frank Gehry that crossed over Columbus Drive.

Sam steered Marley away from the bridge feigning sore feet. He didn't want them caught in the middle with only one way to run. He'd been keeping his head on a swivel and sweating bullets since talking to DeSilva. He was relieved when he finally got Marley into a cab heading back to the hotel.

Sam talked Marley into skipping lunch by promising her an early dinner. Sam hit the bathroom first, and when it was Marley's turn, he slipped his Beretta in the small of his back covering it with his shirt. After they freshened up, they caught another cab to the Wrigleyville neighborhood. Dinner was at his favorite noodle shop from back in the day when he worked the old Area Three, now Area North, homicide team.

The shop sat under the El tracks at Clark and Roscoe which was only a short walk from Wrigley Field. Sam sat facing the door. A habit he had fallen out of since he retired.

After dinner they made the walk to the ballpark. Sam tried to keep them on the fringes of the crowds heading to the game, but the mass of people soon enveloped them. His caution was useless. A wave of anxiety swept over him. Marley must have sensed it.

"Are you okay?" she asked as they made their way from the will-call booth to the gate.

"Yeah, why?" he said.

"You look nervous or something."

"I guess I am. Darvish is pitching today." Good save, he told himself. "It'd be kind to say he sucks."

"Don't worry about it. Just have fun. What's the worst that can happen?"

Sam dwelled on that as he checked the faces in the crowd of people around them.

DARVISH GAVE up five runs by the time the manager pulled him in the top of the third. His relief was coming in cold without having time to warm up, so the ump was granting him extra throws on the mound to get loose.

Marley stood and said to Sam, "I'll be right back."

"Where are you going?" he said.

"Duh. Where do you think?"

Sam popped out of his seat. "I'll show you where it is. Come on."

"You don't have to. I can find it."

"I might as well go too." He wasn't going to let her walk around by herself. He started shuffling his way down the row of people to the aisle.

He led her all the way and told her to meet him right there at the entrance to the women's bathroom. He watched her go in, slipped into the men's room, and pulled out his phone. He dialed DeSilva's number and she picked up after only one ring.

"Laska, I was just going to text you," she answered.

"What's going on? Please tell me you have something."

"Nothing on Nichols. I was going to tell you we're in Chicago. We landed about an hour ago."

"That makes me feel better, but only just a little. I'm walking around like a human bobblehead."

"I wish I could tell you to relax but I can't. Keep your eyes open."

"What's your plan going forward?"

"To be truthful, we're still working on it. Trying to track his burner."

"That's not really helpful."

"I know. How about I talk to the FBI and marshal's supervisors and see if we can get some bodyguards for you? You haven't told Marley yet, have you?"

"No, and I was hoping I wouldn't have to."

"I'll tell them the bodyguards need to be low profile. Just shadow you. Are you at your hotel?"

"No, we're at a ball game."

"What the hell? What were you thinking? That's one of the worst places you could be. There are too many people around. The crowd is great cover."

"I know. But we made the plans before you told me Nichols was in town. I couldn't beg off without Marley getting suspicious."

"Alright. Hopefully I can get some people over to your hotel tonight."

"That'd be great. Listen, I gotta go. Marley's in

the bathroom, and I've gotta meet her when she comes out."

"Okay, I'll text you later."

Sam walked out and stood watching the door to the ladies' room. The call with DeSilva made him feel only slightly better. The bodyguards were a relief, but he still had the rest of the evening to get through.

He stared at the door and continued waiting. And waiting. He looked around, thinking she may be standing somewhere else. Nothing. He moved closer to the door and waited again. The door opened. A pair of girls came out. He stretched his neck trying to look over them hoping to get a glimpse of Marley. The door closed. He stepped closer, tempted to open it and peek in. He thought better of that and stepped back. He stuck his hands in his pockets and took them out again. He looked down the hall again. First to the left and then the right. He shifted his weight from the left, to the right, to the left again.

He moved to the door and thought again about peeking inside.

"Hey."

It was Marley's voice behind him. He turned and saw her walking towards him. A Cubs cap on her head and another in her hand. He exhaled deeply. "Where did you go?" he said when she was close enough.

She held out a cap. "Here," she said with a smile on her face. "You weren't around when I came out, so I went to get you a beer. I changed my mind and bought these instead."

"I was worried. I thought...you were lost."

"Well, here I am. Come on, let's get back to our seats. And, you're welcome."

"For what?"

She began walking towards the bleachers. "Your new hat. Put it on."

Sam tried to relax and enjoy the rest of the game. The Cubs mounted a comeback and had the bases loaded with two out in the bottom of the ninth. But Bryant struck out, and they fell short losing to the Cards by two.

Sam tried to talk Marley into heading back to the hotel, but she insisted on seeing the party scene around the park. He bargained her down to one drink at the Cubby Bear, which was one of the more popular spots in the area.

It was after midnight when the cab dropped them off at the Peninsula. Walking through the lobby on the way to their room, Sam noticed a couple of guys lounging in chairs trying to look inconspicuous. Their military flat-tops gave them away. He caught the eye of one and they exchanged barely perceptible nods.

A half hour later he slipped into bed next to

Marley. He held onto her, feeling better – safer – now.

A FEW MILES away at the Best Western motel in the River North neighborhood, DeSilva walked into her room. The marshals secured the entire top floor for their people while the FBI took rooms at a different motel. McCarthy reminded her that the marshals and the FBI didn't play well together, and distance was the best way to avoid potential dick measuring contests.

They spent the hours after landing at O'Hare airport unloading bags and equipment and reloading it into vans and SUVs provided by the local marshal's and FBI offices. The first stop was the Dirksen Federal Building in downtown Chicago. The Chicago FBI provided empty offices and conference rooms and the deputies and special agents immediately set about organizing the spaces. The local FBI also fed Dunlop and secured him in a holding cell close to their offices making him available for immediate access.

Instead of standing around feeling useless, DeSilva figured it was a good time to get Laska up to speed. Before she had a chance to reach for her phone it began buzzing in her pocket. It was Laska.

Their conversation lasted only a few minutes, and after she hung up she went in search of McCarthy.

She found him in a small kitchenette off a conference room making a pot of coffee.

"Hey," she said, "we have to talk."

"What about?" he said without turning away from the brewing pot.

"We should put some guards on Laska and his girlfriend."

He grabbed a Styrofoam cup from a stack on the counter, filled it, and turned around. "Great minds think alike. I'm going to sit down in a few minutes and work out a quick assignment schedule. It was part of my plan."

"I talked to Laska a few minutes ago. He doesn't want the girlfriend to see them. Can we do that?"

"Yeah, of course. I'll put my best two men on it."

"I was thinking more like six people."

"Four."

"Sold," she said.

He took a sip of coffee and looked at her over the rim. He put the cup down on the counter. "You only wanted four all along, didn't you?"

"Yep. You're getting to know me better."

When she finally got to her room later that night, she showered and slipped between the sheets. She looked over to the nightstand where she placed her weapon and the silver Special Deputy Marshal's badge McCarthy gave her. She picked up the badge and looked it over. She fell asleep with it still in her hand.

40

SAM AND MARLEY

Marley set a plate down on the table and sat. She piled it high with fresh fruit, cheese, and what looked like blintzes dripping with a strawberry compote. She looked across the table at Sam and grinned.

"I know. You're eating for two now," he said.

They were at the Peninsula's Sunday brunch in a dining room adjacent to the lobby. It was another beautiful room with crystal chandeliers, oriental carpets, linen tablecloths, and gold-plated cutlery. Marley munched on a cube of watermelon. "What are we going to do today?" she said.

"Considering that's your third plate, I think we should go for a long walk. Let's go down to Michigan Avenue, maybe head to Water Tower Place and check out the bar on the 95th floor of the Hancock building. After that we can catch a cab and go to the observation deck at the Sears Tower."

"I like it. And after that?"

"Well, if you're not too tired, I was thinking we'd take the car and I can show you the neighborhood where I grew up."

"Your house too?"

"Yeah, of course."

Marley finished her plate, decided against a fourth, and they headed out. They walked a few blocks down Michigan Avenue and back up again. Marley showed Sam the shop where she bought his present and promised she'd revisit it when he wasn't around. They each had a virgin Bloody Mary at the 95th bar followed by a cab ride over to Willis Tower.

Sam lectured the cab driver on why he could never call it anything but the Sears Tower. "You just don't change the original names of landmark buildings," he insisted.

On the observation deck Marley ran to The Ledge, which was a glass box, including the floor, that jutted out from the side of the building. She was like a little kid standing on the glass floor mesmerized while staring straight down from 103 stories high. Sam wouldn't get anywhere near it and couldn't watch as she did a little tap dance on it.

He stayed in the center of the room near the elevators refusing to go anywhere near the perimeter of glass walls looking out over the city. After what seemed like hours to him – it was only twenty minutes - he finally coaxed Marley off the glass. He put up with her ribbing him over his fear of heights, and they took the elevator back down. Sam hailed another cab, and they settled in for the ride back to the hotel.

He directed the cabbie to the Peninsula and sat back next to Marley. "What do you think?" he said. "Are you up for a ride to my old 'hood?"

Marley made a face. "Your 'hood?"

"Yeah, my old neighborhood. Where I grew up."

"I know what the 'hood is. It just sounds weird coming out of your mouth."

"Are you making fun of my whiteness?"

"No, your age."

"Ha ha. Funny," he said poking her with his elbow. "So, what do you think? Want to take a ride?"

"Definitely. I want to see where you became you."

THEY PULLED up to the hotel and Sam paid the cabbie. He dug a valet ticket from his wallet, handed it to the door man, and waited only a few minutes before a carhop pulled in front with Sam's Infiniti. Minutes later they were cruising along on I-90, the Kennedy Expressway, headed to the Edison Park neighborhood on the far northwest side of the city.

Marley flipped down the sun visor and peered into the mirror on its backside.

"No need," Sam said. "You look great."

Marley pushed the visor back up. "You want to tell me what's going on?"

Sam glanced over and back again to the road. "What do you mean? I'm trying to compliment you."

Marley stared at Sam. "That's not what I'm talking about."

"What are you talking about?"

"Why are people following us?"

Sam felt an icy chill run down his spine. "I don't--"

"It started last night after we got back to the hotel. I saw you give a little nod to some guy in the lobby. At first, I thought he might have been someone you met in the bar or something. Then this morning you did it again. To two different guys.

"Those same two guys followed us on our walk and tried to look inconspicuous at the bar in the Hancock building. And now they're following us in a big black SUV."

Sam checked his rearview mirror.

"They're three cars back," Marley said. "Busted."

Sam slumped his shoulders. "They're federal agents. Assigned to protect us. I'm sorry, I should have told you."

"Yeah, you should have."

"I didn't want to worry you. I wanted you to enjoy this trip."

"Tell me what's going on."

Sam glanced over to her again. "You would have made a great detective."

"A damn fine one. Tell me."

Sam exhaled slowly. "Jesse Nichols is here. He followed us."

Sam laid it all out for her. From the lawyer Dunlop giving Nichols their address to the burglary of her condo and the theft of her laptop.

"He apparently went through the search history and found out we're here," he said.

"And he knows where we're staying?" Marley said.

"Yeah."

"And your friend DeSilva followed him here. With federal agents?"

"Yeah, the FBI and US Marshals."

"What's their plan?"

"Nichols has a burner phone. They can track his location with it, but only when it's powered on. And he only does that when he makes a call, which is hardly ever. They're waiting for that. For him to make a call."

Marley sat back and stared out the window. They both sat quietly.

"Please don't be mad at me," Sam said breaking the silence.

"I'm not angry, Sam. I'm disappointed. Wait, no. I am angry. You shouldn't have lied to me."

"I didn't lie. I just didn't tell you. Like I said, I didn't want you to be frightened or worried. I was trying to protect you."

"Same thing, Sam. You should have told me."

"I'm sorry. I promise, I won't do it again. Ever."

"If we're going to spend our lives together, there can't ever be any secrets. Understand?"

"Loud and clear."

Marley checked the mirror on her visor again. "I do feel better knowing they're looking out for us." She flipped the visor back up. "How's my condo?"

Sam looked over to her. "We're gonna need a new TV."

41

SAM AND MARLEY

Sam pulled off the expressway at the Harlem Avenue exit and took Marley on a tour of his old neighborhood. He showed her the Catholic church and school he attended and the park where he played little league. He pulled onto Northwest Highway, the main thoroughfare in the neighborhood, and drove past the small Italian grocery store and bakery that had the best lemon knots in the world. He pointed out the restaurants and bars he loved, the ones that he hated, and the new ones that had opened since he left.

He took a right turn. Halfway down the block, on a sleepy residential street, he pulled to the curb. He stuck a finger out.

"That's where we lived. That's where I grew up."

It was a simple blonde brick home with a green shingle roof and hunter green trim around the doors and windows. It was a style of house called a Chicago bungalow.

"It's pretty, Sam," Marley said. "And look," she pointed to a sign in the front yard. "It's for sale."

"Hmm," he said. "I wonder what they're asking for it."

Marley looked from the house to Sam. "Are you thinking you might want to move back here? To Chicago, I mean."

Sam paused, staring at his old home. "No," he finally said. "my home is in Sarasota with you."

He pulled away from the curb. "I don't know about you, but I'm getting hungry again."

"I could eat," she said.

"I know the perfect place."

Minutes later he pulled into a spot in the Superdawg lot. Superdawg was a classic 1940s style drive-in where car hops still brought the food to your car on trays that hooked onto your window.

Marley looked over the menu board on the post next to their car. "Seven dollars for a hot dog?" she said.

"No," Sam said with a grin. "Seven dollars for a Superdawg."

Sam pressed a button on the intercom attached to the post and ordered two Superdawgs and two chocolate shakes.

"Make mine a malted," she said.

Sam spent the time waiting for their food to

arrive explaining the components of a Chicago hot dog. "It starts with a steamed poppy seeded bun, then a pure beef hot dog in a natural casing is nestled in the bun. They top the dog with yellow mustard, chopped white onions, neon green sweet pickle relish, a dill pickle spear, tomato wedges, and sport peppers. Finally, it's sprinkled with a dash of celery salt."

"No catsup?"

"Blasphemy," Sam said. "Never, ever do you put catsup on a Chicago dog. There are hundreds, maybe thousands, of hot dog stands on corners everywhere in the city. None will ever put catsup on a hot dog. Catsup is for the fries only."

The carhop brought their food. Sam watched Marley as he ate his. "What do you think?" he said.

"It's alright, I guess. I like the malted."

Sam shook his head.

"Are you disappointed?" she said.

"No, not really. I was hoping you'd like them more but I probably expected too much. I grew up with this food. It reminds me of good times. When I was a teenager this was a regular spot for us. I'd bring girls here after a ball game or movie or something."

"Big spender."

"I'll ignore that. I think I brought every girl I dated back in high school here at one time or another. And after we ate we'd drive across the street to the county forest preserve." He pointed out the windshield. "See it there? We'd park in a dark spot in the lot and...steam up the windows."

"Did you take a lot of girls there?"

"I don't know. What's a lot for a teenager? But I had a little streak going." He crumpled up his empty cup and tossed it on the tray hanging from his window. "Do you want to know about my old girl-friends? There's not much to tell. I never had a serious relationship before you came along."

"I don't think I want to know." She slurped up the last of her malted through the straw. "But I wouldn't mind you taking me over to the forest preserve. We wouldn't want to break your streak, would we?"

He smiled. "What about our friends in the SUV back there?"

"Dang, I forgot about them. I guess we'll just have to go back to the hotel."

"Another time."

"Promise?"

"Promise."

It took them longer than Sam thought it would to get back to the hotel. Rush hour traffic going into the city was a mess. When they finally arrived he saw the street blocked off near the parking garage by several marked and unmarked police vehicles. Yellow plastic tape crisscrossed the garage entrance.

"What's going on?" Marley said, not really expecting Sam to know.

"Nothing good," Sam said.

He circled around to the other end of the block and pulled into the valet station. He handed the keys over and asked the valet about the police presence.

"I'm not sure," the kid said. "But I heard someone got shot."

Sam said nothing. Thoughts of Nichols cornered near the hotel by the feds and losing a gunfight flashed through his mind. But he dismissed it. The agents tailing him and Marley would have heard about it and let him know.

He walked over to Marley who was waiting just inside the hotel's door.

"Hang on a second," he said. "I want to let our friends from the SUV know you made them."

"Don't embarrass them, Sam. Just tell them you let me in on it."

"Okay, I'll do that. Go on ahead. I'll meet you by the elevators."

Sam watched her walk away and waited for the two feds. When they came through the door he stopped them. They looked surprised and both looked past him. For Marley, Sam thought.

"Don't worry, she knows about you," he said.

"You told her?" the man on Sam's left said.

"Yeah, but only after she made you."

"You're kidding, right?" the man on the right said.

"No, but it's okay. You don't have to play hide-and-seek now."

"Shit, we're sorry," he said.

"Don't worry about it. It was going to happen sooner or later." Sam looked back to Marley waiting at the elevators and then to the two men again. "Did you hear what's going on down the block? By the parking garage? It doesn't involve Nichols, does it?"

"We haven't heard a thing. And we would have." He tapped his ear indicating they both wore a well-hidden earpiece. "It's probably some local bullshit. Maybe some wife confronted a cheating husband coming out of the hotel."

"Yeah, maybe," Sam said. "Anyway, thanks for watching over us."

"No problem. That's what we do."

Sam thanked them again and left to join Marley. As he got close he nodded towards the bar. "Want to have a drink before we go upstairs?"

"You mean do I want to watch as you have a drink? No, thanks. It's late and I'm really tired."

He winked at her. "Not too tired, I hope."

"I think I am, Sam. I'm sorry."

"Don't be, we've got all the time in the world." He pushed the elevator call button.

42

LASKA AND STAFFORD

L aska woke up to the sound of a telephone. It wasn't his cell but the hotel's phone on the nightstand. He looked at the clock. It was 8:30 am. Marley stirred next to him and murmured something that sounded like "you get it." He propped himself up on an elbow and grabbed the handset. He cleared his throat and hit the talk button.

"Hello?" he said.

"Laska? Finally. It's Rebecca Stafford. Get to my office now."

He rubbed the sleep from his eyes with the heel of his hand. "I'm sorry, I'm confused. You want me--"

"In my office now. Yes."

Coming to, he said, "Is this about the deposition? I thought it was later in the week."

"I don't want to talk over the phone. Just get here."

The line went dead. He yawned again and rolled out of bed wondering what the hell was going on.

He showered, shaved, and dressed. He slipped his Beretta in the small of his back again and went to the bed. Marley hadn't moved. He bent over and kissed her on the cheek. She stirred only slightly.

He wrote a note on hotel stationary and left it on the bathroom sink where he was sure she'd see it.

In the lobby he located the marshal's assigned to the bodyguard duty and let them know where he was going. He accepted the offer of a ride on the condition two of the four men stayed to look out for Marley and that they stop along the way so he could grab a coffee to go.

He arrived at Stafford's building twenty minutes later. The marshal's waited in the lobby while Laska took the elevator up to Stafford's office.

Rebecca Stafford was on the phone but cut it short with a "I'll call you back" when Laska walked in.

"Sit," she said pointing to one of the chairs in front of her desk.

"Good morning to you too," he said as he sat. "What's this about?" He sipped his coffee.

Stafford leaned back in her chair and folded her arms. She turned her head and stared off into space for a moment, thinking. She turned back, exhaled deeply, and leaned forward on her desk.

"I'm your attorney. That means anything you say to me is protected by attorney-client privilege. You understand that, right?"

"Yeah, of course. Again, what's this about?"

"You don't have anything to say to me? There's nothing you want to tell me?"

"No." Laska put his coffee cup on her desk and leaned forward resting his arms on his knees. "And unless you want me to walk out of here right now you'd better tell me what's going on."

Stafford paused, then said, "Kevin King is dead."

Laska straightened up. "What?"

"His lawyer is in critical condition."

"Jesus," Laska said. "What happened?"

"They were shot yesterday evening. In the parking garage of the Peninsula hotel."

Laska slumped back in his chair, thinking. He stood up. "Now I get it. Now I get this attitude from you. You think I had something to do with it. You think I did it."

"You're saying you didn't?"

"No, I didn't."

"Please lower your voice, Mr. Laska. And sit down."

Laska ran his hands through his hair.

"Please sit," Stafford said.

A light bulb went off in Laska's head. "Wait a

minute. How did you hear about this already?" He plopped down in the chair.

"I got a call from the police this morning. A detective. Just before I called you."

"Why would the police call you?"

"They're looking for you. You're their only suspect."

"How could that be?"

"You sent King's lawyer, Darren Jordan, an email requesting he and King meet you at the Peninsula. The police already have a hard copy from his firm."

Laska's phone began buzzing in his pocket. He pulled it out. Marley was calling. He looked at Stafford. "I have to take this," he said.

"Wait a minute. Don't--" Stafford said.

Laska punched the 'talk' button. "Marley?"

"Sam, the police are here. They're looking for you. What's going on?"

"It's okay. I'll tell you all about it when I get back. Did you tell them where I'm at?"

"No, but..."

"Good, don't. Do whatever else they say. Answer any of their other questions. Tell them the truth. Except about where I am. I'll be back in a little while. Oh, and don't leave the hotel."

"Wait..." she said.

Laska punched the off button and smiled at Stafford.

"What are you smiling about?" she said. This is serious."

"I know it is. But I'm not worried. I didn't do it."

"The detective confirmed your email address with me. You sent the email."

"I didn't." Laska grabbed his coffee and took another sip."

"They recovered a weapon at the scene. A Glock pistol. The detective said it was registered to you."

Laska's brow furrowed. "Now that's a twist. But, thinking about it, it makes sense."

"Not to me."

"Did they tell you I reported that gun lost months ago?"

"No."

"They would know. It's in the NCIC database."

Laska's phone buzzed in his hand. It was Marley again. He held up a finger to Stafford who shook her head in disgust.

"Marley?" he said.

"Sam, the police found your note. They know where you are."

"Are they still there?"

"No."

"Thanks, honey. I'll talk to you soon." He disconnected the call and looked at Stafford. "Let's take a walk."

"Why? Where to?"

"Anywhere. The police are on their way here."

"No, we should stay. If you're really innocent like you claim we should take care of this now. As your attorney I'm advising you to surrender to them. I'll be here for your arrest and any interrogations. You don't talk to anyone but me."

"I'll turn myself in when I think the time is right. There are people I have to talk to first."

"Who?"

"The FBI and the US Marshals. And you."

Stafford sat staring at him.

"We don't have much time. Do you want to know the whole story or not?"

"Shit," Stafford said. "let me grab my purse."

Alone in the elevator, Laska pushed the button for the second floor. "We'll take the stairs from there," he said. "We don't want to run into the arriving troops."

As the elevator car sped down he asked Stafford to open her purse.

"Why?" she said.

He pulled the Beretta from his pants. "I want you to hold this for me. Just in case."

"What are you doing with a gun?"

"I'll explain it all after we get out of here." He held the gun out for her.

"Shit," she said opening her purse. "Shit, shit, shit, shit."

Laska deposited the pistol in the bag and said, "Oh, one more thing." He pulled out his phone and placed it in her purse. "If the police see us, if I'm arrested before we can talk, go into the recent calls list. Look for the name DeSilva. Call her and tell her what's going on. Tell her I'll meet you both at Area North detective division."

"DeSilva? Who's she?"

"She's working with the US Marshals. She'll be able to fill you in on everything."

THEY SUCCESSFULLY AVOIDED any arriving police units by exiting the building through a service entrance in the rear. The downside was he couldn't get to the marshals in the lobby. They walked south to Lake Street and then east. Laska said he remembered a coffee shop nearby and hoped it was still there.

It was. They both got coffee at the counter and grabbed a table in the back.

"Okay, Laska," Stafford said. "Spill it. What the hell is going on?"

Laska began explaining. Starting with Jesse Nichols' escape, the murder of two US marshals and Nichols' pursuit of Laska. He explained the FBI and US marshal's investigation, the burglary of Marley's condo and the theft of her computer, the same computer Sam used for sending and receiving email. He gave Stafford background on Nichols, his connection to the crimes of the Cordele family in Arcadia, and Laska's role in Nichols' arrest.

"So, he blames you for getting caught and he's looking for revenge," she said. "And you think he sent the email to Jordan pretending to be you?"

"Yeah," he said. "I think he read all the emails between you and me. Including the entire file on Kevin King and saw an opportunity."

"What opportunity?"

"To set me up. To put me through the ringer."

"But he had to know it wouldn't stick. He's got to know you'd have an airtight alibi."

"I don't know. Maybe just to play with me."

"It doesn't make much sense." She took a sip of coffee. "What about your gun? The Glock?"

"I lost it on the Cordele property the night Nichols and the Cordeles got busted. One minute I had it, then I didn't. Someone obviously found it and passed it to Nichols somehow."

"And you said that you reported the gun lost?"

"Yes, to the DeSoto county sheriff's office."

"And who's this DeSilva person you wanted me to call?"

"She's a detective lieutenant with the DeSoto sheriff's department. She's working with the US marshals. They're in Chicago now. Probably working out of the federal building." Laska took a sip of coffee. "And on top of all that I just told you, we've had deputy marshals, body guards, assigned to tail us everywhere. I couldn't have done it without them seeing me do it."

"Iron clad alibi witnesses. Where are these bodyguards now?"

"Two are with Marley. The two that came with me to your office? Probably standing in the lobby of your building acting very confused."

Laska looked over to the counter. A uniformed police officer had come in and ordered himself a cup of coffee to go.

"I think you're all caught up now," Laska said. "Any questions?"

"No," Stafford said. "I don't think so."

"Alright. I'm going to go now. We'll talk again in a little while. Call DeSilva for me. And maybe you can find my bodyguards and fill them in too."

"Where are you going?" Stafford said.

Laska got up and walked over to the uniform. He held his hands up. "Excuse me, officer," he said. "My name is Laska and I'm wanted for murder."

43

LASKA

Laska sat alone in an interview room on the second floor of the Area North detective division headquarters. The stunned uniform he surrendered to handcuffed him and transported him there on the instructions of the investigating detectives. The uniform marched him into the Area, still handcuffed, past the front desk, up the stairs, and across the floor full of detectives. Many of whom Laska knew from his time there. Some he didn't. The detectives he knew and that knew him stood stone-faced watching him as he was paraded through the offices and deposited in the interview room.

He waited in the small room with its walls the color of old bones. Ironically, it was the same interview room Kevin King and he had their altercation. It hadn't been repainted since that day and Laska swore he could see a faint smear of old blood where King's head hit the wall.

Sooner than he thought it would be, the door opened and two detectives walked in. Ed Charles, a salty old-timer who Laska knew, and a younger detective Laska assumed was a recent promotion.

"Eddie," Laska said, "how're you doing? I'd shake your hand but, you know." Laska jiggled the handcuffs binding his wrists.

"Sam," a frowning Ed Charles said with a nod.

"Where's Tony?" Laska said. Tony Chinn was Eddie Charles' regular partner when Laska last worked in the Area.

"Retired. Last year," Charles said.

"Good for him. Who's this?" Laska said tipping his head to the other detective in the room.

"This is Detective Rodriguez," Charles said as both detectives pulled out chairs and sat across from Laska. "Sam, I wish we could catch up. I wish we bumped into each other in a tavern somewhere and had the time to knock back a few beers and talk. But we've got a job to do here. You understand, right?"

"Sure, Eddie. I understand."

"Okay. Now I'm going to read you your Miranda warnings. I know you know them by heart but I've gotta do it." He pulled a small booklet from his sport coat's pocket.

"I waive them all, Ed."

Detective Charles glanced at Laska and down to

the booklet. He began reading. He recited each of the warnings and Laska replied to each with an "I understand."

When he finished delivering the warnings Charles slipped the booklet back into his pocket and said, "Do you waive the rights I just read?"

"Yes," Laska said.

"And you'll talk to us now?"

"Yes."

"Without an attorney?"

"Yes."

Ed Charles folded his arms across his wide chest. "You're acting pretty nonchalant about all this, Sam. Okay then, why don't we start with this? Tell me what happened. Why did you shoot Kevin King and his attorney?"

"I didn't shoot them. I was nowhere near the scene when they were shot."

"Sam, we have a copy of an email you sent from your account to Attorney Darren Jordan requesting he and Kevin King meet you in the parking lot of the Peninsula hotel. Jordan's brother, his law partner, gave it to us."

"Can I see the email?"

Ed Charles pulled a paper from another pocket and unfolded it. He slid it across the table to Laska.

Laska began reading.

Mr. Jordan, I'd like to arrange a private meeting between myself, Mr. Kevin King, and you. I can't afford any financial judgements against me and would like to work out a deal. I think I can arrange my testimony so that there would be no doubt as to the city's liability. All I require is that you don't ask for any punitive damages from me. I'd also like Mr. King to be present at the meeting so that I can apologize to him personally.

Meet me on the second level of the parking garage next to the Peninsula hotel Sunday evening at 7:00 pm. If Mr. King does not appear neither will I. Do not contact my attorney. She cannot know about this as she will make any and all attempts to prevent our meeting. Please acknowledge your attendance by replying with one word: yes.

--Sam Laska

LASKA SAID, "I guess King and the lawyer showed up." He slid the paper back to Charles. "What a slime ball. He could get disbarred for agreeing to that meeting."

Det. Charles continued. "We also know you're currently registered as a guest at the Peninsula. On top of that, we recovered a Glock model 17 9mm pistol at the scene. The gun is registered here in Chicago. Do you want to guess who it's registered to?"

"I don't have to guess. It's my pistol. It was my duty weapon when I worked here. I reported that weapon lost months ago."

Rodriguez hitched his chair closer. "Just because you reported it doesn't mean you really lost it. Anyone can…"

Ed Charles held up a hand cutting Rodriguez off. "Sam," Ed Charles said, "you can keep denying…"

He was interrupted by a knock on the door. It opened and a familiar face, Sergeant Jim Gibbons, walked into the room. Gibbons had worked Homicide in the Area back when Laska was assigned there. He was one of those supervisors that detectives said had 'the right stuff'. A supervisor who walked the walk.

Gibbons looked at Laska. "Sam," he said in greeting.

"Jim," Laska said. "Good to see you."

"We'll talk later, okay?" Gibbons said. He turned to Charles and Rodriguez. "Come on out here. We need to talk."

The detectives followed Gibbons out of the room and locked the door behind them. Laska sat alone again. *I guess the cavalry's here,* he said to himself.

LASKA SAT in the room waiting and thinking. Nichols was trying to set him up. But the setup was obvious and flawed. Deeply flawed. And Nichols had to know it. So why bother? Just to mess with Laska? It didn't seem worth it. Nichols followed them, Marley and him, to Chicago for a reason. Was this the best he could come up with?

His thoughts moved to Marley. She was probably sitting in the hotel alone and worried. It was hours ago that he last talked to her. He needed to call her.

Laska sat up when he heard the click of the lock. Sergeant Gibbons walked in the room with a hand-cuff key in his hand.

"Jesus, Sam," he said as he unlocked the cuffs. "You're a magnet for trouble."

"Did the FBI and marshals show up?"

"Yeah, and your attorney too. They're all in the conference room."

Sam stood and rubbed his wrists. He shook Gibbons hand and gave him a short man-hug. "It's good to see you, Jimmy."

"You too. Sam. Come on, everyone's waiting for you."

Laska followed Gibbons as he led the way past a slew of obviously confused detectives who hadn't yet been let in on recent events. A few who heard nodded and smiled at him.

Gibbons pushed through the swinging double doors of the conference room. Seated around the table were an assortment of people Laska assumed were either FBI or deputy marshals. On the far end seated at the head of the table, the power seat, was Rebecca Stafford. And next to her sat Kathleen DeSilva.

DeSilva walked over to Laska and hugged him.

"Thanks," Laska said to her.

"For what?"

"Looking out for me and Marley. I owe you."

"Nothing ever changes, huh? Come on, time for you to meet everyone."

DeSilva went around introducing the room full of people. She started with McCarthy and the four deputy marshals with him and moved on to ASAC Gleason of the FBI. The two special agents with Gleason introduced themselves after DeSilva apologized for not knowing their names.

"And I guess you know the detectives and your attorney, right?" she said.

Laska gave a smile to Stafford and nodded another hello to Ed Charles, Rodriguez, and Jim Gibbons.

"And now you're all caught up," DeSilva said.

Laska looked from DeSilva to Gibbons. "Am I clear now? Did the feds clear everything up for you?"

"Yeah, Sam," Gibbons said. "Special deputy DeSilva gave us the whole story. This guy Jesse Nichols is our number one suspect now."

Laska looked over to DeSilva. "Special deputy?"

"I'll explain later," she said.

Laska turned back to Gibbons. "How's the attorney? Darren Jordan? Ed said he was in critical condition."

"Out of surgery. Still critical but stable. He'll pull through."

"Good," Laska said. "Do you think he can ID Nichols?"

"We're hoping. He was hit in the abdomen so he was facing the right direction. We'll show him a photo lineup when he's able."

Laska looked around the room. "Okay," he said. "I need to make a call and then I need a ride back to my hotel."

"Marley knows where you are, Sam," DeSilva said. "She knows you're okay. I called her."

"Thanks, but I still want to get back to her."

"Hang on a minute," McCarthy said. "Let's talk this through first. This was a strange move Nichols made. We should try to figure out what he's up to."

"I agree," DeSilva said. "He had to know a murder beef on you wouldn't stick, Sam."

"I think you're giving Nichols too much credit," Gleason said as he leaned back in his chair. "He doesn't seem like a criminal mastermind to me. He was a small town, back-country cop. They don't have a clue how to put together any kind of intricate plan." He looked at DeSilva. "Present company excepted."

Laska turned to DeSilva and hooked a thumb at Gleason. "Who's this guy again? FBI?"

Gleason answered. "Assistant Special Agent in

Charge Ronald Gleason. Federal Bureau of Investigation."

Laska took a step towards him. "You ever disrespect her or any working copper in my presence again and I'll rip your tongue out. Now sit there and shut up. The adults are talking."

Gibbons stifled a laugh and tried to look stern. "That's enough, Sam. Not in my house. You're all here for the same thing. And now, we are too. Let's just get on with it."

"Sorry, Jim," Laska said walking back around the table away from Gleason.

"Same old Laska," Gibbons murmured as Laska passed him.

McCarthy spoke up. "Okay, we don't all agree but the consensus seems to be that Nichols set up Laska knowing it wouldn't stick. At least not for long. He had to have a reason. Anyone have any ideas?"

44

MARLEY JONES

Marley paced across the living room in their suite crisscrossing the sight-lines of the two deputy marshals watching late afternoon television from the sofa. She last talked to Sam hours ago when she called to tell him the police had found the note he left for her. Police officers, detectives in sport coats and suits, had come to her room looking for him. They refused to say why but she knew it couldn't be anything good. Not the way they acted, looking through every room, and the brusque manner they spoke to her. Polite but all business, telling her nothing and asking everything. And when they found Sam's note they rushed from the room with no explanation. After she called Sam, nothing else. Not a word from Sam or anyone else.

She went down to the lobby and found the deputy marshals, the bodyguards, sitting in overstuffed chairs drinking coffee. She hadn't seen the two men before but a third grader could have picked them out.

When she spoke to them they didn't have a clue as to why the local police were looking for Sam. They didn't even know detectives had gone to their suite. That pissed her off.

But the deputies redeemed themselves. They escorted her to her suite and stayed with her. They made calls, using the hotel telephone and their personal radios, but whoever they talked to had no information either.

Finally, the deputy marshals got a message. Sam was under arrest. For murder they told her.

"Where is he?" she asked the deputies.

A police facility at Belmont and Western on the north side of the city, they told her.

"Take me there," she said. But they talked her out of it. They convinced her to wait for more information. They promised her their people were on it and it wouldn't be long before they heard more. They were right.

Marley heard from Lt. DeSilva less than twenty minutes later. DeSilva laid it all out for her, from the email sent to Kevin King's attorney to the shooting in the parking garage and the pistol once owned by Sam found on the scene.

"The deputy marshals are with you now, in your room, right?" DeSilva said to her.

"Yes, do you want to talk to them?" Marley said.

"No, I don't need to. But I want you to sit tight. Everything is going to be okay. It's obviously a setup by Nichols and we have the evidence to prove it. So, don't worry. We're taking care of everything. We're talking with the detectives now and it won't be long before Sam is released."

"Okay, thank you."

"And I'll have Sam call you as soon as he can."

"Thank you again, Kat."

That was nearly two hours ago and Sam still hadn't called. She stopped pacing and stood in front of the television. The deputies looked up at her.

"I'm not waiting any longer," she said. "I'm going to that police station. You can either drive me, or I'll take an Uber. Your choice, but I *am* going."

The deputy on the left stood up. "Ms. Jones..." he began.

"Marley," she said.

"Marley," he continued, "we're going to stay here in your room. It's not a good..."

"Then you can stay," she said. She grabbed her purse, slung the strap over her head and shoulder, and slipped the room key into her jeans. She marched to the door.

"Marley, please..."

She spun around. "Like I said, I'm going. With or without you."

He turned to the second deputy and shrugged

his shoulders. The second man stood and said, "Alright. Let's go."

They rode the elevator down to the lobby. Marley stood in a back corner while the deputies stood in front of the door. Marley said, "I'm sorry, I don't know your names."

The deputy closest to her said "I'm Tallon." The other man turned his head to her and said, "I'm Bielski."

"Deputies Tallon and Bielski, thank you. For driving me, I mean. And watching over us. I didn't mean to give you a hard time."

"That's okay, ma'am. And you're welcome," Tallon said as the doors opened.

They stepped out of the elevator car and headed across the lobby. At the door, Tallon stopped Marley. "Deputy Bielski will get the car. We'll wait inside here until he pulls up."

They didn't have to wait long. The black Suburban pulled to the curb in front of the door and Tallon and Marley stepped outside.

45

THE CONFERENCE ROOM

"Nobody?" McCarthy said. "Nobody has an idea?" He looked at the faces of the people standing and sitting around the table. "Come on, people. Speak up. There are no stupid ideas."

Rebecca Stafford slowly raised her hand.

"You don't have to do that," McCarthy said. "Just jump on in. You have something?"

"Yes, I think so," she said. "Now forgive me, I just heard all this stuff about Nichols and Laska and everything else today. So maybe I don't have a good handle on it."

"But?" DeSilva said.

"Correct me if I'm wrong," Stafford said. "This is all about revenge, right? Nichols wants to get even with Laska for some perceived wrong."

"Yeah," DeSilva said. "He blames Laska for losing his job, his family, and for his arrest."

Stafford continued. "And he is so bent on revenge he followed Laska to Chicago and killed a man and nearly killed another to set him up on some bogus murder charge."

"We know all this," McCarthy said twirling his finger in a 'keep-going' gesture. "Get to the point."

"What happens if Laska gets arrested?" Stafford said. "He's separated from his girlfriend. She's left alone. I think it's possible that's what he wanted. I think he knows the best way to get back at Laska is to go for his girlfriend."

DeSilva shot to her feet. "And maybe draw Laska out into the open."

"Hang on a minute," ASAC Gleason said. "She's got two deputies with her. He's not going to get anywhere near her. If that's even his plan."

Laska stepped towards Stafford. "My phone. Give me my phone."

Stafford pulled his phone from her purse and slid it across the table to him. He grabbed it and dialed Marley.

McCarthy pushed back from his chair and stood. He pointed at one of his people. "Get Tallon and Bielski on the radio. I want their exact location. I want to know if they have eyes on Miss Jones." He pointed to the others. "Call the office. Get people to the Peninsula." He turned to Laska. "Did you get her?"

"She's not answering her cell," he said, louder than he thought he did.

"Try your room. Maybe she's not near her cellphone."

A deputy called out across the room to McCarthy. He held up a handheld radio. "Nothing. I can't raise them."

"Keep trying," McCarthy said, and to the rest of his people, "That's it. We're not taking any chances. Let's get moving." He started to the door.

Gleason called out to him. "You want us to go?"

Without turning around, McCarthy said, "Only if you don't get in the way."

McCarthy and his deputies piled out of the room. DeSilva stood next to Laska and watched him punch the off button. "Nothing?" she said.

"No."

"Come on, you go with me," she said.

"I'm driving. I know the city better," he said. He turned to Stafford. "My gun." She held her purse open for him. He took the pistol and checked the chamber and magazine. "Thank you," he said. "For everything." He looked over to Gibbons who was standing across the room with Ed Charles and Rodriguez. Gibbons looked down at the gun and back to Laska. He said nothing.

Laska tucked the gun in the small of his back and, to DeSilva, said, "Let's go."

Gibbons, Charles, and Rodriguez followed them out of the room to the stairs. "We'll meet you there."

"Thanks, but...,"

"I said we'll meet you there."

46

THE PENINSULA

Marley and Tallon stepped outside. The doorman tipped his hat and nodded to Marley. She gave him a smile and walked toward the big SUV as Tallon walked ahead and grabbed the passenger side rear door handle.

The explosions deafened her. She stood stunned as she watched Tallon fall to the pavement. Someone screamed. People rushed past her running to safety. Someone else yelled "Get down! Get down!" She turned to the voice. Bielski was out of the SUV, pistol in hand and his free hand motioning for her to get down. She lost sight of him, blocked by the large vehicle, as he ran to the rear of the Suburban.

She dropped to her hands and knees landing in a puddle of Tallon's blood. She looked down at him and stared into his dead eyes. More explosions. And more still, from somewhere else. She looked up and saw a man. She had met him only once before years ago. But she remembered him. Jesse Nichols stood on the sidewalk pointing and firing a pistol towards something or someone at the rear of the Suburban she couldn't see.

She scrambled to her feet and ran to the hotel's door, crouching, trying to stay low. She jerked backwards in pain and reached for her head. Nichols had her by the hair. She struggled and tried to pull away. She lashed out, swinging her arms, desperate to escape. Nichols was too strong. He slammed her head into the plate glass door and pulled her away, dragging her stumbling down the now deserted street.

LASKA PUSHED the pedal to the floor, weaving around traffic and blowing through stop lights. "Does this thing have emergency lights and a siren?" he said.

DeSilva, strapped into the passenger's seat, said, "I don't know." She began fumbling around the console and dashboard. She popped open the glove box. "I found it," she said and flipped two toggle switches. A siren began wailing from beneath the hood.

The walkie-talkie clipped to her belt cackled. She twisted the knob to up the volume. She recognized McCarthy's voice. "Shots fired. Chicago police reporting shots fired at the Peninsula. Two down."

She looked over at Laska. He stared straight ahead, his eyes narrowed and jaw clenched. He leaned forward in his seat as if it would close the distance between him and the Peninsula.

"More," he yelled. "More information. Who's down?"

DeSilva yelled into the radio. "Who's down?"

No sound came from her radio.

"Who the fuck is down?" she screamed into it.

"Hang on," came the reply.

NICHOLS RIPPED OPEN the driver's door and shoved Marley inside. *My truck*, she thought, *he stole my truck*. Nichols pushed her to the passenger's side and climbed in. He pointed the gun at her. "You try anything and you die right here," he said.

He cranked the engine. It sputtered but started. He peeled around the corner, turning north on Rush Street.

Marley flattened herself against the passenger's door and unconsciously clutched the purse slung around her neck, protecting it for every useless reason. Nichols glanced at her as he drove. A bell dinged in his head.

"What do you got there?" he said. He tucked his

gun between his legs and grabbed her purse. He pulled at it, yanking her closer along with it.

Her head was nearly in his lap, the gun no more than a foot from her face. She grabbed for it. Nichols was too fast. He closed his thighs, shielding the gun, and pulled her upright by the hair.

He pushed her towards her door. He gripped the gun and pointed it at her. "Bitch, I told you what would happen."

"I'm sorry," she whimpered. "I'm sorry." Tears welled up in her eyes.

Nichols glared at her, still pointing the gun.

"I'm pregnant," she said.

McCarthy's voice came over DeSilva's radio. "Chicago police on the scene. Two male subjects down."

"What about Marley," Laska yelled, more to himself than DeSilva.

Before DeSilva could bring the radio to her mouth, McCarthy's voice came over. "Wanted is a male white subject seen leaving the scene dragging a black female by the hair. Reports say he fled the scene with the girl in a blue and white older model pickup truck. Florida plates. Northbound on Rush. Police issuing an APB on the truck."

DeSilva turned to Laska. His face was frozen in

fear. A single tear ran down his cheek. There was nothing DeSilva could say but she tried. "She's still alive."

"Shit!" Laska screamed. He slammed on the brakes and swerved, narrowly missing a green Lexus making a left turn. Laska floored the accelerator again and punched through the intersection.

DeSilva, with a straight-arm death grip on the dash and her door, knew better than to caution him.

"Where could he be headed?" she said, her voice competing with the blasting siren. "He's north on Rush. Do you know Rush Street?"

"Yeah," he said. "He could be going anywhere."

"He'll want something private. A motel maybe?"

"There are hundreds around the city. Motels, cheap hotels, flophouses. He could be anywhere."

"Goddammit. Think, Sam. It's your city. Where would you go?"

"Ha," Nichols boomed. "That's perfect." He lowered his gun and glanced at Marley. His eyes narrowed. "Boy or girl?"

"I don't know."

"Bullshit. Is it a boy or girl?"

"We wanted it to be a surprise." She wiped the tears from her eyes.

He waved the gun at her. "Don't lie to me," he growled. "A mother always knows. What is it?"

"A girl, it's a girl," she said as she pressed herself against the door.

She saw him relax. His face growing calmer. His thoughts somewhere else as if he was remembering so she went fishing. "Do you have any kids?"

Nichols glared at her. "Shut up," he said.

He made another right turn on some busy street Marley didn't know. Then a left. He was driving calmly now. Like he didn't just shoot two people and kidnap another. But she noticed something. Something about his face.

He took another quick look at Marley and slipped the gun between his legs again. "Give me your purse."

She lifted the strap over her head, slipped it off her shoulder, and held it out for him.

He snatched it from her and opened it. He shoved the contents around and threw the purse to the floor on her side.

"Satisfied?" she said.

"You've got a real attitude for someone with not a lot of time left."

She backed up against her door again. She looked at Nichols. There was a grimace on his face. It had been there all along but she didn't recognize it until now. He was in pain.

She looked him up and down and for the first

time it registered. "Your bleeding," she said. "You've been shot."

"I DON'T KNOW. It's a big fucking city," Laska said. "Get on the radio. Ask if there are any sightings on the pickup."

DeSilva called it in. Twice before anyone answered her. "Nothing," the unfamiliar voice said. Laska pounded on the steering wheel.

"Are you on the scene yet?" DeSilva said into the radio.

A squelch from the radio and an answer. "Just pulled up. Tallon is DOA. Bielski in route to the hospital. Condition unknown."

DeSilva looked over to Laska. "How far are we?"

"Four blocks, maybe." He looked at her. "It's Marley's truck. The blue and white pickup. It was her father's truck."

"We'll get her back," DeSilva said. "And the truck."

Laska sped through the last intersection, yanked the steering wheel into a right turn, and stopped in the middle of the street half a block from the hotel. A mass of police vehicles and gawkers prevented him from getting any closer.

He and DeSilva ran over to the scene. DeSilva

flashed her new badge and they ducked under the police tape.

"There." She pointed to McCarthy standing in a crowd of uniformed police, detectives, and deputies. They weaved through the mass of people and ran over to him.

"What's going on?" she said.

He nodded to Tallon's body lying on the ground.

"I'm sorry," she said. "Any more on Bielski?"

"No." He looked over to Laska. "We fucked up. I'm sorry."

"Not yet, no apologies yet. It's not over," he said.

"You're right. We've got work to do. But I--"

A voice yelled out from somewhere behind them. "Sam." It was Gibbons. He ran up holding a walkie-talkie to his ear. "Hit and run. Blue and white older Ford pickup truck," he called out.

"Where?" Sam said.

"Ashland and Belmont. The truck fled north on Ashland."

Laska looked at DeSilva. He turned and ran to the Suburban. Gibbons followed.

47

A DAMN FINE DETECTIVE

Nichols tucked the gun between his legs again. He reached to his right side, lifted his blood-soaked shirt, and looked at his wound. The deputy's bullet passed through the fatty tissue just below his ribcage. Blood leaked from the wound. Nichols assessed himself. "I'm fine," he said.

Marley looked up from the wound. Nichols' face was fish-belly white. Tiny beads of sweat dotted his forehead. "You're not fine. You're losing blood," Marley said.

Nichols looked at the wound again. "Find me something. Napkins or something."

Marley opened the glovebox and found an old, oily rag. She looked out the windshield. They were approaching a busy intersection. The light turned red.

"Does it hurt?" she said.

"What the fuck do you think," he said. "Gimme that." He reached for the rag.

Marley tossed it in his face and punched his wound. Nichols howled and doubled over. She braced herself against the dashboard as the old Ford rammed the car in front of them. The impact hurled Nichols forward and slammed him into the steering wheel. Even before they jolted to a stop Marley lunged at her door. She grabbed the handle and pushed the door open.

Dazed from the pain ripping through his side and face, Nichols swiped a hand at Marley. He came up empty as she jumped from the truck. She stumbled on a curb, caught herself, and ran.

Nichols turned, wincing against the pain, and threw open his door. A man stepped from the crumpled car in front and glared at Nichols. Nichols looked behind the pickup at the fleeing Marley and back to the man. Cars behind him began blaring their horns. Pedestrians stopped to gawk.

He yanked the door shut, shifted the truck into reverse and stomped on the pedal. The old Ford jerked backwards. He slammed the shift arm into Drive and peeled away.

Marley heard the screech of tires. She looked over her shoulder and saw her truck speeding away. She stopped and watched. Gasping for breath, hands on her knees and her chest heaving, she kept her eyes on the rear of the pickup waiting to see if it turned.

She lost it in traffic and the heavy shadows of the setting sun. She spun around, her head twisting back and forth. She spied a restaurant. A family-type diner. DeMar's, the sign read. She ran inside and began screaming. "Call 9-1-1, call 9-1-1."

LASKA AND DESILVA tore down the street with the siren blaring and headed westbound to Ashland Avenue. Gibbons, lights flashing and siren wailing, tailed them.

Laska tore through intersections, barely slowing, while DeSilva called out the cross-traffic. He slipped between and around cars and cursed them for not pulling to the right.

They were drawing close. "Less than a mile," Laska said to DeSilva as he zipped through another intersection.

Gibbons pulled even with them on the left. His horn blaring between the wails of the siren. Sam looked out his side window and saw Gibbons motioning. Gibbons shot past Laska and cut over into his lane. Ahead, Laska saw a marked squad car, roof lights flashing, double parked in front of a diner.

Gibbons slowed and pulled behind the squad

car. Laska stopped behind him. Gibbons bailed out of his car pointing at the diner. Laska jumped from the Suburban, ran to the door, and yanked it open.

Marley stood in the back, a pair of police officers next to her. She turned to the sound of the opening door and spotted Sam. She pushed through the two uniforms and ran to him with tears in her eyes.

They threw their arms around one another. Sam held her tightly, afraid to let her go. Relieved he had her back.

He broke the embrace but held on to her, his hands on her shoulders. He looked her up and down and saw the blood smears on her jeans and tee shirt.

"Are you hurt? Did he hurt you?" His hands moved over her searching for any injury.

She stared back at him, her eyes damp with tears. Her body trembled uncontrollably. The fear she steeled herself against while escaping from the truck finally overwhelmed her.

"I'm okay. I'm not hurt."

"The blood..."

She began sobbing. "It's not mine."

Sam understood. "It's not your fault, Marley."

"It is. That deputy...he...they didn't want me to leave the hotel. I made them. It's all my fault."

"No, Marley. There's no way anyone could have known." He led her to a booth and had her sit. He slid into the seat across from her. He grabbed a napkin from the steel box on the table and handed it to her. She took it and dabbed her eyes.

DeSilva and Gibbons stepped over. They both knew the conversation needed to change.

"Marley," DeSilva said. "How did you get away?"

Marley looked up at her. DeSilva could see her shifting gears and collecting her thoughts.

"He's wounded. The other deputy...Bielski. He must have shot him. He...Nichols, he said it wasn't bad but I knew it was."

Laska looked up at Gibbons to explain. "She worked in a morgue."

Marley continued. "I hit him. I punched him there, on his wound. He crashed the truck. My truck, Sam. He crashed and I jumped out."

"Smart girl," Gibbons said.

Marley looked at him.

"This is Jim Gibbons," Sam said. "I worked with him. He's a friend."

"Hello," Marley said softly.

Gibbons nodded. "Do you know where he's going? Did he say anything about where he's staying?" he said.

"No," Marley said, "no." She slowly turned to Sam. Her eyes grew wider as she remembered. "My purse." she said. "My purse is in the truck."

"Don't worry about it," Sam said. "It's not important."

"No, Sam," she said raising her voice. "My purse..."

"We'll get it back. We'll cancel your cards."

"Dammit, Sam. My purse. My phone is in my purse."

"We'll get you a new phone."

She slammed her hands on the table and leaned forward. "Listen to me. My phone is on. It always is. Track my phone!"

"Jesus," DeSilva said pulling her phone out.

"Gimme a pen," Laska said to Gibbons. He pulled another napkin from the box and wrote down Marley's cell phone number. He handed it to DeSilva.

He turned back to Marley and smiled, "Damn fine detective is right."

He slid out of the booth. He grabbed Gibbons and pulled him off to the side. They spoke softly, leaning into each other, as DeSilva made her call. Marley watched them from the booth.

"Sam," Marley called to him.

He continued with Gibbons.

"Sam," Marley said a little louder.

DeSilva ended her call. "They've got her number," she said to Laska and Gibbons. "They say they'll have something soon."

"Sam," Marley said getting out of the booth.

He walked over to her. "Kat is going to take you somewhere safe," he said.

"What?" DeSilva said. "No, I'm not..."

"Kat, please," he said. "Take her. Maybe Area North. Or the Federal building. I'll stay here with Gibbons. Call me when you have a location."

"No, Sam," Marley said. "I don't want you to go. Stay with me."

"She's right," DeSilva said. "Wherever he's at, when we get a location we can have an army there in minutes."

He looked at DeSilva. "I didn't make this personal. He did." He turned to Marley. "I have to do this."

He waved Gibbons over and headed to the door.

"No, you don't." Marley called out.

48

THE HEART OF CHICAGO

Gibbons steered the unmarked car north on Ashland, the same street and in the same direction Nichols fled. Laska, in the seat next to him, stared straight ahead.

"She's right, you know?" Gibbons said. "Your girlfriend."

"I know."

"The smart play would be to wait for the troops like DeSilva said."

"When did I ever make the smart move?"

Gibbons chuckled. "Yeah, you're right."

"But that doesn't make you the sharpest knife in the drawer either."

"I came along to make sure you didn't get yourself killed."

"Getting killed isn't part of the plan."

"You have a plan? That'd be a first."

"The plan is to kill that fucker. Or accept his surrender if he's so inclined."

"I always loved a detailed plan."

They drove on. Dusk was fading into night. Gibson flipped on the headlights.

"Why are you doing this, Sam?"

"I told you, to end him."

"No. That's not you. Jokes aside, the Laska I knew would wait for backup. There's safety in numbers. We should wait for them to track the phone, get superior numbers, and overwhelm the bastard. Call the SWAT team if we have to."

"You really want to know why I'm doing this?" Laska said.

"Yeah, I do."

"I'm doing it because for years I walked in the darkness wading through the dregs of humanity. I saw the worst of what people can be. What vile horrors they commit on each other. Horrors I still have nightmares about. And in those nightmares I see unspeakable violence. I see torn and brutalized bodies. I see the faces of men and women. Children and babies. And the faces talk to me. They ask me why I couldn't help them or at least make it right again. Bring them justice. Bring them peace.

"It stains your soul, that much horror. You know this, Jim. You know what the job does to us. So, I tried to fight it. I forced myself to become immune to it. I became numb to it. I isolated myself. I thought that would protect me from the darkness. But in reality, I plunged deeper into it. I believed I didn't deserve to walk in the light again. I was in a shadow world and sinking deeper into it.

"Then I met Marley. She pulled me out of that dark place. She led me back into the light. She showed me a world I thought didn't exist anymore. She's the only thing that keeps me in the light.

"Now, knowing that, what do you think I would do to keep her safe? What would I do to keep her out of the shadows? What would I do to keep her from becoming another face in my nightmares? Tell me, Jim. What would you do?"

Gibbons said nothing. He slowed, pulled into the right lane and then into a donut shop lot.

"What are you doing?" Laska said.

Gibbons shut down the car. "We don't know where we're going. For all we know, we're headed in the wrong direction. Let's get a cup of coffee and wait here."

"Then you're still in? You're with me?"

"I'm with you," Gibbons said.

"Thank you," Laska said. He stepped out of the car. "We'll get coffee and wait in the car, okay?" he said.

They sat in the car sipping their coffee making small talk and waiting. Gibbons munched on a chocolate frosted donut. "Your girlfriend," Gibbons said. "Marley?"

"Yeah?"

"She's hot. How did that happen?"

Laska smiled. "Man, you're busting my balls? It's like I never left the job."

Gibbons laughed. "I'm serious. How did you get her to go out with you?"

"Actually, she asked me out."

"No kidding? She must've felt sorry for you or something."

"You're a funny guy." Laska took a sip of coffee. "She's pregnant."

"Yeah? Congratulations. Boy or girl?"

"We don't know. We wanted it to be a surprise."

"Old school. Nice. You gonna get married?"

"Yeah, but we're waiting. We need to get this lawsuit behind us. My lawyer says--"

Laska's phone began buzzing. He looked at the caller ID displayed on the screen.

"It's Marley's phone," he said.

"What are you waiting for? Answer it," Gibbons said.

He pushed the green button. "Nichols?" he said.

"Laska," Nichols said, "you piece of shit. You ruined my life."

"No, Jesse. This is all on you. You did this. You fucked up. You got yourself tossed into jail and you ruined your own life. And then, by some warped logic, you blame me. How many people have you killed trying to get to me? How many lives did you ruin?"

Nichols coughed. "Fuck you," he said. "You started this. Those people that died? They're on you. You stuck your nose where it didn't belong. All you had to do was go back to Sarasota. But you didn't. Those dead people are on you. You fucked up my life, Laska. I was on top, I had everything."

"Except honor. I'm not gonna go back and forth with you, Jesse. What do you want? Why did you call?"

"I want to talk about your woman..."

"You'll never get close again. Not ever. You're done." He paused and listened to silence on the other end. "Don't bother looking for me anymore," Laska said. "I'm coming for you."

Nichols coughed. "I'll leave the door open," Nichols said.

Laska kept the phone to his ear, hearing only soft wheezing on the other end.

Nichols spoke again. "Laska?"

"What?"

"Your woman is pregnant."

"I know."

"It's a girl." The phone went dead.

What the hell was that? he asked himself as he disconnected and dialed another number. DeSilva picked up.

"Did they get it yet?" he said.

"Yeah."

"Why didn't you call me?"

"Laska, wait for backup."

"Where's he at?"

DeSilva exhaled heavily. "They're telling me the phone is stationary just west of Clark Street on Ridge. South side of the street. Do you know where that is?"

"Yeah."

"They're saying it looks like there's a large building there."

"There's a motel there. The Heart of Chicago motel."

"Wait for us, Laska. We're on the way."

"Fat chance."

"Laska, he made a call to the lawyer...Jasper Dunlop."

"Yeah?"

"He asked Dunlop to find his daughter. To get a message to her. He wanted Dunlop to tell her he loves her and to say goodbye. Laska, he's gonna shoot it out. He's not going to be taken alive."

"I'll be happy to accommodate him." He punched the off button. Gibbons was already pulling out of the parking lot, the car's headlights piercing the dark night and pointing the way.

~

GIBBONS PARKED around the corner and they hoofed it the rest of the way, trying to stay in the shadows and out of the cones of light thrown by the street lamps. The motel was a long, squat two-story building much like every other motel built in the 50s. It had a long main building and a short leg attached. Not like an 'L' shaped building but rather attached at an angle like a checkmark. It was set back on the property and fronted by a large parking lot. A five-foot high brick wall ran along the street-side perimeter and offered great cover.

Laska and Gibbons, their pistols drawn, edged up to the short leg of the building. Laska stole a look around the corner.

"Nothing," he said.

"You're sure?"

"No, he could be behind a car or something."

"Did you see your pickup truck?"

"Yeah, its parked halfway down the long end of the building."

"Office?"

"On the other side of the building."

"We've gotta get his room number." Gibbons said. "But we don't know what name he's using."

"Let's hope a good description works."

"Let's hope." Gibbons nodded to the wall. "You go first."

"Thanks," Laska said. He bolted across the parking lot driveway to the wall, crouching behind it when he reached it. He waved Gibbons over and bobbed his head up over the wall to watch for Nichols.

Gibbons hustled over and crouched beside him. Laska stood peeking over the wall.

"Let's go," Gibbons said.

"Hang on," Laska said.

"What?"

Laska stood to his full height, his pistol trained on the parking lot. "When I told Nichols I was coming for him he said he'd leave the door open. There's an open door. The light is on."

"I hope you're not thinking what I think you're thinking."

"I'm going to check it out."

"Sam, we don't know if it's his room. It could be someone just trying to get some fresh air."

"Or it could be a trap. He could be trying to lure us in."

"Exactly."

"I'm gonna check it out anyway. You wait here."

Gibbons grabbed him by the shirt. "No." He looked at Laska and he knew. "I'm not gonna be able to stop you, am I?"

"No."

"Alright, I'll go with you. Stay low, use the cars in the lot for cover. We take positions on either side of the door. We look before we enter. Got it?"

"Got it. You take the right, I'll take the left.

Let's go."

They darted across the parking lot, staying low and scanning the area for any movement as they ran. They took cover behind random vehicles, pausing and watching and listening for any threat before proceeding. They reached Marley's Ford, the closest vehicle to the open door. Laska took a cautious peek into the cab through a side window.

The driver's side seat was covered with blood.

He crept back to Gibbons who was squatting on his haunches at the back of the truck. "You ready?"

"Whenever you are."

They took a three count and made their dash to the door. Standing on either side of the half-open door, weapons at the ready, they waited. With a single finger Gibbons touched his ear. Laska hesitated and listened. He shook his head.

Laska stood at the hinge-side of the door with the best possible view into the room. Both men understood Laska had the next move. He inhaled and held his breath. He bobbed his head, exposing himself briefly, and peeked into the room. He withdrew to his original position.

Gibbons saw confusion on Laska's face. He mouthed a single word to him: "What?"

Laska repeated the move but instead of withdrawing after glancing into the room his head hung exposed in the opening. He stepped forward and pushed the door fully open.

He looked over at Gibbons. "Come on," he said. Gibbons followed Laska into the room.

Jesse Nichols lay stretched out and face up on the bed. His unblinking eyes stared at nothing. Blood, dark and thick, soaked his clothing and the cheap bed linens around his right flank. Laska, knowing he was gone, still checked his neck for a pulse.

"He's dead," he said, though he didn't need to.

"Are you disappointed?" Gibbons said.

Laska looked at him and hesitated. "No," he said. "I'm relieved. I'm glad this is over."

Laska pulled out his phone and dialed DeSilva.

"Laska," she answered. "Where are you? They're telling me we're only a few blocks away."

"Heart of Chicago motel." He glanced at the door. "Room 114. Nichols is dead. He was dead when we got here." He thumbed the off button.

Laska looked down at Nichols' body. His hand clutched a small wallet-sized photo of a young girl smiling through her braces.

Gibbons came over and stood next to him. "He knew he was dying when he called you."

"Yeah, I think you're right."

Gibbons looked down at Nichols. "They're gonna need to replace this mattress," he said. He looked around the shabby room. "Nah," he said. "they'll probably just flip it."

49

THE BOTTOM FEEDER BLUES

Laska stood with DeSilva and McCarthy in a corner of the parking lot now crammed full with marked and unmarked police cars, government vehicles, and vans. Detectives, special agents, and deputies scurried back and forth. Camera strobes flashed in and outside room 114.

"You don't have to stay, Laska. We can get any statement we need from Sgt. Gibbons," McCarthy said.

"Marley should be on the way to your hotel now," DeSilva said. "We've got her statement and I let her protection detail know it was all clear," DeSilva said.

"Thanks, but I don't have a ride."

DeSilva turned to McCarthy. "I'll take him, okay?"

"Yeah, of course," he said.

"What about Marley's purse?" Laska said. "Can I bring it to her?"

"I'll grab it for you," DeSilva said. "They've gotta be done with it by now."

Laska found Gibbons before he left and gave him another man-hug. They promised each other they'd meet again sometime and share a few adult beverages. Laska climbed into the Suburban next to DeSilva and she headed south to the Peninsula.

DeSilva sensed something in Laska as she drove. "You okay?" she said.

"Yeah, I'm just feeling...what's the word?" He glanced out his side window. "Melancholy," he said.

"Well, snap out of it. It's over. Nichols got what he deserved. You and Marley are safe now."

"Yeah, but I can't help thinking Nichols might be right."

"What are you talking about?"

"When he called me on Marley's phone he said this was all my fault. If I didn't butt in way back when none of this would have happened. All those people, the deputies, Kevin King. They would all still be alive."

"That's bullshit and you know it. This is all on him."

"I guess you're right."

"Hell yeah, I'm right."

They sat quiet as DeSilva maneuvered through

the city traffic. Laska said, "Hey, what was that 'special deputy' stuff about?"

"McCarthy deputized me so I could keep working on the investigation. It's only temporary. But he did say he wants me to apply."

"To be a US marshal?"

"Yeah."

"Are you gonna do it?"

"I'm thinking about it."

"Good. I hope everything works out for you. Did you tell your wife?"

DeSilva hesitated. "Bobbie left me."

"Shit. I'm sorry. What happened."

"I guess...she said my job is more important to me than she is."

"I'm really sorry. Do you think you can work it out with her?"

"I don't know. But I'm gonna try." She glanced over to him. "I screwed up, Sam. Don't let it happen to you."

DeSilva dropped him off in front of the hotel. They parted with a hug and an "I'll call you" and Laska ran to the elevators.

He walked into the room and found Marley sitting on the bed. She had showered, changed, and a packed suitcase was at her feet.

"What's going on," he said, handing her purse to her.

"I want to go home, Sam," she said.

"Okay, whatever you want. You don't want to stay in the city any longer. I get it. I'll get ready."

"No, Sam. I booked a late flight. I leave in a couple of hours."

"I don't understand."

Marley stood up. "Sam, I don't know if I can do this. You're reckless and rash. You can't control your rage. You left me when I begged you to stay with me. You thought only about what you wanted and not about me. I needed you and you left me."

"Marley, I left you to protect you. I had to keep you safe. I didn't want to leave you but I couldn't see any other way."

"And that's the problem. You were so blinded by your anger you couldn't see I didn't need you to protect me. I needed you to be with me."

"Marley..."

"I was taken, Sam!" Her voice filled the room. Tears welled up in her eyes. "I just escaped. I thought I was going to die. I thought our baby was going to die!" Her voice dropped to a near whisper. "And you left me."

She picked up the suitcase. "I have to go." She looked at him through watery eyes. "When you get back I think you should move out for a while."

"Are you saying...are we...over?"

"I don't know, Sam. I need time."

Sam plopped down on the bed, his face contorted in an expression of disbelief and panic. Marley walked to the door. "Goodbye, Sam," she said.

And she was gone.

IN THE MORNING Laska checked in with DeSilva. He didn't mention his last conversation with Marley.

He asked about Bielski.

"He's out of surgery," DeSilva said. "It's still touch and go."

"Let me know how he does."

"I will. Hey, what about Marley's truck and laptop? What are you gonna do?"

"My guess is the truck will be impounded as evidence for a while. I'll have it shipped home when it's released. And when they're done with the laptop, can you can ship it to me?"

"No problem. What about your gun? The Glock?"

"Destroy it."

"Really? You don't want it back?"

"No. It's got bad luck all over it. Tell them I want it destroyed."

"Okay, whatever you want."

"What's going on with Nichols' lawyer?'

"Dunlop? He and his assistant are already charged. We'll see what happens. Do you want me to keep you in the loop?"

"No. I don't really give a shit about them."

"I don't blame you. Anything else?"

"No, Kat. Thanks for everything. I'll talk to you again soon."

He hung up and dialed another number.

"Rebecca Stafford," she answered.

"It's Laska."

"Oh, hi. I heard the news. I'm glad everything worked out. Your girlfriend, is she okay?"

"She's shook up. But physically? Yeah, she's fine. Thanks for asking. Listen, I guess the deposition is off, huh?

"Yes, of course. I don't know if or when things will start moving again."

"Just let me know."

He ended the call, picked up his suitcase, and headed out the door to his car. As he walked he felt the darkness, that familiar shadow world, slowly enveloping him. He exhaled deeply. The drive back to Florida was going to be miserable. And lonely. *Fucking Indiana*, he thought.

ACKNOWLEDGMENTS

Whether by editing, designing, fact-checking, researching, critiquing, or alpha and beta-reading many people help make an author's story come alive. Unlike the author, however, their names do not appear on the cover. They receive no credit for their hard work. To that end, I would like to thank the many who assisted me in getting this book to publication.

Many thanks to my proofreaders, Christie Sergo and William 'Shep' Shepherd. My word processor's spell and grammar check have nothing on you. Thank you to my editor, Miriam Nowon. You make me better.

Special thanks to my illustrator Rachel Larson for the cover art. Her talent is beyond compare.

Thanks to fellow author Bob Weisskopf for his continued support, encouragement, tips and hints.

Finally, thank you to my wife Sharon whose encouragement, suggestions, alpha-reading, and love I could not live without.

ABOUT THE AUTHOR

Richard Rybicki, a former detective, retired from the Chicago Police Department in 2006 and moved to Florida's gulf coast. The Pain Game, his first work of fiction (although many defense attorneys would dispute that fact), was published in 2016 and debuted the Sam Laska Crime Thriller series. His second novel, Where the Road Leads, continues the series. Bottom Feeder Blues is the third book in the Sam Laska Crime Thriller series.

The author lives near Siesta Key, Florida with his wife and dog and numerous bottles of fine bourbon.

ALSO BY RICHARD RYBICKI

The Pain Game

Where the Road Leads

Made in the USA
Columbia, SC
06 March 2023